Among the Ruins

Stephen Williams

Among the Ruins
Copyright © 2014 by Stephen Williams

Cover art and design © 2015 by Mikio Murakami, SilentQDesign.net

Published by **Villipede Publications**

Villipede Publications
PO Box 3643
Idaho Falls, ID 83403
villipede.com

Special discounts are available on quantity purchases by corporations, associations, and others. For details, contact the publisher at the address above or by email.

Printed in the United States of America

ISBN-13: 978-0692553978
ISBN-10: 0692553975

"*Among the Ruins* is horrifying at times in its sensibilities, heartfelt and poetic at others in its examination of the gruesome, but above all the book is damned intriguing from cover to cover. Stephen Williams writes like a seasoned veteran, not only of the intense thriller variety, but a veteran of your worst nightmares imaginable. You don't know where this novel is going to take you and you especially don't know where it will leave you. Highly recommended!"

—Benjamin Kane Ethridge, Bram Stoker Award winning author of *Divine Scream* and *Bottled Abyss*

"Williams writes with the confidence of Shane Carruth. His prose has this weird talent of stealing his reader's ability to breathe. *Among the Ruins* is not only terrifying, but smart, too. You're going to need something a lot stronger than popcorn to survive this one."

—Max Booth III, author of *Toxicity*

"Williams' *Among the Ruins* isn't afraid to jump headlong into the abyss and explore what lurks there. The novel moves at a good pace and includes enough dark twists and unsettling turns to keep its hooks buried in us until the terrifying end. If *Among the Ruins* is any indication, Williams is a writer to keep your eye on."

—Kurt Fawver, author of *Forever, in Pieces*

"This is a nail-biting, 'where the hell is this going to end up' kind of thriller . . . a rollicking ride that will have you clutching your seat with one hand while flipping the pages with the other, and wondering all the while who to root for. This one kicks in faster than a Ramones song and never slows down.

—John Everson, Bram Stoker Award winning author of *NightWhere* and *The Family Tree*

For my parents, Jeff and Pam Williams

Thanks for not kicking my broke ass out of the house

Contents

Proper Foreshadowing . . .

Ryan

❖

NATE DIPPED HIS FINGERS into a jar of petroleum jelly, swirling them around like sausages on ballet. After a few moments, he retracted them, admired his technique, and sat the jar down on the dusty sink.

"Perfect," he said, moving the gray globs around his knuckles. "Just right even."

"You'd almost think that you've done this before."

"Funny how that works isn't it? Experience is the key, practice really does make perfect."

"I hope not," I replied, his grin fading. I could no longer see his two missing teeth. "If that's the case then how well can we possibly hope for the next couple of days to go?"

He put his hand on my shoulder—the clean one—and I relaxed.

"Don't think about it. Trust me, thoughts can only lead to second thoughts—and second guessing went out the window as soon as we finalized the plan last week." He turned away and approached the tub on the far side of the room. "For now, all you have to do is get in the van and not think for twenty-four hours. Can you handle that?"

He turned around to face me, his eyes meeting mine long enough for his sincerity to take hold.

"Sure," I said. "Just jitters I think."

"That's what I figured. I mean, after all, we've been friends for how many years? I'm in a better position than most to know that your ability to not think is one of your best qualities."

"For now I'll just say I'm not about to put that on my résumé."

"Fair enough," he crouched down next to the tub like a parent about to bathe a child. "But to be on the safe side, you might not want to put me on any of those applications as a reference."

"But after tomorrow wouldn't you technically be classified as a prior employer?"

He laughed.

"I suppose that's right, but what jobs are you going to be looking for where 'prior experience with kidnapping and ransom' is a prerequisite—shit, I'm sorry, we're not talking about this, remember? It's subject changing time, come check this out."

I followed the footsteps he'd left in the dust on the yellowed tile until I could see into the basin. Hints of white still existed in the bath, but they were limited to scattered dime-sized splotches (probably from where the roof leaked on rainy days). Instead, the pristine surface of the tub was buried beneath a coral reef of beige grime and what I hoped was some type of dark mold. I found it hard to believe that something built with no other purpose than to hold water could be so filthy—but then I saw the toilet and decided to focus on keeping my breakfast down instead.

Nate took my silence as permission for him to proceed. He slathered his fistful of jelly along the walls of the tub in wide strokes, wrapping all the way along the perimeter. After the majority of it was applied, he smoothed it out until all that remained was a thin sheen, barely visible in the gritty light.

"When are you planning on telling me what this is all about?"

"It's not much," he said. "A little something I discovered a year ago by accident. It's pretty gross but it'll blow your mind."

"And you can't just tell me?"

"That's not a very adventurous attitude, is it? Sorry friend, but you're going to have to wait until we get back from our business trip to find out."

"Oh, I can hardly wait," I groaned. "Wouldn't it be better if you told me now so that we can get the disappointment out of the way?"

"Don't be such a downer. I'm finished," he stood up. "Now for the difficult part, getting this shit off my hand."

He walked to the sink and scrubbed at the remnants of goo still clinging to his palm.

"Shouldn't it be easy for you? I imagine you have lots of practice with getting oily lubricants off your hands—what was that you said? 'Practice makes perfect?' "

"Not funny, but hey, I'll give you a D+ for effort. It's good that you're lightening up a little."

"I've said it a million times, don't worry about me. I'll be fine."

"You always have been when it comes time to do what has to be done. Necessity is necessity, you know?" He shut off the water and checked his reflection in the cracked mirror. "Are you ready?"

"Why wouldn't I be?"

WE CLOMPED DOWNSTAIRS and were about to leave when he stopped in mid-step, about-faced, and headed for the back door instead.

"One more small errand to run before we go," he said. "Don't worry, we'll be quick."

The old screen door shut behind us with a brisk squeal. It was cool for late spring, and there wasn't a cloud in the sky. Nate pointed out past the old workshop at the edge of the woods to a dilapidated road that fit every meaning of the phrase "less traveled."

"You see that back there? That's the closest thing we have to an emergency exit if this thing doesn't go as *swimmingly* as we've planned for. Do you understand?"

"If by 'swimmingly' you mean searchlights and SWAT teams, then yeah, I get it," I yawned.

"It's an old fire trail, at least that's what Uncle Joseph used to say. It snakes back through the woods and comes out on the main road something like six miles down. I have no idea what kind of shape it's in; I haven't walked it in years."

"When was the last time it was used?" I asked. I wasn't really interested in the answer, but any excuse to not get in the van and move one step closer to mayhem seemed like good conversation at the time.

"Shit, maybe the Seventies?" He scratched his chin. "Who knows? We're the only ones out here anymore—it doesn't matter. The point is that if I live here occasionally and barely remember that it's there, then there's a good chance that the cops aren't going to know it's there. But don't worry; we're not going to have any problems, right? We're going to get the kid, get paid, and be done with it."

"I know, all this is a just in case."

"Precisely."

"Can we go now? This waiting around is making me anxious."

"Say no more."

We walked along the back of the house and passed through the side yard where I caught a glimpse of some forgotten relic tangled in the weeds. It was an old Triumph motorcycle painted white with pulsing veins of rust spider webbing their way from the tank onto the rest of the frame. The wheels had gone flat years ago but all of the spokes still seemed to be intact. Nate noticed my staring.

"That used to be mine," he said. "Back when my family came here I'd ride it in the backyard, sometimes up and down the road out front when my parents weren't around."

"Sounds like a blast."

"It was—except for when you crashed. A little case of road rash here and there wasn't enough to keep me away from that thing though. I loved it. Hell, I bet it even still has gas in the tank."

"Ever get the urge to dust it off?"

"Not really. Not because I'm not interested, I just don't think about it often."

"After this is taken care of, we should see if we can get it up and running," I said, testing my grip on the handlebars. "I haven't driven a motorcycle in forever."

"Well, now you have something to look forward to." Nate resumed his walking. "It's easier to go through Hell when you have some sort of light at the end of the tunnel, but I'm sure Madison provides more than enough of that on her own."

"You have no idea."

WE EXITED THE SIDE YARD to find Wesley, Jacob, and Schafer waiting for us. They were all leaning up against our gray van discreetly salvaged from a nearby junkyard. Other than the license plates it had no distinguishing features, and judging by the condition it was in, the plates had probably been obsolete for years. The crackling sound of our footsteps through the gravel of the drive lulled them out of their boredom.

"Was beginning to wonder if you guys were going to show," Schafer said with a scowl. "What took you so long?"

"I had to show Ryan our backup plan," Nate replied.

Schafer sighed.

"Haven't you heard it's bad luck to come up with a backup plan? It takes away some of the urgency, makes you lose focus." It looked like he was gearing up for a tirade, but before he could continue Wesley stepped to his side.

"Relax," he said. "Our plan is bulletproof. We shouldn't be experiencing any feelings of *urgency* to begin with."

Wesley is Schafer's younger brother and the only person that can give him advice; if anyone else even tries he gets defensive, like somehow we're trying to take away his alpha male thunder. Their physical features are almost identical (muddy eyes, matching hair, pronounced cheekbones, and the shadow of facial hair on their chins), with the exception that

Schafer is a head taller and fifty pounds heavier (all muscle) and Wesley wears glasses.

"If you say so," Schafer said turning away. "Did everyone use the can? It's a long way to Seattle."

"How many stops are we making?" Jacob asked nervously, he didn't want to get Schafer going again.

"As few as possible, and the less memorable they are, the better. If you haven't noticed, we're trying to avoid creating eyewitnesses."

"I know, but it still sucks," Jacob replied. "I hate long drives."

This conversation was predictable at best. Jacob always seemed to get the short end of the stick, and Schafer didn't mind beating him with it from time to time. He wasn't blessed with striking good looks—or brains—or even charisma. To be totally honest, if we hadn't felt like we needed another gun, he would've been left behind—the same can be said for if we felt like there was anyone else we could trust with a job of this magnitude. But no, all roads eventually led back to Jacob; and thus, he was brought into the fold. I don't think he's a bad guy and I even like him on some level, but at the same time my feelings mirror the rest of the group's: we don't like long car rides, long car rides with Jacob to be specific.

"Shut up and deal with it," Schafer groaned. "Are we ready?"

We nodded and Wesley took his spot in the driver's seat, we'd elected him as the first spot on our driving rotation—not that he minded. Early in life Wesley had never really fit in like his athletic brother, and while trying to find something to help define his personality he discovered a certain therapy behind the wheel. By the time he was eighteen he was already dominating the local street racing circuit, a life where his geeky looks came in handy. It didn't take long for him to realize that no one thought of him as a threat—until he was crossing the finish line full laps ahead of them, and by then he had already hustled them out of their money. This formula proved so successful he put himself through college with his winnings.

The rest of us circled the van and opened the side door. A two-foot-long king snake dropped out at our feet with a soft plop that accented Jacob's squeal of terror. The snake slithered off across the drive and disappeared into the woods.

"Sissy," Schafer chuckled.

"Do you believe in omens?" Nate asked me.

"Don't get biblical on me."

Schafer crawled in first and grabbed a faded blue tackle box. He popped open the lid so that he was the only one who could see inside, took silent inventory of its contents, and shut it again.

"Are you going to tell us what that's all about?" I asked.

"Nope," he said. "If the need arises then, and only then, you'll find out."

"Not even a hint?"

"Call it a *backup plan*," he rolled his eyes.

"So much for bad luck and superstitions," Nate whispered in my ear. He looked over my shoulder back towards the house and nudged me. "Looks like someone wants a word with you."

My gaze followed his over to the front porch where Madison stood waving.

"Make it quick," Nate murmured. "These other guys aren't going to wait around, and remember, thoughts only lead to second thoughts."

"Don't worry," I said. "She probably just wants to say goodbye."

I approached the house and with each step I could pick out more and more of her expression. She was smiling, though it was obviously strained. I stopped before the porch, out of reach. I knew that if she touched me there was no way I was getting in the car.

"Were you really going to leave without telling me?" she joked, her eyebrows raised.

"Maybe," I grinned. "I guess we'll never know."

"How's that?"

"You stopped me."

"Fair enough," she laughed. "I'm glad I did, because now I get to force you to say goodbye."

She walked down the front steps with three long strides until we were within arm's length. I held my ground.

"You mean try to remind me that everything is going to be okay, even though both of our guts tell us otherwise?"

"Am I really that easy to read?" She played with her long red hair, twisting it around one of her fingers nervously. "Guess I won't become a professional gambler after all."

"I'm sorry," I said after an awkward pause. "You know I'm not thrilled about this, but it's too late to turn back."

"Please don't apologize," she said. "You're sort of doing this for me, in a roundabout way, and how do you think it makes me feel when you apologize for a favor you're doing for me?"

"I'm sorry—"

"There you go again," she giggled. She closed the rest of the distance between us and hugged me. I buried my face in her hair and inhaled. When knights would go to war they'd carry a token of their beloved with them for strength; the soft scent of generic strawberry shampoo would serve as the banner of my lady fair on this damned crusade that was destined to make or destroy the rest of my life.

"No kisses," she said. "You get those when you come back."

"Drats," I mumbled. "Are you sure you're going to be okay all by yourself for the next couple of days?"

"Please, you make me sound like the damsel in distress type," she shot back. "Plus, I'm not really all alone, Nate's uncle is here. Maybe we'll find a checkerboard or something and become best of friends."

"Fat chance, Nate says he hasn't left his room in almost a year. He only sees him when he brings his food in. Kind of a weird guy."

"Eh, he's old; he's allowed to be weird."

"Are you two love birds done making out yet?" Nate called from the open van door. "Time is money."

Madison flipped him off smiling and turned back to me.

"Take care of yourself," she said. "Keep your eye on the big picture."

"I will, I love you."

"I love you more, 'Tall Dark and Handsome,' come back to me in one piece."

"Don't worry about that, Maddy," Schafer shouted out his window. "Even if something does happen, I'll gather up his pieces and bring them back to you. With a little super glue it'll almost be the same thing. The caliber of his personality will remain unchanged at least."

"Oh, because that makes me feel better."

I said one more goodbye that hung in the air between us like a phantom as I walked back to the car. Wesley wrestled the rusted behemoth into drive and pulled out onto the dirt trail leading through the forest. I didn't turn around until we hit the paved road seven miles later at the highway. When I looked back, all I saw was trees.

I

"Now all my nightmares know my name . . ."

Ryan

❖

I KNEW IT WAS A FLASHBACK. Retracing steps, trying to figure out how things could've ended differently—even wishing that they had. But there is one upside to knowing that you're dreaming: you can't be depressed when you emerge again in the empty paleness that we've all come to accept as reality.

I lied. It's still damn depressing.

In the flashback, I'm standing by a window in a generic hotel room with Madison sitting on the bed behind me. I hold my hand out a jagged hole punched in the glass, feeling the moist air and thumbing a cigarette that's been reduced to ashes. The taillights of passing cars reflect coldly off my wedding band. We're on the outskirts of Seattle weeks before the present.

"You shouldn't be smoking," Madison says, her hand stretching across her stomach.

"I'm not," I say, releasing the cigarette. I watch it fall into the puddles two floors below. The dips in the uneven pavement of the parking lot make a fantastic lake.

"Have you decided?" Even her murmurs seem deafening in the quiet room. "Do you want to talk about it some more?"

"I don't know if there's anything left to say," I step away from the window and lay on the bed next to her. "But I have to say something, because we're running out of time, and I've never been very good at coming up with ideas."

She moves her hand to my forehead and strokes my hair; I

don't stop her as my bloodshot eyes trace the lines of the ceiling fan watching over us.

"What do you think?"

"You know what I think," she says sighing. "I like Nate, and he isn't just some thug. If he says he has a plan, it's probably pretty good—but I can't be the one to make this decision—we've been through this."

"I know, but if we're being completely honest," I say as I sit up, touching her naked shoulder. "I wish you'd push me into it already."

"What do you mean?"

"Well if you'd just told me to grow some balls and get it over with, we wouldn't have a decision on our hands," I reply with an exasperated laugh. "That way I wouldn't have to think, you know? Not about the ugly process involved, all of the complications, not to mention my responsibilities as a father if I fail and wind up in prison—I'm not going to leave you to raise a baby by yourself, there's no way . . ."

She looks away, but I know she isn't crying. She's too strong for that.

"But if I forced you into it, would you love me like you do now?"

"Please," I smile as I pull her on top of me. "We both know that it's impossible for me not to love you."

We kiss twice, the first is innocent but with the second our mouths open. I want to make love with her—but the decision is still festering.

"This had to have been fate," I say. "I don't want to be melodramatic, but that's the only explanation I can come up with. Nate and I losing our jobs within an hour of each other, and not even ten minutes after cleaning out my desk you tell me you're pregnant. Desperate times call for desperate measures."

"I'm sorry, honey, but coincidences and fate aren't exactly the same thing. You're distracting yourself with the details again."

"I know, but it seems like an awful lot of puzzle pieces came together all at once."

"Regardless," she says, "a decision still needs to be made. I think we're asking the wrong questions. We shouldn't be focusing on 'What happens if I fail?' but rather, 'If I don't go through with this, what am I going to do instead?' "

Until my "release to pursue other opportunities" I'd been an accountant—on paper at least. The truth was a little more complicated. I preferred to think of myself as a spreadsheet Robin Hood. Adjusting numbers, moving sums between accounts, my real job was to snatch up every penny that nobody noticed and reinvest it in the company. Not glamorous work, but not scrubbing dishes either.

"I could get another job," I reply. "I'm not under-qualified, I have the experience. I'm damn good at what I do."

"You are, you're the best, but you know how the market is right now—and if all of these companies are doing massive layoffs, why would they hire you over someone they already let go? They don't know you like I do, to them you're just another applicant."

It may sound like she was being pushy, but she wasn't—she was being realistic. Her motherly instinct had kicked in and these questions were her own form of insurance. When her baby was born she was going to NEED a roof over her head, she was going to NEED food for the baby, she was going to NEED a warm bed to sleep in. Not that I minded any of this. If she had asked me to die for her, I would've asked for directions to the nearest bridge.

"So you think I should do it?"

"All I'm saying is that with Nate you won't have to wade through résumés, jump through hoops, or get on your knees and beg. And if you succeed, you won't have to worry about working nine to five, you can stay home with me and your new daughter or son."

"If we succeed . . ."

"*When* you succeed. You said it yourself, you're the best at what you do."

The phone rings and suddenly it feels like someone has shoved a fistful of nails into my heart. I watch it for a second on the bedside table, vibrating across the fake wood finish as the little red light on top blinks away like a cop in hot pursuit. I stand up, take one last look at Madison and pick it up. There's no remorse on my face, just the side effects from more than forty-eight hours of hard calculations.

"Hello Nate," I say, followed by the code we agreed on ahead of time if I was good to go. "What wonderful weather we're having."

"That's a relief," he replies. "That means the roads should be clear. I'll see you in a week at Uncle Joe's house. Tell Maddy I say hi, take care of yourself."

I hang up before he does, but the conversation is over anyway. We'll plot out our course of action face-to-face, it's too risky to discuss it any other way—too many chances for eavesdropping.

Madison nods and kisses me. We both know I made the right decision—the only decision—but it doesn't make me feel any less horrible.

NATE WAS THE ONE to shake me awake. The ugly atmosphere of the hotel room, which minutes ago was so real I could taste the dried up coffee and blood stains on the carpet, peeled away. I stretched and let out one more yawn.

"Well look who decided to join us?" Schafer crowed. "I was beginning to think that you were going to miss the whole operation."

"Whatever," I groaned. "Give me a break, I haven't been sleeping well."

Nate shot me a nervous glance; I could tell he was thinking too much into it. I waved his worries away and changed the subject.

"Did I miss anything?"

"Not really," Wesley called back from the front seat. He looked down at his watch. "We're almost there, but I'm going to take the long way around. I don't think school officials would take too kindly to a sleazy van just hanging around the exit waiting for the kids to get out. If we were going to do that, we might as well dress up like clowns and start handing out *free candy* if you know what I'm saying."

We turned and coasted through an upper class neighborhood. Large brick homes lined both sides of the road; each had its own motorcade of Cadillacs and Range Rovers in the driveway. We were definitely getting close.

"I want to suggest that we go through the plan one more time," Nate said. "A quick checklist of everything so there's no last minute memory lapses."

"Cool with me," Jacob said, pulling a piece of paper out of the glove compartment. "This is our target."

While talking, he handed the magazine clipping to us. It was bright yellow and in puffy letters at the top read: "Billionaire Heartthrobs!" In the center of the page was our boy, Edric Samuels. He looked like a typical sixteen year old—what these rags would have you believe a typical sixteen year old should look like. Long brown hair, perfect teeth, thin frame and no acne. If teenagers were supposed to have some kind of awkward phase, this kid missed the memo. Other than his "boyish good looks" (let's face it, magazines targeted toward teen girls aren't about inner beauty) he looked like an average kid to me—a kid who was going to have the bad luck of being in the wrong place at the wrong time in about ten minutes.

"Still not impressed," I mumbled.

"I don't care if you like him," Schafer said. "We like his dad, software CEO Victor E. Samuels. *Forbes* recently estimated his net worth at twenty-two billion dollars. That's billion with a 'B,' pal. B as in Benjamin Franklin, B as in breaking the fucking bank."

"I'm not you, I can spell, thank you," I sighed. "Carry on, Jacob."

"Anyway, we'll be grabbing him from his private school a few blocks over when they get out at 3:15 on the dot," he said.

"Security?" I asked.

"Not much," Wesley said. "A couple of guards, but none of

them are armed. It's a school, not a bank."

"And are we expecting much resistance from the kid?" Nate said, feeding us questions that we all already knew the answers to.

"You never know," Schafer said. "The plan is to put the fear of God in him right off the bat. With a little luck he'll be pissing in his tighty whities and be a good little prisoner during this whole ordeal."

"Which leads us to the kidnapping itself," Nate said. "When we scouted last week we saw that there was a small through street right across from the front entrance. It's virtually an alley, we're going to park the van there with the back door facing the school, that way we can just throw him in and take off, no three-point turns involved."

"Thanks, I love you guys too," Wesley said. Everyone knew he liked to go fast; the less turning involved the better.

"Have you guys reconsidered?" I teased. "Are we going to do this quietly?"

There was a pause before the van erupted with laughter.

"Definitely not," Schafer said. "The more violent we seem, the more scared everyone will be, which in turn will create chaos—chaos creates mistakes, and in this context, mistakes are a very, *very* good thing. And don't worry about artillery, that's Nate's department. Take it away, Nate!"

"Thank you, Schafer," he said like a phony game show host. "I've got prizes for everyone! First, on crowd control I have Jacob and Ryan! Can I get a round of applause please?"

We looked at each other a little confused before he continued, elaborate arm gestures and all.

"As we all know, on crowd control, you want to be able to hold down the fort against many aggressors at once, so for you two I have matching Mossberg Mavericks! That's a twelve-gauge shotgun, my friends, each loaded with a full eight rounds—more than enough to take off limbs, heads, or whatever the fuck you feel like!"

He handed us our guns. I clicked the safety off and checked to make sure it was loaded, you can never be too careful.

"It's a little heavy," Jacob groaned.

"Deal with it! Up next, we have the kidnapper himself, the big, the bad, Schafer!"

"Thank you very much, Nate," he said. "It's a pleasure to be here, what do you got for me?"

"Well, as the one physically grabbing this poor defenseless child,"—this line dripped with sarcasm— "you're going to need something both intimidating and versatile. Designed by Mikhail Kalashnikov himself, weighing in at nine and a half pounds, let me introduce you to the AK-47!"

"Nice," Schafer smiled as he took his weapon. He looked down the sight and checked the tension on the trigger.

"I like his," Jacob said. "Can we trade?"

"Fuck off."

"What about me and you?" Wesley asked.

"You and I both get Glocks," Nate said contentedly.

"What? Is that some kind of joke? Why?" Everyone could feel his disappointment.

"I'm taking a pistol because I'm going to have to carry the half of a sixteen year old that Schafer isn't, and you're staying behind the wheel the whole time so you don't need to be out in streets firing something big and scary."

"I guess . . ."

"Look at it this way," Nate was frustrated but he was doing a good job of keeping it under control. "If anyone decides to go vigilante and try to pull you out of the seat before we make our escape, you just lift your Glock to the window and, abra-cadabra, they suddenly don't have a face anymore."

"If you say so." Wesley was getting anxious. "We're within a couple blocks, guys, let's finish this powwow up."

"Consider it done, cabby," Jacob replied.

"Call me that again and I'll test my Glock, just to make sure it isn't going to misfire," Wes snapped.

"Sorry. Anywho, once Edric gets halfway across the street we burst out of the van. Ryan and I are crowd control. We make a V formation as we cross the street so that we can part the crowd like a ski mask wearing Moses while Nate and Schafer blitz up the middle to our target. Schafer will knock out Edric with our good buddy chloroform, they'll grab him, drop our ransom note and we'll take off. Something important to keep in mind: just because we're not trying to shoot anyone doesn't mean DON'T SHOOT. We're trying to create a panic, and for that the only thing better than the media is gunfire."

"Sounds simple enough," I said. "And after we have the package our fate rests in the hands of Wesley?"

"Wow, no pressure or anything," he said. "Don't worry about it, I have a route in mind, but if that doesn't work it's still no big deal. I've driven around Seattle enough to know where I'm going. Our ultimate destination is a parking garage fifteen miles away, far enough to escape the scene but not far enough for the police to get their choppers on our ass.

"Once at the garage we're going to trade our van for a different one—one the cops and any AMBER Alert do-gooder fucks won't be looking for. After that, we're home free—taking lots of back roads of course."

"Well I would expect nothing less," I said. I was still a little scared, but after laying out the plan again I was feeling much more confident in our chances of success. "For good measure, let's go over how payment works after we get the kid back to the house—we have time to kill."

"Let's not get ahead of ourselves," Schafer said. "But it's funny that that's actually the easiest part. On the note we're leaving there's a number to a cell phone that Wes has attached to a fake signal in Wisconsin. The cops will try to track it but end up on nothing more than a wild goose chase. After that we're banking they'll play ball. We're only asking for ten million, that's pocket change for daddy."

"Two million apiece isn't a bad week's work for anyone," Nate said. He really had dotted all of the Is and crossed every T, but there was still one question that was nagging me.

"How are we going to be able to collect the money? They aren't just going to hand it over and let us go," I said. This made Wes laugh.

"That's my favorite part; we're going to bluff them. There's an old pawnshop that's been abandoned on the outskirts. It has a great four-inch-thick sheet of bulletproof glass separating the customers from the clerk. We're going to put a fake bomb vest on the kid, get him behind it, and break the locks. By the time they find a way through the glass and we give the okay to quote unquote 'defuse the vest,' we'll be in Canada buying Aston Martins. We're here."

Our van passed the front of a large building surrounded by an ivy coated iron fence. Where the street stopped, ancient cobblestone began running all the way through the front gate up to the entrance of the school. Two pudgy security guards who wore pepper spray holsters but had probably never fired a gun before in their lives unlocked the gate. It wouldn't be much longer.

Wesley parked in position and we began to get ready. We all pulled ski masks over our faces and slid on disposable latex gloves. Then we passed around a container of shoe polish.

"Rub this around your eyes and mouth," Schafer said. "But make sure you have the gloves on first, we're not trying to save the pigs a step by giving them our fingerprints."

It smelled awful but I went along with it, smearing greasy trails of black around my eyes. I had a flashback of dressing up like a skeleton for Halloween when I was five years old.

"This wasn't in the plan," Jacob said.

"Another precaution I thought up," Schafer said. "There's a small chance that someone will get a good look at us during our escapades, but with everyone running around like their dicks are on fire, some people might actually confuse us for being African Americans instead of the White boys we are."

"I don't know," I said. "I wouldn't say shoe polish is a convincing way to disguise our race. They're more likely to think we're coal miners or chimney sweeps."

"Come on," he groaned. "We're not trying to actually be Black; it's just an extra layer of confusion for the detectives to wade through, a smokescreen."

"I get it," I said as I finished. "When you wet the rag, don't do it in here, the fumes are bound to knock us all out—that'd be embarrassing. I'm in no hurry to end up on one of those 'America's Dumbest Criminals' shows."

Schafer grabbed the chloroform, which he'd put inside of a vintage whiskey flask. The fancy cursive monogram on the front seemed to suggest that its previous owner had been Uncle Joe. He popped his window and wet the rag on the outside grumbling all the while. Wes checked his mirrors.

"Looks like they're getting out early, are we ready?" he asked. We nodded and got into position at our respective doors. "You guys know what you're doing, there's no reason to get flustered, just get in and out nice and clean. Safeties off, let's do this thing."

There was a metallic buckling and the doors dropped. Sunlight rushed into the van momentarily blinding us as our shoes hit the pavement.

We had reached the beginning.

II

Anesthesia

Edric

❖

THERE WAS SO MUCH I was thinking about. The look Shawnee Scott gave me in biology, for instance. A quick glance from underneath her eyelashes was all it took to get my attention. I wanted to say something a little too smooth to get her to giggle (if you can make a girl laugh, she's yours), but before I could, I felt her leg creeping up mine from beneath our granite topped lab table. This may have worked against me because by the time I picked up a scalpel and peeled open my frog, I realized that I hadn't completely sedated my patient. Oops, frog guts hopping all over the table. At least that got a couple laughs.

After class, I asked if she wanted to study with me. She blushed but she had to be faking. Someone who has the confidence to grope me while making frog sushi shouldn't have an issue looking me in the eye when I'm asking them out. She said she'd think about it, to which I replied my father was going to be at a golf tournament for the week and that I'd have the whole estate to myself. This may have tipped the scales in my favor.

Whatever, even if she flaked I'd find someone else to help keep me busy. I wasn't about to waste a week to celibacy.

After the bell rang I swung by my locker. I grabbed my headphones, slid them over my ears, and cranked the sound up loud enough to forget about homework. It was going to be another one of those unproductive evenings. Sure finals were coming up and I couldn't afford to fail math, but at the same time another night of falling asleep in a pile of textbooks wasn't a top priority.

After closing my locker I was the only one left in the hallway. Students say that the school is haunted, and it's old enough for me to believe them. I shivered, even though the place is more likely to have mysterious clouds of asbestos instead of poltergeists (the former being much more deadly and a lot less stupid). Plus if I were to get possessed at least I'd have a story to pass around and impress some girls with.

I pushed the front doors open and smiled up at the sky. Even if I would have to inevitably do homework or miss my chance to fool around with Shawnee, it was going to be a glorious afternoon. Springtime Washington can be so amazing when it isn't rain delayed.

With my headphones on and my eyes on the clouds, I didn't notice the screams.

Ryan
❖

THERE WAS SO MUCH I was thinking about—all of it leading to potential disaster. I tried to focus on the plan, and I must have been to some degree because I was going through the steps as methodically as we'd laid them out in the car. But at the same time, my churning guts were tricking my brain into loops of desperation.

At what point should I decide that the operation had failed and I needed to jump ship? And even if I came to the conclusion we weren't going to be able to recover, what should I do? Should I run? Where would I go? How would I ditch the gun and disguise myself as anything but this shoe-polish skeleton? How would I get back to my wife but not drag her into this mess . . .

No time for that, too much to worry about now.

I hit the ground in stride, and focused on my job and my job alone. I took the left flank while Jacob hit the right running twice as fast as me, his nerves getting the better of him. Timing was critical and I prayed that he wasn't going to do anything stupid; but it was too late to call out to him, so I moved my vision back down my iron sights. Schafer and Nate took their positions by the back of the van and opened the doors before wading into the mass of teens flooding from the front gate. It was like the school had dammed up these children and now that 3:15 had rolled around they were free to rush the street, filling the gutters and sidewalks.

One scream was all it took, and soon the visual language of the spectacle matched the growing intensity of our mission. Kids dropped backpacks, duffle bags, and anything else keeping them from running full speed away from us. A few stood frozen in place or dropped to their knees with their hands spread out in front of them, but not nearly enough to slow our progress across the asphalt. It was an orchestra of panicked shouting with a nice background harmony of whimpers and cries for help. I was beginning to think that drawing the crowd control straw had been a blessing in disguise: if our target waited long enough, we wouldn't have a crowd left to control.

The only thing missing was gunshots. We all knew they were coming, I just didn't know who was going to be first. I was betting on Schafer, he seemed like the type to want to set the bar as high as possible, which was fine with me. I wanted to save my ammunition in case I needed it later.

Jacob, bobbing and weaving between kids, reached the security guards within seconds of our leaving the vehicle. It wasn't really part of the plan but it seemed like a reasonable enough first step. He cocked his shotgun once, ejecting a perfectly good shell into the air, and pointed the barrel at their chests.

"Get on the ground," he said calmly. "If you ever want to eat another doughnut again, you fat bastards, do it now."

One guard wasn't having any part of it. Even before Jacob finished his threat he ran back towards the entrance of the school so fast he split his pants. He almost tripped on the front steps but managed to keep his balance long enough to get inside.

"Wee wee wee all the way home, eh?" Jacob smiled, pointing the gun at the other gentleman who still hadn't complied with his one easy to follow request. He was fingering the pepper spray on his belt, getting ready for a quick draw.

"Are you serious?" Jacob moaned. "Don't make me shoot you!"

But he wasn't listening; adrenaline had shut down his common sense indicators.

"Screw it," Jacob said. He took the butt of his shotgun and shoved it into the guard's stomach with bone splintering force, creating tidal waves of flab across the khaki, ketchup-stained fabric of his uniform. The spray rolled from his hand across the cobblestones, clinking over each one before it came to a rest in a nearby patch of grass. The guard's dreams of receiving the key to the city for bravery vanished with his ability to stand up.

Schafer was the first to shoot.

He took his AK and sprayed the face of the school with a hail of random gunfire. Two windows broke and bullets pockmarked their way along the brick sending a small shower of red chips and dead ivy down to our level. He only let off a short burst, but it was more than enough for those that hadn't started running already to take off.

Whether it was the gunfire or screaming kids running in every direction, I'll never know. But my attention wasn't just on our flank anymore, because after Schafer turned what used to be such a nice school into a shooting gallery, a strong, slender, pillar of navy rounded the corner. It was a cop, his gun was drawn, and I would have bet anything he was itching for target practice.

And I was even beginning to think that everything was going to go according to plan.

I wasn't facing him head-on, but I was close enough to know his service pistol was aimed at me. If I'd moved to the right even a foot he would have been forced to take the shot (I would have in his position). I assumed no one else in our posse noticed him because there was no shouting, taunting, or anything, just eerie quiet leading up to a "You have the right to remain silent" or "Drop your weapons!"

I turned towards him, and oddly enough I didn't think about what I was about to do (my heart was beating too loudly for me to hear the angel on my shoulder). Instead I was only curious if he'd even bothered to call for backup before rushing in here like some kind of idiot hero.

I don't know who was more surprised by my first shot, him or me. The crack from the barrel echoed off the nearby buildings and the recoil made me check my footing. The buckshot ripped the gun from his hand, taking three of his fingers with it. He went pale as his blood splashed against the ground ruining the bottoms of his pant legs—that's when I fired again.

The second blast was nastier than the first. His vest shredded, leaving his uniform oily with blood as it seeped out from half a dozen holes. Even worse though was somehow my shot had tore into the left side of his face, pulverizing his cheek and popping his left eye in a jet of yellow jelly. He was dead in seconds, but that didn't stop me from running to his corpse and dropping his gun and radio down a nearby storm drain in case anyone else got smart.

I should have been horrified at what I'd done, Jacob sure was. I could see the pinpoints of his eyes from thirty feet away. He looked like he wanted to puke—but at least he was professional enough to keep his forensic evidence down. I turned back towards Schafer to see what he thought. He shrugged nonchalantly before returning to his post.

Necessity is necessity, after all.

My stomach clenched. Had we missed our target? A lot of kids had already fled the scene, and there was always the possibility that we'd got our description from an out of date picture. But then, like a sign from God, he emerged from the front gate, eyes closed, bobbing his head to his music. Schafer soaked the rag again using the rest of the chloroform, and with Nate backing him up, they ran at Edric with their guns in the air.

Edric

❖

AN INTENSE DRUM SOLO—followed by a sudden impact that almost knocked me on my ass. I thought I'd been hit by a car, which then made me wonder how I was going to explain crossing the street with my eyes closed to my lawyers. But as the seconds passed I realized that I was okay and took a look around.

Two armed men were standing on opposite sides of me. The larger one had moved to my back and wrapped me in his arms while the other kept his gun aimed at my forehead. I was going to struggle; I assumed that if I kicked the man with the pistol between the legs I'd still have enough time to squeeze out of the more muscular one's grip. But by the time he finished locking his arms, I knew it was pointless to fight. It's like getting in an arm wrestling match, and as soon as your rival's muscles tense, you know it's only a matter of time until you're pinned.

Plus, missing my kick and getting shot in the face wouldn't make a very compelling story, now would it?

"Let me go!" I spat. There was no harm in trying.

"Get it over with," the man in front said. "He's making me nervous and the cops are going to be here any minute."

The one behind me loosened his grip enough to reach around and force a white cloth over my mouth, the texture grating my lips as his palm pressed into my face. Amazingly I managed to stay calm, somehow accepting that this guy was too strong to fight helped me relax. I continued to breathe out my nose while keeping a tight seal on my mouth until the man in front shook his head.

"You have to get his nose too otherwise he's not going to go under," he said. "Let me help."

So much for that.

Using his free hand, the front gunman arranged the cloth so that it was covering both of my nostrils. As soon as he felt that he'd done a satisfactory job, the man behind me tightened his grip.

I knew what was happening but I still got the first wisp of whatever was on the rag. It made me want to gasp for air, like bobbing for apples in a bath of photo chemicals, but I remained calm.

Hold your breath I told myself. If they think you go under, they'll let you go. Houdini could hold his breath for almost four minutes, you can handle a few seconds. I knew I had to make it convincing, so I kicked my legs and thrashed before having my eyes drift closed in a toxic coma. I made myself as limp as a corpse and waited for their next move.

Ryan
❖

THERE WAS NOTHING TO WATCH on my side of the street except for the collapsed mess of the cop I'd slaughtered. His blood continued to empty into the street, stretching out in a crimson wave on all sides of his body. Soon it would dominate the intersection in an ocean of congealed red. I tried to keep my eyes peeled and my ears perked up for sirens, but instead my vision kept finding its way back to that huddled pile of shredded cloth and flesh.

Did he have kids?

I didn't want to think about it, but in a way it was the most rational thing to pass through my mind since waking up. I had to keep my head on straight until I was back in Madison's loving arms, and knowing Schafer as well as I do, I knew that if I showed any signs of weakness he would leave me and my regret behind. Either way it was too late to do anything, so I turned my back on my handiwork.

Nate and Schafer were finishing up. The kid was incapacitated and as complacent as all teenagers would be in an ideal world. They laid him down on the ground and, using a combination of ropes and belts, secured his ankles, wrists, and legs. The way his body was perfectly still with his cheek pressing into the asphalt looked almost peaceful. No sign of terror, no struggle—too perfect.

"Are you all ready?" Nate called to the rest of us. "It's time to go."

Jacob and I fell back to Nate and Schafer as they dropped the note, lifted our package, and carried him back to the van.

"He isn't as heavy as I thought he'd be," Nate said.

"That's because you have the feet," Schafer groaned. "How should we get him in here?"

"Lightly toss him," Nate said. "He's going to be out for at least another twenty minutes, he won't feel it."

They counted backwards from three, rocking him back and forth to build momentum. They released him and he tumbled in an awkward somersault inside with a heavy plop. He looked contorted and uncomfortable on the rusted metal floor, but it would have to do until we swapped cars in a few miles. We shut the doors.

We were beginning to get back into the van just in time for one more surprise.

"Hold it right there!"

From the entrance of the school came the security guard who'd run off earlier, a woman in a pinstriped suit and heels carrying a baseball bat, and a thin elderly gentleman holding a revolver in a shaky hand. They were at least a hundred feet away, but even an amateur could tell they were out of their league. The security guard had a large wet spot around the crotch of his pants, the woman was holding her bat with both hands like it could fly away if it suddenly became self-aware, and the old fogy had large, horrified blue veins protruding from his forehead.

"Leave this to me, guys," Nate said. "Get in the car. I'll take care of these jokers."

I didn't like the thought of leaving Nate alone, oftentimes amateurs with guns are more dangerous than veterans because they lose their cool easily, but the calm in his voice convinced me to join Schafer and Jacob.

"Sorry, not today," Nate said raising his Glock towards the entrance. He kept firing until the slide slammed back indicating he was empty, but it didn't matter. The school officials or whoever thought they were coming to save the day had taken cover out of sight where they would later tell the police that they had tried to stop us, but were powerless. Nate tossed his empty gun inside and followed it.

"Drive," he said before shutting his door. It had been exactly four minutes since we opened them with guns drawn, ready to go for broke.

Wesley hit the accelerator and screeched out of the alley into a neighborhood going twice the speed limit. I moved to take off my ski mask but Nate grabbed my wrist.

"Wait a mile," he said. "We don't want to risk anyone seeing our faces fleeing the scene of the crime."

I set my gun on the floor and stretched. The van was silent —except for a soft squeaking coming from where the backseat should have been.

"Do you hear that?" I asked.

"Yeah," Schafer said. "Is something wrong with the car?"

"No," Nate replied. "Even though it looks like it's held together with chewing gum and rubber bands, I checked it out before we left and everything seemed solid. Plus, if something was wrong there'd probably be some sort of rhythm to it, machinery is like that. That's something else."

The three of us turned our heads to discover that our captive wasn't exactly as docile as we'd hoped. Using his hands alone he was scooting his way towards the back hatch. The sound we'd heard was from the button on the front of his jeans scraping up against the bare metal of the van floor. What he was planning to do once he reached the back door was anyone's guess—but it didn't matter, Schafer saw to that.

"You tricky little bastard," he said, climbing over our seat and grabbing Edric by the foot. With one hand Schafer flipped him over and pulled him back to his starting point. Looking more like a worm than a teenager, Edric wiggled his foot free.

"Let go of me!"

"Shut up," Schafer scowled. "Just shut your mouth and play nice. You understand?"

"Go to Hell! I don't know what you have planned, but it isn't going to work. You honestly think you're going to get away with this? Give me a break! You aren't smart enough."

"Smart enough, huh?" Schafer chuckled. His face was still obscured by the ski mask, but I could tell something dark flashed across his expression. It was in his voice. "Well I guess you're right, maybe our plan had some holes in it. Like we thought that we'd be able to grab you and everything would be cool. You'd just go along with it, seeing how we're bigger and stronger than you. And had that been the case, we wouldn't have had to hurt a hair on that precious *teen heartthrob* head of yours. But then you had to go and get funny, didn't you? Thought you could play a little practical joke of your own on my friends and I. Sure wasn't very nice of you now, was it?"

For the first time since the start of the mission, Edric looked scared. As he spoke, Schafer sat down on the boy's rigid legs and scooted his way up so that they could look each other in the face. He pulled one of his latex gloves off and clenched his hand a few times to readjust to the naked feeling. He popped his knuckles.

"What are you doing?" I asked breathlessly.

"Plan—Fucking—B."

Edric

"**OH GOD, PLEASE** don't do this. I'll pay you, I'll do whatever you want, just please don't do this . . ."

Ryan

BY THE TIME THE REALITY of the situation sunk in, it was already over. Schafer raised his fist into the air and brought it down across Edric's face with a sick, wet packing sound. It was the same sound a thick slab of raw meat makes when it's dropped onto a cutting board. Edric coughed in pain and disbelief, twisting his face around, trying to get his words back.

"Please," he cried. "I'll shut up."

"You see, now he's making fun of me! I must not be a *real man* if I can't take him out in one punch, right, guys?" Schafer laughed. "Fuck you, rich boy!"

He swung again and this time it made his lips burst open, spritzing two lines of blood spatter onto the rust below. Had his fist been one inch further north he would've broken his nose. Schafer wiped his hand off on his shirt and grabbed Edric by the collar, shaking him violently.

"Hello? Anyone awake in there? Who's smart now, asshole!"

"What the fuck is going on back there?" Wesley called from the front seat, too intent on keeping us out of traffic accidents to follow along play-by-play.

"He's beating the shit out of him!" I yelled. "Cut it out, he's done; you're going to kill him!"

"Don't tell me what to do, Cop Killer!" he growled. "Plus, it looks like he has something to say. If he can still talk shit then I haven't been hitting him hard enough. So what do you want to say, kiddo? Say it loud say it proud so we can all hear you!"

Edric wasn't going to last much longer under the circumstances, but from the way he had articulated himself I knew that he wasn't an idiot—far from it. Even with his brains jostled he was still plotting. He knew that pleading wasn't going to get him anywhere; the last punch in the face confirmed that much, so with his last fiber of consciousness he went with a more satisfying approach.

"Just you wait," he smiled. "You'll see soon enough how big of a mistake you've made, you fucking moron."

Before the last punch came he spit a slimy glob of blood with a splintered toothy center onto Schafer's chest. Schafer wound his arm back so high it brushed the ceiling before he smashed it into the side of Edric's head. He probably would've hit him a few more times for good measure had Nate and I not restrained him. He only fought us for a moment, but with Nate on one arm and my hand working into the pressure point on the back of his neck, he gave up. He sat back down next to us and remained quiet for almost a whole minute before laughing nervously.

"Buckle up guys," he said. "It's a long ride back to base."

Edric

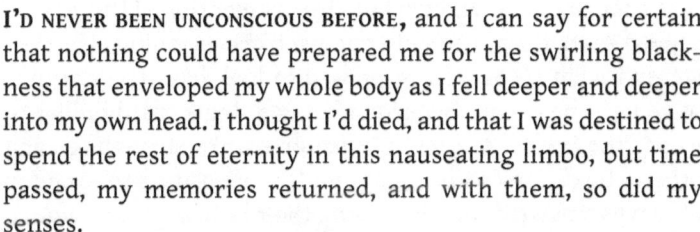

I'D NEVER BEEN UNCONSCIOUS BEFORE, and I can say for certain that nothing could have prepared me for the swirling blackness that enveloped my whole body as I fell deeper and deeper into my own head. I thought I'd died, and that I was destined to spend the rest of eternity in this nauseating limbo, but time passed, my memories returned, and with them, so did my senses.

First came the scent of fresh lawn clippings, sweet and fresh. I took as many deep breaths as I could without choking, filling my lungs with the brilliance of the smell. Next, my ears were greeted with the sound of birds coupled with the faint wind blowing through the grass and trees; it was reminiscent of the tide rolling lazily over a forgotten beach. I could feel the rough ridges of unfinished wood beneath my back and the cool breeze on my face. I opened my eyes.

Royal blue shocked all of my senses and fried my retinas. I shut my eyelids again, but the damage had been done and tears poured down my cheeks in an effort to console my aching corneas. A few moments later I tried again, this time sliding them open a sliver at a time so I could adjust to this new world.

The sky was a deep blue, had no clouds, no contrast, and despite there being no sun in sight, was bright beyond belief. I was lying on a crudely built wooden cart with large wheels that had probably been salvaged from an old covered wagon. Whoever had abandoned me didn't want me to get very far, because each of my hands were bound to the cart with heavy shackles.

I sat up as much as the chains would allow and rubbed the sleep from my eyes. I was positioned at the top of a hill in the middle of a rocky path. Off in the distance was a small farm. It had a wooden shack with tools scattered around it. Even further out was a large stone waterfall emptying into a lake. I knew there had to be more than I was seeing, no landscape, not even a national park, is as seamless and beautiful as the world that was spread out before me. However, the oppressive sky made it impossible to distinguish detail, so for the time being I was stuck with a postcard.

Other than the landmarks I already mentioned there were a few trees dotting the fields, but just like everything else, they weren't what trees were supposed to look like. Their trunks were light beige and instead of being a single sturdy pillar of wood, they were a mash of smaller trunks strangling each other. The canopies were the complete opposite, a solid clump of leaves smashed together doing their best impression of an umbrella; great for shade, not for climbing.

Most unnatural of all though was the grass. It rolled along unbroken all the way to the horizon and was a mellow, earthy green. It was thick, easily as wide as my thumb, but still swayed in the wind effortlessly; and despite there being acres all around, I could visualize every separate blade. Imagine being in the center of a sea anemone as its tentacles comb the tide for its prey, that's what it felt like.

I could have spent eternity there. Every time I thought I had found the end, something new would spring up; but it wasn't meant to be. I'm not sure how I feel about fate, but sometimes you can't help but imagine things are too strange to have happened on accident.

"You're awake," an unfamiliar voice said from behind me. "For a while there we thought you were a goner."

"You're not the only one," I said, my voice clogging up my throat.

"What brings you all the way out here?" the voice continued. "We don't get many visitors."

"To be honest, I don't know."

"Don't know? Well, let's have a look at your noggin; I'm sure we can solve this mystery."

A hand grabbed the hair on the back of my head and ruffled

through it. I reached up to stop whoever it was, but the shackles kept my hands in place.

"Yeah, seems like you got a couple of lumps, that'd do it."

"Knock it off!" I yelped. "What's going on? Who are you? What am I doing here?"

"Oops, sorry about that," the man said retracting his hand. "Like I mentioned before, we don't get very many visitors. I'm afraid my manners may have suffered a tad because of that."

Two figures stepped into view; the first was a head taller than me and was wearing a brown leather coat, faded jeans, and a black hat with a wide brim. He couldn't have been as old as my grandfather, but his face was pitted and wrinkled with years of experience nonetheless. He had huge hands, menacing eyes, and didn't have to flex for me to know that his body was little more than solid muscle from years of manual labor. The other was a boy no older than seven. He had delicate features, messy blonde hair and terrifying blue eyes. At first I didn't think he had any pupils, but closer inspection revealed they were there, just pinpricks.

"My name is Asclepius," the old one said. "And this here is my son Sigmund."

"Nice to meet you," I said, trying to remain calm. "You too, Sigmund."

He said nothing, only continued to stare into me. I looked away.

"You'll have to forgive Sigmund," he said. "He doesn't talk much."

"It's alright," I lied. "I used to be shy when I was his age."

Asclepius opened his mouth to say something, but thought against it.

"You wanted to know why you were here?" I nodded. "Well, heck, you're the only one who can answer that. But I can help point you in that direction. Usually when someone comes plopping down on my farm, they have a problem that needs solving."

"Problem?"

"You betcha, so think—but not too hard, can't have you

blacking out again."

I laid back down on the cart and covered my face the best I could (damn shackles), and the more I wracked my brain, the more tears rimmed my eyes until they spilled over the edge and onto the bed of the cart. The faint smell of dust and musty wood wafted to my nose.

"Come now," Asclepius said. "Whatever it is, it can't be that bad."

"Oh it is," I grunted between wheezes. "I've been kidnapped, I think, and I don't know what they want, but from what they said it sounded like ransom and—and—and . . ."

I sniffled away my tears as much as possible, it was getting embarrassing.

"Calm down now," he chuckled. "And what?"

"A long time ago," I said, "my father was reading the paper about some casino owner's son who'd gotten snatched up, and the whole time he was shaking his head. I was pretending to eat my breakfast, but secretly I was watching him. Then out of nowhere, he slammed the paper down and started to laugh."

"Laugh?"

"Yeah, he said that dumbass was actually going to pay them off and he couldn't believe it. Then he told me if that ever happened to me, I was shit out of luck—not because he couldn't afford it but because he couldn't afford to look weak in the eyes of his competitors. I know, it sounds like a joke, and I think he may have even thought it was—but it wasn't. I could see it in his face."

I turned away from them and sighed, frustrated.

"In other words, I'm as good as dead, I'm all alone, there's nothing I can do."

Even though I wasn't watching him, I could feel Asclepius's eyes on me, prying into my heart and mind, sizing me up, seeing if I had what it would take.

"Okay, you've convinced me," he said as he pulled a large silver skeleton key from his jacket pocket. "I'll take you on. We'll begin immediately."

"What do you mean?"

"Believe it or not, I've got some years under my belt," he said. "And I'm going to teach you what you need to know."

He slid the key into each of the locks binding me, and faster than I could blink, the chains dissolved into black grains of sand. I rubbed my wrists in amazement, unable to comprehend what was going on.

"Why did you chain me up?"

"I didn't know if you were dangerous or not, and you don't get to be as old as I am by taking chances."

"Fair enough," I finished drying my tears. "You said you were going to teach me—what exactly do you have in mind?"

"That all depends on your ultimate goal," he said. "Lesson one, I don't give a shit what kind of mess you're in or how you got there, I only care about the future and what you plan to do about it. You were saying that you're all alone, and that this is too daunting, whatever. Newsflash, kid: we're all alone, and the sooner you realize that and become self reliant, the better off you'll be and the easier this is going to come to you. So, what's it going to be, kid? What do you plan to do?"

I didn't even have to think about my reply.

"I'm going to kill them all."

III

Hypnagogia

Edric

❖

"I KNOW IT LOOKS LIKE A BIT OF A HIKE," Asclepius said. "But don't let me catch you complaining. You could use a little conditioning—I can't take on a slab of blubber as an apprentice, after all, not with what you want to accomplish."

Freed from my shackles, I was standing to the right of him while Sigmund stood on the left. I tried to get his attention, but it was no use; his eyes remained fixed on some distant point miles away. To him, I didn't exist. I was a figment of my own imagination.

"I don't mind walking," I replied. "Do you have a spare pair of shoes I can use?"

"Nope, but I'm sure we can find some back at the house, and the faster you walk, the faster we'll get there."

The trip was short but hard. The path was made up of cold, packed mud, the kind that feels gritty underfoot but doesn't make your feet sloppy. However, this mild inconvenience flipped as soon as I found out that the cool ground was the only reprieve I had from the sharp, flinty rocks that littered the trail. I yelped in pain once when my big toe crashed into a jagged stone sliver. Asclepius's only response to this outburst was a slap to the back of my head—from then on out, I restricted my cries to the occasional wince.

"Beautiful day, isn't it?" he said.

"I suppose so."

"I hate to break this atmosphere, but duty calls and I think we need to fit in as many lessons as possible."

"Agreed." I swallowed a lump remembering the smack, I didn't think Asclepius understood the concept of constructive criticism (though I would've settled for *nonviolent criticism*).

"How many of them are there that you know of?" he asked.

"I saw four," I replied, "but I think there might be another, because I didn't see anyone climb into the front seat—which means they probably have a driver."

"Very observant of you." He smiled and I loosened up a little bit. Maybe this wouldn't be so bad. "That'll serve you well, later. Five is tough—but there are ways around numbers. Ah, we're home."

We stood in front of the farm I'd seen earlier. The main residence was small and looked to only be one room with a roof made from wooden beams and bundles of straw.

"Sigmund," Asclepius said. "Go get our new friend Edric here a pair of boots."

Sigmund nodded, and with his eyes still zoning in and out, walked through the front door. I went to follow, but Asclepius's firm hand fell on my shoulder with a clap.

"While we wait, I'll teach you a couple other things. Do you have any idea where they're taking you?"

"No clue, I'm not even sure who these guys are yet."

"I figured as much, but I also figured that there's no harm in asking."

I nodded and Sigmund exited the house carrying a pair of light boots that looked like they were made from deerskin. He handed them to me and I thanked him.

"They aren't super fancy like something you'd usually wear," Asclepius said, "but I don't think you'll mind."

"Anything to help keep the rocks out is much appreciated," I said, dropping to one knee and tightening them. "What's next?"

"Good to see your enthusiasm!" he exclaimed. "Nothing personal, but I think I'm going to wade you into this, you know, start small and work your way to the harder stuff later. It's like learning to drink. Have you ever killed anyone before?"

"No," I laughed, but the humor seemed lost on him.

"Well it isn't easy, but once you know the basics, it'll be just like turning on a light switch—in more ways than one."

"How's that?"

"On one side is the physical aspect: what weapons to use, where to strike, when, how deep to go, etcetera. On the other hand, most people have a mental block that keeps them from killing. I'm going to teach you how to tear down that wall."

"Cool," I smiled. "That sounds interesting, can we learn that first?" He hesitated.

"As much as I would like to, you're not ready. As your teacher, sensei, master, whatever, you're going to have to trust me on that. When I think you're ready, or if necessity dictates, we'll get to the nasty bits. Do you trust me?"

He extended his hand and I took it.

"I have no reason not to, where do we start?"

"Here," he said, gesturing towards his house. "The reason I asked if you knew where they were taking you is because I was curious what kind of a building they were using for their base of operations. Whenever you have an elaborate scheme with multiple steps, set up a base somewhere that you can return to to regroup. For your training, this will be our base of operations."

"I understand, but there's a problem."

"That is?"

"I don't know where they're taking me. But setting that aside for now, how am I supposed to establish a base while in their captivity?"

"Don't you see? That's the beauty of it. They won't be expecting you to be so well prepared right under their noses. It's genius, really. And you're not playing Capture the Flag; you don't need to build a high-security multi-room bunker, you just need a hiding place—like a crawlspace, or a shed, or something."

"But if you're going to go through that much work to begin with, wouldn't it be better to escape?"

"Nope," he grimaced. "No siree, that's not what you told me you wanted to do. You said you wanted to make them pay."

"And I still do. Sorry, I was being curious."

"Don't worry, I'm going to teach you how to escape also, it comes as part of the package. But remember: if you trust me, you'll make it through."

I was going to have to stop questioning him if I wanted help. No matter how strange it all seemed, I swore to myself at that instant that I'd follow him no matter how crazy his lessons were. After all, even if he only had a brief understanding of combat and survival, that was already more than I knew on my own.

"Okay, I'll establish my own base the first chance I get," I replied. "This revenge thing is easy, what's next?"

"I'm afraid it's only going to get harder from here," he chuckled. "Do you have any acting experience?"

"A little, I spent a year in drama club."

"Better than nothing," he said. "Different people are going to respond to you differently, that's just the way of the world. What you need to learn to do is understand how certain people are going to react to you, and then use that to your advantage. In other words, acting scared and defenseless, and then turn around and be ruthless when they let their guard down. Remember B.E.E. yourself: Body language, Emotion, Expression. Let's practice. How do you think these guys see you?"

"Hard to tell, it's early, but so far I'd say I look an awful lot like a paycheck."

Asclepius laughed.

"What about that one that put those welts on your head?"

"Quick temper, seemed upset by my money . . ."

"If you can make someone mad at the drop of a hat, then you can control them. Do you think the others feel the same way as him?"

"I doubt it. If they did, they probably wouldn't have pulled him off me."

"You see, in a way, you already know these guys. The goal is to be unpredictable in an otherwise predictable climate. I'm impressed, Edric. I think you've got this, but let's roleplay a little just to make sure. I can't stress enough how important it is to your success . . ."

Ryan

❖

"I THINK WE'RE AS CLEAR as we're going to get for now," Wes said. "Let's get rid of these masks."

"About time," Jacob wheezed. "I was beginning to think that I was going to suffocate in this thing."

"Suck it up," Schafer replied. It was the first thing he'd said since punching Edric out. Even his voice made me sick. I couldn't look at him.

"You can't understand," Jacob mumbled. "My claustrophobia keeps getting worse, and believe it or not, having my head crammed into a glorified tube sock doesn't help."

I pulled my mask off and balled it up. Looking at it, I spotted a few random smears of blood that I could only assume had hit me when I shot the cop. I rubbed one of my hands through my sweaty hair, trying to make it look natural again.

"Take some of this," Nate said as he handed me a bottle of water. "For your eyes, I mean."

I opened the cap and drizzled a small stream of it onto my ski mask (on the opposite side of the blood) and began to scrub away at the shoe polish on my face. It was slow going at first, but eventually I scoured away most of it. There was still a slight hint of gray ringing my eyes, but it would have to do until I found a proper shower; and if I absolutely needed to I could lie and say I was one of *those* guys who thought that mascara helped complete their look.

"How's the driving treating you?" Nate called up to Wes. He shrugged.

"For the most part it's been pretty average, other than that first set of cops, of course. And by the way they sped past us, I think it's safe to say no one called in a description of our vehicle."

"Even so," Nate said. "Don't get too comfortable. I want all of you as alert as mongooses on speed until we get back to the house."

"Don't worry about it," Wes said. "I haven't screwed up yet, right? I've been stopping at every light, not making eye contact with our other motorist friends, and even pulled out of the way like a good citizen when those cops appeared out of nowhere. Satisfied?"

No one could deny that. So far Wesley had performed his job to the letter, but as he tried to put us at ease, he'd made an interesting point. Two minutes after we exited the neighborhood across from the school, two patrol cars sped past us heading in the opposite direction. As soon as I caught that shimmering glare of red and blue through the windshield, my heart sank. I could've sworn we were finished, but it didn't get to Wesley. He merely pulled over, waited for them to pass, and then continued on his merry way. At the time my adrenaline was pumping, so I didn't pay it too much mind, but as the seconds ticked by inside the quiet van, my curious nature got the better of me.

"I have a question."

"Go for it."

"You've been in high speed chases, right?"

"Correct."

"And you've never been caught?"

"Also correct."

"Well I was wondering, when a cop is all lit up and speeding towards you like that one a few minutes ago, how can you tell that he's on the way to another call and not after you?"

Wesley paused thoughtfully as he cut through two alleys and merged back onto a main road, passing diners advertising specialty chilies and fresh seafood.

"Like most things it depends on the situation," he replied. "For instance, we weren't speeding, so they weren't going to pull us over for that—and had they known who we were—that is, rotten kidnapping bastards—they probably would have pulled into our lane head-on to block us. Not to mention, even if they had pulled us over, I would have waited until they were out of the car and approaching my door before taking off—this van isn't going to be able to outrun a Crown Victoria, so I'll take whatever head start I can get."

"That makes enough sense."

"If experience has taught me anything," Wesley continued, "it's that the most important thing to learn on the road to becoming a successful criminal is to improvise and think on your feet."

"Survival of the fittest," I murmured.

"Exactly."

Edric

WE FINISHED MY EMOTION TRAINING and I felt drained. I would have been content to pass out on the spot, but Asclepius perked up and I knew my day wasn't finished. No rest for the wicked.

"Good news," he said. "You may not know this, but even though your brain is sleeping, your ears aren't—let me guess, you're a light sleeper?"

"Yeah, how did you know?"

"Even though you may not be technically conscious, I know everything that's going on around you, I can sense it."

He walked over to me, crouched down, and drew in the sand at my feet.

"What does this have to do with my ears?"

"Since your nap started, I've learned all of their names."

He stepped back and five portraits stared up at me from the ground. I knew he'd composed them from nothing more than sand and stones, but they were vivid, to say the least. The way the wind swirled made them come to life, blinking and breathing.

"Pay attention," he said. "By learning their names you add yet another layer of personality to yourself and it'll make it much more difficult for them to treat you less than human.

This is Ryan, Jacob, Nate, Wesley, but his friends call him Wes, and Schafer."

My eyes froze on the last portrait.

"What's the matter?" he asked.

"That's the one that put me here."

"Oh really?" Asclepius said. "Then you're going to love this. Compare these last two portraits."

I scrolled between the images of Wes and Schafer, the resemblance was uncanny.

"They're related, aren't they?"

"That's a good guess," Asclepius said. "I imagine they're brothers, and you know what that means?"

"That's another weapon in my arsenal?"

"Precisely, you can use one to get at the other if the need arises."

Everything was beginning to come together. In retrospect my plan seemed pretty half-assed: how on earth was I, a teenage boy, going to break out and then seek revenge on my oversized captors? But now that my training had begun and Asclepius seemed dedicated to the cause, I had hope.

Then I was hit with a splitting headache that radiated from the back of my eyes all the way out the top of my skull. When I regained focus, the whole world shifted on its axis below my feet.

"What's happening?" I said, trying to keep my balance.

"Relax," Asclepius said, wiping the portraits in the sand away with a single sweep of his hand. "You're leaving is all, it isn't a big deal."

The air got thick and warped, everything looked like I was viewing it through a pane of glass smeared with grease. My eyes fluttered as voices and sounds from the outside ripped their way into existence all around me. I didn't know how much longer I was going to last.

"Leaving?" I called. "But I still have so much I need to know! Please, I can't go yet!"

"Don't worry," Asclepius replied. I could barely make him out through the haze, but I could see his grin literally stretching all the way between his ears. "You'll be back."

"How do you know?"

"I have a really good feeling is all. Remember, trust me."

Ryan
❖

OUR VAN PULLED DOWN a deserted avenue lined with chain link fences, spools of barbed wire, and dilapidated warehouses. At the end of the street, looming like the derelict skeleton of some extinct creature, was a morbid gray parking garage. It looked dirty, like decades of grime and pollution had decided to cling to its carcass, parasites of the surrounding city.

"That's our destination straight ahead," Nate said. "And not a single soul in sight, how perfect could this be?"

"Remember to take your own advice, please. *Stay alert.*" Schafer shook his head. "I don't need to tell you how pathetic it would be if it was our mastermind of a leader who was the first one to get caught."

"Relax, I haven't popped the cork on the champagne yet."

Shadow rolled over us as we entered the complex and began the steep climb up to the third floor. The wheels squealed as Wes steered frantically, trying to make our spiral up the ramp as smooth as possible. I looked out the window at the black swirls of graffiti, interlaced with violent shots of sunlight from the porthole windows jammed into the walls of the structure. As we reached our destination, the van gave one more squeak before dying; we rolled to an abrupt halt. Wes cranked the key three times, but it was no good.

"Just be lucky it happened here," Schafer said. I'm not sure who this was supposed to be a threat towards, or if anyone else even registered it as one.

"Okay, everyone, we move the kid last. The less time he's exposed the better off we'll be," Nate said.

"Are we leaving everything?" Jacob asked, unbuckling his seatbelt.

"No, we're taking it with us. The less evidence the cops have to go off, the better. I want to be back on the road within five minutes—only bad things can come from having a random passerby call in some suspicious individuals hanging out in an abandoned garage. Am I clear?" Nate's voice was serious, but his expression had lightened considerably since the day started. He'd never admit to it, but I think even he was surprised that his plan had gone off so flawlessly.

We opened our doors, lifting the curtain to reveal our new ride. It was another full-size van, the kind that's designed to hold families who don't know when to stop having kids. It was the color of red wine and had limo black tinted windows. I didn't need to have the back door opened to know that its backseat had been removed also.

We started by moving our disguises and weapons, then made sure all of our guns were reloaded and hidden underneath their owners' seats, just in case things got messy on the way back to base. Opening the new van was like opening a sarcophagus; it was empty, quiet, and cold on the inside. Nate did a quick walkthrough of the first van, cleaning up any obvious evidence (like Edric's blood). The last piece of equipment to make the trip over was Schafer's blue tackle box.

"So when are you going to tell us what's inside?" I asked.

"Only if and when I need to."

"Ryan, do me a favor and open the back door, would you?" Nate called to me.

I made my way over and popped open the back. The hold was carpeted and more expansive. Edric would have the room to stretch out and sleep for most of the trip, which is the least he deserved after the hell we'd put him through so far. One other detail caught my eye: a piece of carpet on the right side had been pulled up to reveal a metal bar set into the floor.

"Who's going to move him?" Nate asked.

"I vote you and Schafer," Jacob replied. "There's no sense in any of us leaving DNA on him, you guys have already grabbed him once."

Nate and Schafer shrugged.

"He has a point," Schafer said.

They rolled him to the edge of the back, and once again with Nate at the feet and Schafer at the head, they carried him across the parking lot. He groaned groggily.

"I think he's waking up," Schafer said.

"Let's hurry," Nate replied.

They tossed him in the back and Nate followed.

"Give me your knife," he said.

Schafer reached in his jeans and brought out a large pocketknife with a fake wood finish. Nate unfolded the blade and cut Edric's restraints.

"Jacob," Nate called over his shoulder. "Bring me the cuffs."

Jacob came around the corner and handed Nate a pair of handcuffs and leg irons, and they weren't the cheap kind you can pick up at a sex shop for ten bucks. These were police grade through and through. He tore Edric's shoes off and slid on the leg irons; they were a snug fit but didn't seem too bad. Then, he contorted Edric's arms so that he could loop the chain of the handcuffs through the metal bar in the floor before clasping them on his hands.

"Do I want to ask where you got those?" I said.

"No," Nate replied. "Not really. Let's get out of here."

The doors shut.

Edric

THE IMPACT OF MY HEAD on the carpet was the last shock I needed to wake up, but for some reason my limbs wouldn't do what I was telling them. Something, an invisible cloud, had wrapped my body in numbness, making it impossible to move. I felt the straps that had cocooned me give way, then heard the methodical metallic clicking of the new restraints being put in their place, followed by six loud slams as my mobile cell was secured once again.

Worst of all though was how I felt. My head was still sore from the punches, but that was just the start of it. Every pore on my body prickled with iciness, like someone had rolled me in a pit of vodka and needles. Was this a side effect of leaving Asclepius and Sigmund, or do all people feel this way after being knocked out? Through raw willpower alone I was able to open my eyes.

The first thing I saw was a large caramel colored cockroach a couple of inches away from my face, staring at me while it kissed my exposed cheek with its flickering antennae. Whether it had hitched a ride on me from the previous car, or been in this van all along, was something I didn't feel like thinking about. I blew at it until it scurried off to hide in a corner.

I tested the handcuffs on my wrists; whoever had put them on was kind enough to leave a little breathing room (the same couldn't be said for the ones around my ankles). I moved into a crouch and tested the chain; it held. I let out a deep sigh and plopped back down on the van floor. Wherever they had planned to take me, it looked like I was along for the ride.

I didn't think my crash landing had been that loud, but apparently it was, because no sooner had my body settled into its new resting place that one of my captors shuffled around in his seat to have a look at me. I recognized him from Asclepius's sketch as Ryan. We made eye contact, which was strange, because instead of snitching on me outright he waited, like he was deliberating whether or not it was worth sounding the alarm. After what seemed like an eternity (but couldn't have been more than two seconds, tops) he shut his eyes and turned around.

"He's awake," Ryan said.

IV

Atropos

Ryan

❖

WE WERE LEAVING THE CITY, only the highest points of Seattle's skyline found their way past the lip of the back windows. It should have been a relief; there hadn't been any roadblocks or highway side marquees lit up with recollections of our visit (two things Nate had mentioned he was worried about). But with one ordeal behind us, a much more immediate one was revealed.

"Group meeting," Nate said. He motioned for all five of us to lean into a huddle; it was the most privacy we could come up with. "We might have a problem."

"How so?" Schafer glared.

"I didn't think Edric would be conscious so soon."

To illustrate this point, Edric groaned from behind us.

"Why is that a problem?" I asked.

"We haven't hit the back roads yet," Wes whispered over his shoulder. "Shit, Seattle is still in view. This kid isn't dumb. The longer he's awake, the more clues he's going to have to backtrack to our hideout after we've handed him over."

"But, if we're sticking to the plan," I retorted, "then it shouldn't matter. After we hand him over we're leaving anyway."

Nate thought this over then shook his head.

"If he leads them back to the house, they might still find something that can point them in the right direction."

"Fine." I threw my hands up. Sometimes it's obvious when you're outnumbered, and I was angry. "But just talking about it isn't going to help, indecision stands a better chance of getting us caught than that kid back there. So what are we going to do?"

We all looked at Nate, curious how our leader would handle this new wrinkle in his plan.

"I know this was my idea and I'm the one who's responsible," he mumbled. "But I'm not going to come to a decision about this one by myself. We all have to agree, alright? This blood is on all of our hands. It wouldn't be right for me to say, we're going to do *this*, or to tell someone that they don't have a say. My recommendation is we put one of the ski masks on him backwards. It won't make him blind or anything, but it'll be enough to obscure his vision so he can't read road signs."

"SOMEONE HELP ME!" Edric screeched from the back. "SOMEONE PLEASE! LET ME GO YOU BASTARDS!"

"That's a good enough plan," Jacob said. "But what about that? We can't stop somewhere if he's going to scream—I guess we could gag him underneath the mask?"

"Nope," Schafer frowned. "I refuse to gag a hostage."

We all turned in shock. Schafer, the man who punched out a sixteen-year-old earlier in the day apparently had some kind of code of ethics when it came to kidnapping. He laughed at our expressions.

"Don't think I'm soft or anything," he started. "I had some friends kidnap a fourteen year old girl a few years back; she wouldn't stop screaming either, so they gagged her . . ."

"GOD DAMN IT! DO YOU KNOW WHO I AM? LET ME GO!"

"So they left her alone to go do, I don't know, something—and when they came back she was dead . . ."

"THESE CUFFS ARE CUTTING INTO MY WRISTS! PLEASE, I'LL DO WHATEVER YOU WANT! JUST—LET—ME—GO!"

"When they undid her, they found that the gag had been forced back into her mouth and that she had choked on her own tongue."

"That's impossible," I said.

"That's what I thought too," Schafer continued. "But apparently one of the guys had punched her once or twice and her teeth had cut the thing that kept it anchored to the floor of her mouth. It was nasty, man. He had a picture of her in his wallet. From her collarbones up she was black, like someone had smeared ink all over her. Her throat was all contorted too, bulging with veins sticking out everywhere. After seeing that, I swore I'd never use a gag on someone."

"Ah, you really are just a big sweetheart," Jacob smirked.

"I guess," he shrugged. "That and corpses don't have a very high rate of return."

"Any other ideas?" Nate said, rubbing his temples. Nate is as mentally tough as anyone, but the laundry list of stressful issues that kept popping up was wearing on him.

"I could always go with the fisticuffs approach again," Schafer said.

"Definitely not," I spat.

"Why?" Wes called back. "If he keeps this up, it's going to turn into a situation where it's either him or us, and fast."

"And you don't find the brutality of it sickening at all?"

"We never actually promised that we wouldn't rough him up . . ." He shrugged.

"Well I vote NO," I said. "And I'm not going to change my mind either. Next?"

There was silence as we all weighed the possibilities.

"Guys?" Edric called, sniffling. Was he crying? "My father won't pay you, he's too fucking stubborn."

"He'll pay," Schafer said. "Even if we have to start sending fingers to him first class mail in little padded envelopes."

This shut him up—but we still didn't have a solution.

"So that's it then, seriously?" I said. "We either strangle him or beat him senseless? Great plan, guys."

"There is another option," Schafer said. "I didn't want to suggest it, but here goes nothing."

Schafer pulled his cerulean tackle box onto his lap and opened it up. Inside was a neat little line of syringes, and opposite of them, a handful of glass vials holding some kind of clear liquid.

"I'm afraid to ask," I said. "Is it heroin?"

"Not at all," Schafer laughed. "This is atropine, a drug made from deadly nightshade—among other things."

"And this will solve our problem?" Nate said skeptically. "Getting Edric fucked up on this? Sounds dangerous."

"You guys worry too much," Schafer chuckled. "Just because it's made with nightshade doesn't mean it's lethal. Legit hospitals use this stuff every day."

"Where did you get it though—that's the real question—and the needles? If it's mixed with something else, we're screwed," Jacob said.

"I made it myself." He rolled his eyes. "You know how our little home away from home in the woods serves as more than just a base of operations for this mission? This is another one. I got bored one day and flipped through some medical and chemistry books until I found something I could make from the local flora."

"Have you," I started, trying to find my words. "You know—tried it?"

"Well, yeah," Schafer laughed. "Remember how I said I was bored? Necessity is the mother of invention. It wasn't too bad, just made me drowsy with some minor hallucinations. Wes can vouch for me here."

We looked to the driver's seat. Wes met our stares with a shrug and a smile.

"It actually feels pretty good, and I'm a grown man. Edric would probably float the rest of the trip if we shoot him up."

"And you really don't think it'll kill him?" I had to make sure; by then I'd made it my personal crusade to make the rest of Edric's time with us as pleasant as possible. Wes and Schafer nodded.

"I vote we do it," Jacob said. "It beats the crap out of the alternatives."

Wes and Schafer quickly followed with their votes—and then Nate did as well. It was up to me. Reluctantly, I gave my approval. I would be lying if I said that the whole affair didn't make me nervous, but I wasn't about to give Schafer another chance to get punchy.

"That settles it," Schafer said, looking around at the other lanes for cops before unbuckling his seatbelt. "This is a two-man operation. Ryan, do you want to inject or restrain?"

It's strange; even though I'd shot and killed a man earlier, the thought of stabbing someone with a syringe and pushing the plunger turned my stomach.

"I'll hold him down," I said. "Wait to load the needle; we don't need to get stuck by accident when he's thrashing. I'll go in first, you follow."

I climbed over the seat. Edric had his eyes shut tight with a small pool of tears moistening the carpet below his head. I put my hand on his back first so I didn't startle him.

"Relax," I said. "We're going to give you something to help take the edge off."

"I don't want it," he mumbled. "Leave me alone."

Schafer had finished loading the needle. I saw him spraying a thin line of fluid onto the ceiling of the van, checking it. I nodded at him and he climbed over also. Edric took this as a sign to start struggling. I repositioned so that my knee was in his back and I held his arms down.

"Relax," I repeated.

"We're not going to be able to do his arm," Schafer said. "Not with him struggling like this."

"Is that a problem?"

"Not really."

"What are you doing?" Edric screeched through gritted teeth. "What are you giving me?"

Schafer jabbed the needle through the seat of Edric's pants, paused for a second, then pressed the plunger down.

"A lullaby," Schafer said.

Edric

I'M NOT SURE HOW MUCH of the pain from the needle was mental, but it was enough to make me gag and start coughing. After they'd finished, Schafer and Ryan crossed back over the seat, taking the needle with them. I guess they didn't want to give me a weapon, or risk me picking my cuffs. I hoped—no, *prayed* —that the needle was clean; I didn't want to escape only to die from infection or disease later.

I could actually *feel* my pupils dilate, and as the seconds ticked away, the air conditioning vents emptied more and more purple and black smoke into the car. Soon I couldn't see anything, and all of the sounds of the road disappeared, camouflaged by the beating of my own heart. My back lifted off the floor, and then I found myself standing in an empty dark void.

"Hello?"

"I told you you'd be back soon," Asclepius said. He stepped out of the shadows no more than five feet away. He had been there all along, but remaining so perfectly still that I hadn't noticed.

"Thank God," I replied. "I thought I was stranded. Are we in the same place?"

"You betcha, it's nighttime is all. Sigmund is in bed, he won't be joining us. Lights!"

At this, a massive glowing moon appeared in the sky, spilling a wave of pale light into the center of the field a few hundred feet away. We were still in the dark, but at least I could see my hand in front of my face.

"That's amazing . . ."

"Get used to it. I only have a couple of lessons for you tonight, easy stuff. Think you can handle it?"

"I've been doing pretty well so far, haven't I?" before I could finish I felt his hand come down across my face.

"Arrogance makes you stupid," he said. "Even if it's true, don't lure yourself into thinking that way—it'll only make you careless. Understand? It's better to prove it than talk about it."

I agreed before wiping the blood away from my nose on the back of my hand; it left sticky, rust colored streaks.

"Tonight we're going to learn about the dark, and how it can be your best ally. Remember how I revealed myself to you? If you need to hide, find a dark place and don't move, shut out all distractions, only expose yourself and run if someone is literally breathing right on top of you."

"What if they're coming for me, wouldn't it be better to get a head start?"

"Not necessarily," he said. "The dark also works against you, it plays tricks on people's eyes. Someone might start walking towards you because they think they saw something—but that doesn't mean that something was you, get me?"

"Don't come out of hiding unless I need to."

"Perfect," he smiled. He pulled a six-shooter from the holster on his belt, popped open the cylinder, and loaded three rounds. "Let's practice."

"What do you mean?" He thumbed back the hammer.

"You should hide now, if you'd be so kind."

He lifted the gun in the air and fired over my head. The muzzle flash illuminated the surrounding field, making the shadows come alive in the grass. I dropped to the ground and scurried away on my hands and knees.

"One and a two and a three," he laughed.

I moved in a zigzag pattern initially, but soon realized I was almost straight ahead from where I started. That wouldn't work, not if I wanted to stay alive.

"Fivesixseveneightnineten, ready or not!" He fired again; this shot shredded the grass five feet to my left. I could feel the impact the hot lead made with the ground. I dropped to my stomach and began to slide slowly to my right.

"Not bad, kid," he called out. "I half expected you to jump up and take off."

I didn't answer, just held my breath.

"Oh, have you gone quiet on me? Eh, we're almost done anyway. One to go . . ."

I could hear the hammer click back again, then the trigger, then the soft hiss of the firing pin. The bullet flew past me, I don't know how close it was, but it left a small charred streak on the back of my shirt—I didn't move.

"Okay, we've finished that lesson. Olly olly oxen free!"

I found my legs (they were below me and shaking) and walked back to Asclepius. He looked pleased. I vomited a little and wiped away the remnants; the streaks of bile matched the blood.

"You've exceeded my expectations," he said. "Good work."

"Those weren't real bullets, were they?"

"What do you mean?"

"Never mind. What should I do next?" I wasn't looking forward to risking my life again—but then I remembered the oath I had taken; I'd trust Asclepius no matter what. At least I felt alive.

"Only one more for tonight," he said. "And it's just rein-forcement of the whole stay-out-of-the-light thing."

"I don't know," I chuckled. "That wasn't enough reinforce-ment?" He slapped me again.

"There's no such thing." His focus moved to the distance where the cylinder of moonlight had fallen on the field. Instead of the green grass that had been there before, there was only a charred circle of fire. "And this will be good for your condi-tioning."

The ring of light began to creep slowly towards us.

"What do you want me to do?" He pointed in the opposite direction.

"I want you to run—and don't stop. Remember, light can be both detrimental to your goals and your health. Good luck, until next time . . ."

The light was beginning to pick up speed. I decided to get whatever kind of a head start I could and took off. The grass wasn't easy to run in. Sure it was softer on my feet than the rocky path had been, but every time my hands dropped, my fingers and knuckles scraped against the deceptively soft blades. It was like getting wicked paper cuts.

Soon I was sprinting, but the searing glow continued to get closer and closer. I didn't know how much longer I was going to last, but I remembered Asclepius's advice and kept on running. The flames licked at my heels as the field spontane-ously combusted in a wave of golden sparks. I was about to give in to my screaming muscles when suddenly my feet failed to find the next step and I was falling through the air. I had stepped off the edge of the world.

As I fell, I turned around to face the burning mass of earth suspended in space and caught one last glimpse of my tormenter. It hadn't been the moon—it was a giant magnifying glass.

Ryan

WE EXITED THE HIGHWAY and a lush green forest met us. Somehow the claustrophobic nature of the trees on both sides of the road was comforting. Everyone in the car let out a collective sigh of relief, the hardest part was behind us. Edric had been quiet since Schafer dosed him with the atropine, peaceful even. I hated myself for thinking that drugging a defenseless boy had been a stroke of genius—but it was hard to argue with the results.

"How are you doing, Wes?" Nate asked.

"I'm okay, could stretch my legs though. Do you want to make a stop?"

"I want to make THE stop," Nate corrected. "There's a gas station about five miles up ahead, the one we stopped at on the way here. I'm thinking we grab some food, refuel, and then drive the rest of the night. We should be home by tomorrow morning at this pace. It's also probably best to do this while Edric is still in dreamland. Any objections?"

For the first time during the trip there was no grumbling.

"Good," Nate smiled. "Let me be the first to congratulate you all. By this time next week, we'll all be millionaires."

V

Narcolepsy

Edric

THE PRICKLY CARPET against my back reassured me that I'd landed safely. It might sound like a small blessing, but with being ricocheted back and forth between Asclepius's quality time and the wringer of reality, I was more than willing to take whatever mercies I could get.

The van had stopped moving.

I winced and took a quick look around. From my position on the floor all I could see was a lone street lamp with a collection of moths hovering around it. Had we reached our destination already? If so, why hadn't they moved me? I could tell they were still in the car, but I wasn't about to peek over the seat to find out what they were doing. Being that curious was like asking for another black eye.

There was a swarm of mumbling, but I couldn't make out a syllable. All I could do was hope that they weren't discussing where to hide my body if things got nasty.

Ryan

"I TRUST YOU ALL NOT TO DO anything stupid," Nate said; Wes screeched the van into park. "This is a quick trip. Remember, grab whatever you're going to need for the rest of the car ride, stretch your legs, then let's get back on the road."

"Someone's in a hurry to start counting his money," Jacob said. We all laughed. I smiled; it felt like it had been forever since my last.

"One of us should stay behind and keep an eye on him just in case. Any volunteers?" Nate eyed the rest of us. I was about to raise my hand but Schafer beat me to it.

"I can babysit," he said. "Should be a breeze, I can still hear him snoring."

"Okay then," Nate said. "Let's go, I'm starving."

We all hopped out of the van. I had a blinding, momentary flash of the kidnapping but shook it away. No one else seemed to notice my pained expression.

"I'll get the gas," Schafer said. None of us objected. "Pay for it with cash at the counter—pay for all of it with cash. I hate paper trails."

"Do you want anything?" Wes asked.

"As long as it's sweet I don't care. None of what they try to pass off as meat in there, it really screws me up."

We nodded and walked across the parking lot. I could faintly hear the gas cap pop off and fuel flowing as the little bell rang over the top of the entrance, announcing our arrival to the clerks.

The inside had probably once served as a general store and tourist trap all rolled into one, with its wooden shelves and pleasant old men working behind the counter. The tall coolers lined with fluorescent soda bottles and greasy metal rollers rotating hotdogs and sausages seemed almost alien in the nostalgic glow of the overhead lights. Wes picked up a candy bar in each hand and debated which to bring back to his brother.

"What are you having?" he asked, like somehow my tastes would help solve his chocolaty dilemma.

"Something warm," I said. "Actually, can you get me a pretzel or a burger or something? I need to take a piss."

"Yeah, if we're not still in here meet me back at the car."

The bathroom was tucked away at the end of a long hallway out of sight. The walls were a vortex of wood collapsing into a montage of glossy porn magazine clippings that'd been glued and laminated to every surface. This swirl of flesh ended at a lone, bright red door with a unisex placard in its center. I nudged the door open with my knuckles (any opportunity to avoid leaving fingerprints) and stepped into the empty room.

I stared into the mirror, turned on the faucet, and scrubbed away the rest of the shoe polish crust caked around my eyes. Something about seeing my reflection made me lose control, it all suddenly felt so concrete, and before my legs could completely disintegrate, I grabbed the rim of the sink with both hands and puked hot foaming bile into the basin.

"You can do this," I said with a half laugh, trying my best to keep my sweaty hair from tickling my face. "You're almost there. You're almost home."

I wiped my mouth and returned my gaze to the mirror. Once the blood vessels in my eyes softened and I could pass as a weary traveler again, I left the bathroom, and the last traces of spit and acid trickled down the drain.

Edric

I COUNTED MY CAPTORS as they left the van on my fingers (a one and a two and a three and a four and one potato more). They all got out—had they really left me alone? My heart leapt—only to be crushed again when I recognized my personal favorite, Schafer, had been left behind to make sure I didn't get too clever in their absence. I sagged back to the floor as he unscrewed the gas cap and shoved the nozzle into place.

"Think," I muttered to myself. I knew talking was risky, so I kept my voice low and out of the danger zone. "I can't make a run for it, I'm still stuck in these damn cuffs, and Schafer is probably faster than me. It looks like escaping is out for now."

I peeked out the window again. The gas kicked off. Schafer grabbed the hose and attached it back to the side of the pump. That's when it hit me: just because I couldn't escape didn't mean that this was a wasted opportunity. If I was going to seize it, I'd have to act fast.

I took my fingertips and tapped them on the window next to Schafer's head. At first he looked around trying to find the source of the noise. Once he realized it was me, his features hardened. I grinned even though he couldn't see me through the smoky glass; this would be easier than I'd thought. Initially he was going to open the back to talk to me, but then, thinking better of it, he walked around to the side door and climbed into the middle seat.

"Hello, Edric," he said. "How's it hanging, buddy?"

"Buddy?" I smirked. "So we're friends now, is that it?"

"I just thought maybe you weren't in the condition to be yelled at."

"I feel fine," I said. "And Schafer? You and me will never be friends."

"How do you know my name?"

"That isn't important. The only thing you should be focused on right now is how fucked you are. You're so stupid you haven't even realized the gravity of this situation yet. But trust me, you'll know before this is over, when it's all raining down on your empty—little—head."

"What did you say to me?" Believe it or not, this was actually a question. He was in total disbelief.

"You heard me fine, but don't feel bad; I know I threw some big words out there and you're just too retarded to grasp the full meaning of them. Should I repeat myself?"

"No." Schafer's mouth twisted into some inhuman smile. I was *so* close.

"That's too bad," I replied. "I feel like repeating it anyway, and there's nothing you can do about it. You see, let me start by saying you're an idiot."

He climbed over the seat, grabbed me by the shirt, and flipped me onto my back. With my hands bound above my head I looked like some kind of trophy wench from an old barbarian comic book. I was helpless—perfect.

"Are you going to continue?" he asked. "Or did I come all the way back here for nothing?"

"I'm just getting started."

All of the color drained from his face, and what could have been considered a smile was gone; only hard lines of intense hatred remained carved into his cheeks and forehead.

"When I was in highschool I once hit someone so hard that they were hospitalized," he said, looking his right hand over. "They weren't released for like three weeks, you know? I jostled his brain and he needed stitches, and all of that."

"Is there a point to this?" I groaned.

"The point is that three weeks is a long time—and I'm aching to see if I can break my record."

Ryan

❖

I REJOINED NATE, Jacob, and Wesley at the front counter, huddled around our food like a campfire. The cashier was ringing it up one item at a time, and he wasn't in a hurry.

"You fellas must have worked up quite an appetite," he said. "Did you have a long day?"

"You know it," Nate smiled.

"Do you guys got it, or do you need me to spot you some cash?" I asked.

"We're cool," Wes replied as the geezer scanned the last item. "We're also paying for the gas on pump one."

He gave us our total and Wes dropped a wad of wrinkled money on the counter.

"Good thing payday is coming up," he whispered to me. "This is the last of what I've got."

Nate and Jacob each grabbed a stuffed paper sack and we left, the bell ringing a goodbye behind us. I should have been in a more cheery mood, the old man didn't seem to expect a thing, and we were about to get back in our safe, warm van. More importantly, I'd get to see Madison soon and finally know that she was safe.

But something was very wrong.

I think I knew for certain when I didn't see Schafer by the car, but what really sealed the deal was the subtle rocking of the suspension. You wouldn't have noticed if you weren't looking for it, but sure enough, it was there. That's what propelled my walk into a sprint, kicking up loose gravel and broken glass as I ran to the wide-open side door.

Schafer had again mounted Edric's chest and was wailing on him with both fists. There were three or four open cuts on his face, and every time Schafer hit him, blood would splatter onto the carpet around his head. Thank God Edric was unconscious, he was oblivious to the pain. I didn't have time to fully crawl over the seat, so I motioned for Nate to hurry up, balled my fist, and hit Schafer in the nose as hard as my odd angle would allow. He stopped mid-punch and grabbed at his face.

"Knock it off, man, unless you want some too," he growled between his fingers.

"Get off him!" I snarled, my fist coiled and ready to strike again.

"I'm serious," Schafer said, getting ready to continue his assault.

"So am I!" I spat back and swung again. This time my fist hit nothing but air before connecting with one of the van's windows. I got lucky, it didn't crack.

"What in the hell is going on?" Nate said, tossing the bag in next to me. "Holy shit—is he even alive?"

"I don't know," Schafer chuckled. He leaned down near Edric's face before nodding. "He's still breathing, so I guess that's a yes. What did Wes get me? It better not be some sort of jalapeno cheese hotdog."

I grabbed him by the shirt and pulled him in deadly close.

"I knew working with you was a bad idea."

"Oh yeah?" he replied. "If it wasn't for me this plan would've never worked in the first place, *Cop Killer*. None of you got any balls. Get the fuck off me."

He climbed over the seat and wiped his gory hand off on his pants.

"Jacob," Nate said quietly. "Get back there and see if you can clean him up, stop the bleeding if possible. Wes, start the car, we need to get out of here. And Schafer? You ever do anything like that again, I'll kill you myself. Understand?"

I saw Schafer ball his fist—then it relaxed. If he wanted to get paid he was going to have to put up with Nate until the ransom was collected.

"Whatever," he said. "If he didn't want some of my own personal anesthesia then he shouldn't talk so much. By the way, do you guys have any idea how he knows my name?"

"Your name? I don't know, maybe he overheard us talking or something. Who cares? Get in the car, we're leaving," Nate said.

"So did you guys get a new ride? Pretty nice, if I do say so myself," an unfamiliar voice said from behind us. We froze and turned around slowly.

The voice belonged to a greasy gas station attendant dressed in worn overalls and a red hat smudged in a dozen different fluids. He was eyeing us curiously, not suspiciously (a good start).

"What do you mean?" Nate asked.

"The other day you were here and you had an old rust bucket, right? If I'm not mistaken that is. Not many people come through these parts, I'm pretty sure it was you folks."

"Oh, yeah, that was us," Nate recovered. "The other one finally decided to die on us, so we picked this one up in Seattle. It wasn't cheap, but it's been worth it."

"I'll bet, how much about?"

"Around twenty thousand, I can't remember the exact price."

"No shit, that isn't too bad at all. Would you mind if I took a look inside? I've never been in one of those big passenger vans."

He went to climb in; Nate was at a loss for words. Before he could see anything incriminating, I grabbed his shoulder and spoke up.

"Actually, we're in a hurry and my son is incredibly sick in the back, so it's a huge disgusting mess. I just want to get home."

He paused before nodding.

"So that's what all the commotion was about. I was a little worried someone was dying."

"Nothing like that," I forced a laugh. "But I think he might have the flu, so the sooner we get him out of here the better."

"Yeah, it's probably better I don't poke my nose in there, I'm on the clock anyway and the bathroom isn't going to clean itself. You folks have a safe trip."

"See you later," Nate and I said, waving in unison, realizing how massive the bullet was we'd just dodged.

"How does he look, Jake?" Nate called over his shoulder.

"He's a mess, but he'll live," he said, buckling his seatbelt. "We should probably bandage him up when we get back though."

Nate turned to me.

"Are you surviving?"

"Yeah, but I need to stop thinking for a little bit," I replied. "Wesley, I'll drive this next leg."

Edric

WHAT HAD ONCE BEEN tinted windows with a fading sky melted together to form a solid stone wall. The smoothness of the glass shattered and crumbled into dust, giving the cave texture. I could hear water dripping somewhere, but behind that was the roar of some unseen river. The dark room had a dim orange glow thanks to a solitary lantern hung on the wall with a railroad spike. Everything smelled like a coal fire.

The sound of crying hinges yanked my attention to the other side of the room as Asclepius entered from a hidden door. Its face was flush with the rock to my right, almost impossible to see.

"How are you this fine evening?" he said with his character-istic scowl. "You sure didn't take your time getting back here."

"Call me an eager learner," I replied.

"I guess it beats the alternative," he concluded. "Today's lesson is a combination of things. At its purest though, you'll be learning how to escape from an enclosure. I don't need to explain why this one is important, do I? You're not that dense."

"No, I think I got it. Where do we begin?"

"We already have," he said, walking back to where he'd entered. "This isn't rocket science, kid. You get out, you pass—if not, then you fail and I leave you in here to rot."

"Oh thanks," I groaned, as a serious wave of déjà vu rolled over me. It seemed like risking my life was going to be a reoccurring theme whenever I was blessed with Asclepius's presence. "No words of wisdom before you go?"

"Well, since you're being so pushy, consider this: you've already been taught everything you need to know to get out of this place. Examine your surroundings and you'll find your way."

With this, he bowed to excuse himself and left through the door. This was followed by the metallic clicking of the entrance's inner workings sealing me in. I stood up and pulled the lantern off the wall; I wasn't going to wait around and find out what other encouragement Asclepius had left for me. By "encouragement" I mean that the room was bound to start filling with leeches or acid any second.

First, I examined the door. It was made from thick planks and was sturdy, but didn't look impenetrable. I sat my lantern down and walked back to the chair I had been sitting in and lifted it. I knew Asclepius wouldn't want me to use brute force to pass one of his challenges, but it was worth a shot. It's always better to be scolded than dead.

Like a batter stepping up to the plate, I wound back and swung the chair. The legs buckled as soon as it made contact and the rest was reduced to splinters. I picked up a couple of pieces to get a better look at them, someone (and I don't have to tell you who) had sawed each part of the chair most of the way through. I probably could have broken it over my own back without injury.

I was about to continue my search when the flame in the lantern started to flicker and burn low. Asclepius hadn't even given me a full five minutes worth of oil. I silently swore at him, and using my teeth, ripped a length of cloth from my shirt. Then I wrapped it around one of the discarded pieces of chair and dipped it inside. It's amazing how resourceful you can be when you're alone, in the dark, and fearing for your life. My torch caught, but I didn't know how long it would last. I'd have to hustle.

Among the loose black stones I found a pile of human bones made brown and brittle from age. For the most part, they were unorganized and scattered about; ribs next to femurs next to fingers next to spines. However, the skulls were stacked in a neat little pyramid; their empty sockets stared at where I'd been sitting before. I counted fourteen, but the gritty crunch of teeth under my feet as I crossed the room suggested many more out of sight. I imagined they were Asclepius's failed protégés, but there'd be time for figuring that out later.

As my light passed over the forgotten graveyard, I caught a glimmer of what I was looking for. There was a shaft cut into the wall a foot and a half above the top skull in the pyramid. It was made from some sort of black metal and looked almost like an archaic mail slot. In the past it had probably served as a dump chute for whatever was being mined up here, but today, it would be my emergency exit.

Much to my surprise, it made no sound when it opened. Instead, a cool rank draft hit me in the face. Something was rotting below me. I leaned into the chute, but couldn't see how deep it went.

"I know you're not supposed to put all of your eggs in one basket," I said, leveling my torch over the opening. "But I don't have much of a choice."

I released the torch and it tumbled through the darkness, illuminating the roughly hewn walls as it fell. Much to my luck, it came to a rest in a pile of sand somewhere around twenty feet below. The flame winked at me once, twice, three times before it dropped to a cool blue and snuffed itself out. It was discouraging, but my disappointment would have to wait.

Twenty feet is a rough landing, but survivable depending on the surface. From where I was it looked like beach sand. Deciding to risk it, I contorted my body so that my feet went in first, held my breath, and let go. I would have shut my eyes, but it wouldn't have done any good. I couldn't see anything. My legs were as straight as a stalactite as I fell, but my hands hit the walls a couple of times. The first scraped my knuckles; the second felt like slivers of stone had worked their way into my palms (under the skin and into the soft meat beneath). I finally landed; unfortunately, my only welcome party was a hollow pop from my hip. It echoed through the cave, followed closely by my scream of agony.

I felt around limply in the dark looking for my leg. Somehow, it had bent in the wrong direction at the pelvis and was now twisted behind my ass. It felt numb and cold to the touch. I shuddered and rolled on my back, trying not to pass out from the pain and mental image alone. I thought I was seeing stars, but then I realized it was the reflection of a flashlight coming down the passage on some glittering minerals stuck in the ceiling.

"It wasn't the prettiest landing, but at least you're out of the prep room," Asclepius said as he bent down next to me. "Nice leg you got there."

He jiggled it at the knee and my muscles flapped like jelly in response, confused, wondering where they were supposed to be attached.

"Not funny," I winced. "I need help."

"I'll say!" he laughed. "But the show must go on! Do you remember what I said about being self-reliant? This is just another case of that. Shit happens in the field, and the better you learn to cope with it, the better off you'll be. We're not blessed you and I, we don't have a support group. We have to be soldiers and medics all at the same time."

"That's great," I cried. "Just tell me what to do, *please*, I'm going to faint."

My eyes fluttered and he slapped me.

"The first thing to do is remain calm." He smiled while moving to my leg. He gripped it with his heavy hands. "If you scream, they'll hear it. The next thing you need to remember is that your body is like a puzzle: everything has its proper place. It wants to fit together. And the last step is to tug and twist . . ."

There was another pop as he wrenched my leg around; the tingling pain was released all at once with a single intense motion, like being stabbed. I stood up and tested my weight on it.

"If it doesn't hurt anymore," he concluded, "then you did it right."

"That's amazing! Maybe I'll get into medicine when all of this is over."

Asclepius shrugged and handed me his flashlight.

"This isn't over yet. If you can find your way out of these mines, *then* you'll pass."

I flashed the beam down the tunnel—no daylight.

"Any hints?"

"God you're whiny," he grumbled. "Sure, since you were such a trooper with your leg. You're going to use senses other than your vision. Good luck."

With that, he stomped off around the first bend and was gone.

"Other senses," I muttered. "He's right, using your vision doesn't make much sense when you can't see—and touch doesn't really work either, because all of the stone down here feels the same."

Then my nose picked up the smell from before, the smell death makes as it cannibalizes its victims. The stench was much stronger behind me where the earth sloped further down into the mines. I didn't really have any indication that the opposite direction was the right way, but I wasn't in the mood to find what secrets were lurking below. So, I set off at a reasonable pace away from the depths. Soon, I caught the sweet scent of the fields again, and following my nose, I was in the sunshine within twenty minutes, at the base of the large waterfall.

"Good work, my boy," Asclepius clapped. I could barely hear him over the pouring water. "You showed a great deal of perseverance today."

"Well," I laughed, "I didn't have much of a choice, did I? You would have left me to die."

"Most certainly," he replied without missing a beat. "Striving for realism is a personal goal of mine."

I was ready to tear into him, and I would have—if my leg still hurt. It was strange; other than the memory of it happening, there wasn't any sign of my injuries at all—not even my hands that I had scraped during the fall hurt. It happened —right? I decided to change the subject—but he beat me to it.

"I want to show you something."

I followed him around the back of the waterfall to a long staircase carved out of the mountain. At the top of the stairs was the wooden door to where this lesson had started.

"What are we doing back here?"

"Remember, examine your surroundings." He lifted one of his hands, and with a soft push on the face of the door, it opened unhindered. It hadn't been locked all along. My brute force approach would have worked—if I had been on the opposite side. My jaw dropped and he burst into laughter.

"Look at the bright side, at least now you know how to play doctor if you need to. Follow me, I have one more thing I want to teach you before you go—and don't worry, this one is easy."

VI

Hypnic Jerk

Ryan

❖

NATE SUGGESTED THAT WE get some rest. With guarding Edric and always keeping an ear open for sirens, it would be a while before we all got true conjugal visits from the Sandman. Nate, Schafer, and Jacob took this advice to heart while I drove and Wes accompanied me from the passenger seat.

It was nice to finally get some peace and quiet. Traversing Washington's back roads (keeping a careful eye on the speed limit) was therapeutic. Sometimes you have to trudge through something mindless as a break from the unpredictability that comes with everyday life. I was feeling at ease thanks to the greasy gas station food massaging its way through my digestive tract and the twisting labyrinth of pavement ahead.

"So you're not going to sleep?" I asked Wes. Neither of us had spoken in over an hour, we were in our own separate worlds.

"I can't," he said. "I get nightmares—plus, I've never been able to get comfortable enough in a car to sleep. Feeling the rumble of the engine, like when I press my face against the window, makes me anxious—like I need to get up and go someplace. I can take over if you want to get some shut-eye."

"It's okay," I said. "It's keeping my mind off things. What are your nightmares about?"

"Nothing in particular," he replied. "It's more the feeling of the nightmare than the actual boogeyman. Kind of like I'm being chased by something. I don't know what it is and I'm too afraid to look behind me and see, but I know something is back there, and being caught by it wouldn't be good for my health."

"You've never looked, even out of curiosity?"

"Nope," he said thoughtfully. "It's probably better that way. You know when you're doing everything you can to avoid something, but deep down you understand that the ending is already decided? That's what my nightmares feel like. With every step away from this thing I can feel my body age and all of the hope I have just kind of melts away. When it becomes too much, I wake up covered with sweat and sometimes I throw up. I know it's just a dream, but sometimes that doesn't help."

He sighed heavily.

"I've never told anyone that before, keep it under your hat," he said, and I agreed. "Do you have nightmares?"

"Not really," I replied. "Not since I was a kid."

"Did you just grow out of them?"

"Kind of, it's hard to explain . . ."

"I've got time," he said.

"No kidding." I rubbed the bridge of my nose, trying to put my thoughts into some coherent order. "When did your parents tell you that Santa Claus wasn't real?"

"I was ten."

"And was it traumatic for you?"

"Not soul crushing," he said. "But memorable enough for me to remember my age."

"Exactly," I replied. "My parents told me when I was four, and it hurt. Not because there wasn't some fat jerk in a red suit shoving packages under our tree; no, it was because the illusion of him and his magic all went right back up the chimney. It caused a chain reaction and I started to think, well, if Santa isn't real, then what else isn't? Once Santa was debunked, so were vampires, ghosts, heroes, and everything else that went with them."

"In other words, your parents fucked you up."

"I don't blame them," I continued. "I think society did it. With science constantly trying to prove everything and religion desperately attempting to fill in the gaps, there just wasn't anything left hiding under my bed. Every time I'd have a dream with a monster or something, my brain would tell me to stop being so stupid and I'd wake up. I'm sorry if that's vague, I think it's the best I can do."

"No worries," Wes said, turning to look out the window. "You'll hear no arguments from me; mysticism was dead even before Freud told us we all want to fuck our moms."

"Plus, when the real world is as frightening as it is, do we really need to invent any other terrors in our heads?" I yawned.

"Exactly."

Edric

ASCLEPIUS AND I WALKED back to his farm to find Sigmund waiting for us out front. While we were away, he'd set up a heavy wooden chair (it looked more like an electric chair than a throne). It had straps on each arm, down the legs, and across the back.

"Thank you, Sigmund, you read my mind. Funny how that works, isn't it?" Asclepius turned to me. "Well, what are you waiting for? Hop in."

"There's no way in Hell I'm getting in that thing."

"Oh come on, don't be such a spoilsport." Asclepius clapped me on the back. "Have I ever lied to you?"

"Lied? No. Deceived—well, do I really need to answer?"

"You need to relax, kid. Remember, I said this lesson was easy."

"Is it your easy, or my easy?"

"Let's agree to disagree and say halfway between the two."

"Whatever." Defeated, I threw my hands up and sat. Asclepius and Sigmund went through and strapped me down. There were seven of them in all (one on each limb and three across the chest).

"What do I do now?"

"Much like today's earlier escapades, all you have to do is escape and you'll pass."

"Okay," I said. "Let's have it."

"Huh?" Asclepius grunted.

"Aren't you going to light the chair on fire or something?"

He paused before bursting into suffocating laughter.

"I'm not going to do that, you joker! That'd weaken the integrity of the chair! Plus, you learned how to put yourself back together today; don't you think that's enough?"

"As long as you do, I guess. How should I get started on this one?"

"There are a few things. For one, most restraints are built to keep people from struggling. So if you're whipping all over the place, you're just going to get more stuck, if that makes any sense. The trick is to learn the difference between constructive and harmful movement. For instance, slowly working your arm in and out in a punching motion won't cause it to swell too much, and it'll begin to loosen up that strap. And all you really need to do is free one hand to be in the clear."

I did as I was told and soon it started to loosen.

"The other lifesaver, in situations such as these, is sweat—or as I like to call it, the body's natural lube, though spit works too, you just have to be damn accurate. You could practice that now if you want."

I tried to spit on my wrist and only got my crotch. Asclepius laughed again.

"Wrong appendage, but I think you're getting it. Keep going."

Even though I thought the leather was rubbing me raw (I kind of wish it had, blood would've made it a breeze), I made it out after ten minutes.

"Piece of cake," I said, removing the last strap from my ankle.

"Remember, don't get cocky. Chances are you're going to have to pull this off on a pretty strict time limit, so make sure you practice."

"No problem," I said.

"Perfect," Asclepius slithered through his teeth. His skin started to glow a brilliant orange. "Just like I planned, you're turning out quite marvelously."

Sparks leapt off of his shoulders and raced down his pants, thin flickers of blue spreading out in all directions around him.

"What's going on?"

"You should be used to this by now." The world ignited with roaring flames. They were deafening as they shot hundreds of feet in the air. It felt like I was in the eye of a mushroom cloud.

"What do I do? How do I escape? We'll be burned alive!" He chuckled at this.

"You won't! You've reached the point of no return, my apprentice. Until we meet again . . ."

He waved goodbye as the tsunami of flames barreled towards me. I covered up with both my arms just as all of the flesh melted off my face. I could feel the heat recede as my bones and muscles were exposed to the open air—and it kept getting colder and colder.

This time I made my exit in a sudden blast of light, like staring into a solar flare or the heart of a magnesium flash-bulb. My pupils spun back in my head, burning beige and red shadows onto my eyelids. When the dim cabin of the car became concrete again, I pulled my face off of an air condi-tioning vent. Then, my gaze fell to my sore hands. My palms were as bleach white as they'd always been, but my right wrist was puffy, red, and free from its shackle. My physical move-ment had been translated back to reality.

If I wanted to, I could've kicked out a window or used the emergency latch to spring the back doors—but closer exam-ination revealed no lights other than stars outside.

There was another option: with my hands free I could reach the guns a couple of them had stashed underneath the back-seat. I extended one of my arms and felt the butt of a shotgun, wondering if they would hear me cock a shell into the chamber in time. It would be so easy. The bastards had actually fallen asleep; I could press the barrel to the back of Schafer's head and splatter his brains through his face and onto the windshield. With any luck, Wesley and Ryan wouldn't even notice until bits of skull and meat were sneezing into their hair. The whole experience was almost erotic. Revenge was something I'd been lusting after ever since they'd forced that disgusting rag over my mouth.

Had it only been twelve hours ago?

I retracted my hand and slid it back into place. Better to play it cool for now. I couldn't rush revenge, and just like making love, the longer I waited, the more satisfying the release would be.

Ryan

I COULD FAINTLY HEAR METAL CLICKING; it was the sound a fork makes when you accidentally drop it in the garbage disposal. A moan followed. I pulled my sight from the road long enough to peek in the rearview mirror.

"Is that you, Edric?" I called out. It was little more than a whisper; I had to compensate for the whirring of the air conditioner.

"Yeah," he groaned. I could tell his throat was dry and scratchy.

"Are you okay? Do you need me to get you some water?"

"No," he whimpered. "I think I'll be alright—but I really need to use the bathroom."

He let out a hacking cough and I glanced over at Wesley, looking for advice. He shrugged.

"Can we pull over?" he continued as weakly as before. "I just have to pee. I'll make it quick."

"Can you go in a bottle?" Wes replied.

"I don't think so," he said. "My hands are still stuck at a weird angle, I couldn't, you know, hold onto it . . ."

"Well then can you go back to sleep?" I suggested. "We'll be back at the house in less than six hours."

"Sorry," his voice was more urgent this time, squeaky and a little embarrassed. "I can't wait that long."

"He has been back there for a while," Wesley said. "Stopping for two minutes isn't going to throw off our schedule. We haven't even seen another car for more than two hours."

"Okay. I'll stop, but you have to take my side when everyone starts giving me shit for it."

I gradually pressed the break until we slid to a complete stop on the gravel shoulder. The change in momentum made the other three stir and rub their eyes.

"We're not home, are we?" Nate said, lolling his head back and forth to get his bearings.

"What's going on?" Schafer asked drowsily.

"Edric needs to piss."

"Like hell he does." Schafer closed his eyes again. "Keep driving."

I nudged Wesley in the ribs and he cleared his throat.

"No. He's been locked up all day. I think letting him stretch his legs could do some good—maybe make him more compliant."

"Or maybe," Schafer shot back, realizing he wasn't going to get anymore sleep, "stretching his legs is just code for running, and I don't know about you, but it's too damn late to get in a marathon."

"He's not going to run. Are you going to run, Edric?" I asked the rearview mirror.

"Wasn't planning on it, I have too many concussions to find my way through the wilderness in the dark anyway."

"Let him go," Nate said, handing me the key to his handcuffs. "I don't want any puddles of forensic evidence on the carpet."

"I have a bad feeling about this," Schafer said. "Let's all get out and keep an eye on him, I think we could all use a stretch."

I kept the car running and we opened our doors. The air outside was stifling compared to the artificial cold of the air conditioner. Even before I'd reached the back doors of the van, the humidity had already made my pants stick to my thighs.

I'd parked at the edge of a large field with waist-high grass still trying to regain its color from winter. The scattered trees

in the distance appeared dead and barren, their dark silhou-
ettes scratched at the sky with rotten leafless branches. Above
them, a dozen or so bats danced in circles, dive-bombing the
occasional moth or mosquito unlucky enough to buzz past. I
knew that the area was alive with wildlife; cricket chirps and
owls' thunderous hoots echoed around us. But for some reason,
everything felt like death. A solitary chill found its way
through the midnight heat to crawl up my back. I moved to let
Edric out, but Nate stopped me.

"Allow me," he said, pulling the doors open. Edric was
already crouched and ready to go, squirming a little and pinch-
ing his legs together the best he could.

"I know you've already said you aren't going to run and I
trust you," Nate said. "But there are a couple of other ground
rules we need to get straight before we give you your
freedom—even if it's brief."

"Hurry, I don't know how much longer I can last."

"As I'm sure you can tell, we're in the middle of nowhere,"
Nate continued. "Civilization shouldn't come knocking out
here. However, if a car does decide to peek its headlights over
the horizon, you either get back in the van or down in the grass
by the road. I don't care if you're halfway through and you got
your pants around your ankles, you hustle your bare ass back
here. Got me?"

"Yeah, I understand, can I please go now?"

"If you fail to comply and some looky-loos even slow down,
we will kill all of them and it'll be your fault. Don't drag anyone
into this that doesn't have to be. Read me loud and clear?"

"I already said yes, please, let me out."

Nate nodded at me and I slipped his cuffs off.

"Nice and slow," Nate laughed. "We don't want to accidentally mistake your eagerness for an escape attempt."

Edric hopped out of the back and the van's suspension reset
to its original position, it deserved a break too. He carefully
waddled around to the side and was about to unzip when he
bumped into Schafer—who just so happened to have one of our
shotguns slung over his shoulder.

"What's with the gun?" I asked.

"Not much," he said. "I just wanted to give our pal Edric here a little more incentive not to take off. I'm not the best shot in the world, I can admit that, but I can aim low and steady enough to take out a kneecap if I have to—and whatever else happens to be in the way."

Edric examined him nervously and Schafer didn't like it. He lowered the gun so that the barrel kissed Edric's chin, but he didn't back down. He stood as stiff as a tombstone.

"You know, I don't need the whole ten million to be happy. We could probably hand in your corpse for half the price—at least there'd be some satisfaction in all of this trouble."

"You wouldn't dare . . ." Edric said.

"All I need is a reason, remember that." He cocked the shotgun quickly and Edric jumped. "You should have seen the look on your face."

"Asshole." Edric turned around and prepared to do his business, but Schafer interrupted him again.

"Oh Edric, my boy, what are you doing?"

"You're honestly asking me?"

"No, I got the mechanics of it down, don't worry about that. I was wondering why you're doing it here on the side of the road. You have to do it in front of the car in the headlights, bro. We don't want you to accidentally slip into the shadows, now do we?"

"Come on, man, just let him go," Jacob interjected, but Schafer cut him off with a snarl.

"Shut the hell up. Get your ass in gear, Edric, we don't have all night."

He let out a deep sigh, and with his head down in shame he made his way to the front of the van and dropped his pants.

"Isn't this excessive?" I asked.

"I'm teaching him a lesson for waking me up. We're the ones who kidnapped him, not the other way around."

The headlights washed out all of the color from Edric's face as his shadow stretched down the empty road, leaving this horrible place behind. His cuts seemed deeper and pressed into the contours of his skull. The sweat on his temples and the glossy stains of tears sparkled. Despite the temperature, the fresh piss steamed off the asphalt. He finished and climbed back in the car, unable to make eye contact with any of us. We repositioned his hands and cuffed them again. I was about to get back behind the wheel when I got an idea.

"Edric?" I asked. He kept his back to me. I could hear him sniffling. "Do you want us to give you some more medicine? It'll help the pain."

"No," he said. "Nothing else for me. I need to go back to sleep, just let me sleep please."

I paused for a second; hopelessly praying that he'd change his mind—but he refused to say another word.

VII
Atonia

Ryan
❖

NIGHT LAPSED BACK INTO DAY and the turnoff for our hideout was in sight. It sat wedged between thickets of trees on both sides of its mouth; the first bend in the road blocked all view of the path ahead. I wanted to do nothing more than hit the gas and coast all the way to the driveway on cloud nine—but instead I slid the van into the shoulder and kicked it into park.

"Almost home," I said, staring out over the top of the steering wheel.

"Why did you stop?" Nate asked. His head darted in every direction, trying to find any clue that could have tipped me off to a police barricade down the road.

"Relax," I sighed. "I was thinking that maybe giving Edric another dose before we get to the house might be a good idea."

"Why is that?"

Oh Nate, you make my life so difficult sometimes. Now I had to think up a pleasant way of explaining myself, one that didn't include the statement, He might run, and if he does, Schafer *will* kill him.

"We don't want him to see where we're going."

"He's asleep, he won't know—and even if he did wake up, if he could find his way back at this point we'd be screwed anyway."

"True, but we're also going to have to move him into the house," I continued. "And if he's under, there's less of a chance of him getting hurt in the process. Not to mention if he looks like he's sleeping there'll be fewer questions asked from Uncle Joe if he's up."

"Uncle Joe is bed-ridden. You mean Madison—you don't have to sugarcoat it."

"What do you think?" I concluded. "Should we take a vote?"

"Is there a need?" Nate replied, looking at each of us; it was the first time he'd been outnumbered since the start. "Let's just get it over with, this isn't my favorite part."

Schafer opened up his box of treats and prepped the needle. He was both graceful and methodical, and probably could have been an excellent nurse except for the whole criminal record thing.

"Wait," Schafer said. "It's your turn."

He flipped the syringe around and offered it to me plunger first. I looked from it to Wes, and then finally into Nate's concerned face. I could tell he thought I was about to snap, and he knew that when I finally lost it, the little disagreement that Schafer and I had back in the gas station parking lot would look like afternoon tea. But little did the rest of my compatriots know, I had had a lot of time to think during my full night of driving, and was beginning to warm up to the situation.

We'd already kidnapped Edric, that's a minimum ten year sentence. I had also already shot and killed a cop in cold blood —another twenty-five years at least (though the gas chamber would be a more likely destination at the end of my Yellow Brick Road). Now, the police wouldn't be able to prove that I was the one who did it, and while I trust Wes and Nate with my life, I wouldn't put it past Jacob (kidnapping and prior convictions) and Schafer (kidnapping, assault, battery, and prior convictions) to rat me out if it meant them seeing the light of day again. Better to be a good boy and go along with it until all of the nastiness is taken care of, not give anyone any reason to doubt my commitment.

"It's cool, I can do it," Nate said.

"Bullshit," Schafer replied. "It was his idea; he has to get his hands dirty."

"Don't worry," I said. "It isn't that big of a deal as long as he's sleeping. Plus, I honestly believe this is for the better."

I unbuckled my seatbelt and crouched my way to Schafer.

"Watch where you're pointing that thing," I said. "I hate needles."

I crawled over the seat and spotted my landing carefully so that I didn't disturb Edric; I wasn't convinced I'd be able to carry out the procedure with him struggling and begging. Schafer gave me the needle.

"Where should I stick him?"

"Just put it in one of his ass cheeks again," Schafer said. "That way you don't have to find a vein and the effect will be more mellow. Hell, unless you want to get him high. We could pump him full of this stuff—think about it. After we collect we'd probably have to pry him off of us. It would make controlling him a lot easier . . ."

"I'll pass."

The car got quiet again and I repositioned myself so that I wouldn't have to stab him at a weird angle (it would've been embarrassing to go in at a diagonal and give him a piercing instead of an injection). As I moved, the carpet below my hands and knees moved with me and I couldn't help but think that Edric knew I was there, hovering over him. He either didn't care or wanted the injection. The thought that maybe he was getting addicted gave me chills, but this idea replaced itself with something else. Was he beginning to trust me? I could understand why he wouldn't trust Schafer (obviously), but maybe because he was being treated so terribly he had subliminally attached himself to me, the only person who'd showed him kindness during this whole ordeal.

"What are you waiting for?" Schafer grunted. "Don't tell me you've got cold feet. Nate, you might need to get back there and give your buddy some encouragement. Maybe a little back rub or a foot massage if he does a good job?"

"Shut up," Nate replied. "Hurry up, man, Madison is waiting for you back at the house."

That was all I needed.

Like a sniper cuddling up to his scope, I made a quick accurate jab, and as soon as I knew it had gone deep enough, I dropped the plunger.

"Forgive me, Edric. Everything is going to be okay."

Edric

"**What about vehicles?**" Asclepius asked, but I didn't register it. I was staring up into the sky mindlessly. At some point my eyes had adapted to this new place and the shocking blue no longer made my corneas blister.

"Hello in there?" He snapped his fingers in front of my face and went to slap me, but I ducked out of the way in time. "Getting faster and sneakier, are we?"

"Only out of necessity. I'm sick of getting hit."

"Well, if you paid attention then I wouldn't have to give you a little positive reinforcement from time to time." He smirked. "At least you've learned something though, for a while there I thought I was spinning my gears."

It's hard to explain, but this last bit hurt me. Here I was thinking all along that the progress I'd made over our past sessions was monumental. So clear and impressive that even a mentally ill blind man would applaud me if he happened to walk by as I escaped from yet another room, or a set of shackles, or endured the agony that comes with resetting bones. Sadly, Asclepius continued to be oblivious; he wasn't exactly a "baby steps" kind of guy. Anything short of a complete and total holocaust of the men responsible for this nightmare would be a failure; and only after I had felt their blood run through my fingers and pushed the last corpse into the waiting mouth of a furnace would any celebration be allowed.

"So, what about vehicles?" he repeated. You had to listen for it, but the tinny venomous sound of expectation was there, daring me to talk back or challenge him again. There was no sense in risking it; I'd fulfilled my boldness quota when I twisted away from his calloused palm earlier.

"What vehicles?"

"General vehicles. Cars, bikes, boats, you understand."

"Not really," I shrugged. "What about them?"

"Easy stuff, like how to drive and parallel park . . ."

I said nothing.

"Come on, that last one was a joke! You need to lighten up, kiddo."

"Sorry, this is serious business is all, and I'm not quite sure yet when I'm allowed to laugh." I smiled but it felt horrible on my face.

"Use your best judgment and I'll let you know if it's inappropriate."

"Anyway." I decided it was a good time to get back on track. The less time Asclepius and I joked about me getting my face beaten in, the better. "I'm comfortable with cars, I think. My dad used to let me practice driving up and down our long driveway. I'm not a pro, but I'm good enough to get to the nearest payphone."

"Can you drive both automatic and stick?"

"Yeah, when my father would leave for business trips I'd take his Lamborghini out for a spin—until he started checking the odometer. You could teach me how to hotwire if you really want to though—or how to cut the brakes or the gas line." He shook his head.

"There'd be no point," he said. "You're going to be in the wilderness, so you'd only be shooting yourself in the foot by taking out any possible means of escape. Also, when you're finished, they're all going to be dead. You can just take the keys."

"You're right, as usual."

We had finished a lap around Asclepius's farm when I finally worked up the courage to speak my mind. I knew there was a high chance of disaster, but the feeling in my gut told me that I was going to have to take action before it was too late.

"I've been thinking," I started. I had only known Asclepius for a short time but he didn't strike me as the type to tolerate bullshit. It was better to get it out as straightforward as possible.

"And?" he raised his eyebrows.

"You know I trust you and this process you're putting me through. I wouldn't have agreed if I didn't."

"Go on . . ."

"I think it's time we get more serious with my training. I feel that my foundation on how to escape is solid—but I still have no experience for after that."

"So you think you're ready for the real shit, am I right? You think you can finally handle everything that I plan to dish out?"

"Yeah, I mean, in moderation of course. The last time I was here you said that there was no turning back. I like how you waded me in before ramping up the difficulty. As long as we stick with that approach, I know I can handle anything you throw at me."

He smiled an evil grin and my insides went cold. For a moment I had been so wrapped up in my plea that I'd forgotten who I was talking to. Asking Asclepius to take my training to the next level was like stripping down nude and lathering up in barbecue sauce in front of a starved cannibal. He nodded his head towards the front of his house.

"Okay," he replied. "Let's get to the real reason you're here. Do you see that axe over there?"

How could I not? The thing had been looming dangerously in my peripheral vision ever since we'd finished our walk along the grounds. It had a double-sided blade and a smooth wooden handle. It bit deeply into the top of an old, scarred tree stump. Even if the tree had found some way to beat the odds and survive being chopped down (its roots running deep, searching for a cold, quiet place to recover), it was certainly dead now. I shivered at the thought of what trials Asclepius had put it through in its long, evil history.

"Yes," I replied weakly. His eyes narrowed to fluorescent slits while his smile widened to reveal four rows of jagged fangs.

"Bring it to me."

VIII

Our Little House in the Woods

Ryan

❖

OUR VAN CIRCLED INTO THE QUIET DRIVEWAY so that it faced the road.

"When I was younger my father used to take me target shooting," I said. "And every time he would park the car facing back towards the city, and every time he felt the need to explain to me why. It was so if anything went wrong we wouldn't have to worry about backing the car out—not that it made any difference, I would've been too young to know how to drive anyway."

I popped my door open and listened for any cars coming down the road, but there were none.

"Looks like we're clear," I said.

"Welcome home, guys," Nate said. "Ryan and I are going to undo Edric's restraints and we'll carry him up to his room. I want both Schafer and Jacob to flank us on the left, and Wes on the right. Not only will that give us a little more coverage in case someone comes snooping around, but it'll also be a little insurance in case he wakes up and takes off."

"I don't see why two of us have to be on the same side," Jacob whined. Schafer shut him up with a slap to the back of the head.

"It's because the forest is closer on that side, numbnuts. Lighten up, will ya? It's payday."

"He's right," Nate replied, while neglecting to comment on the slap. "It shouldn't matter much anyway; we just put him out. In any case, let's hurry. The less opportunities we give for someone to see him the better off we'll be."

We got out and opened the back doors. Nate whispered Edric's name but he didn't move.

"Good sign," Nate said. Schafer looked disappointed, but I didn't want to think about the reason why.

Nate and I disconnected his cuffs and pulled him from the van. His weight was manageable with the two of us. We all moved into formation and made our way to the front door.

We were finally back.

Edric

WITH EVERY STEP I TOOK TOWARDS THE STUMP, the rotten wood slithering toward me with its deathly gray roots, the axe grew more intimidating. The shadow of its handle stretched out over my face as it seemed to rip towards the sky. I gripped the wooden shaft with both hands and rocked the blade free as whispers of dust circled into the air, set free from their deep resting places. It was heavier than I thought it would be.

"I'm going to regret asking this—" I smiled at Asclepius. I was out of his reach so I would at least have a head start if he tried to hit me. "What do I do next?"

"Back behind my home sweet home here is a wood pile. Maybe you saw it on our walk?"

I didn't remember but I nodded anyway.

"I want you to bring those logs out here and chop them into kindling for my woodstove. Not having a real sun makes it awfully chilly at night. Every log should make about four perfectly sized pieces."

"And how many would you like me to butcher?"

"All of them, of course," he said. "Silly Edric, you'd better get moving if you want to finish before sundown, I know I would. Just because we don't see them doesn't mean there aren't things living in this field—and you better believe they get bolder around people at night—hungrier too."

I gulped and stuck the axe into the stump again before scurrying as fast as my feet would take me to the back of the house. Once there, my newest challenge wasn't hard to spot. The woodpile turned out to be a wood mountain; either by magic or some kind of miracle I hadn't been able to see it from the front. It was disorganized and unstable. By prodding one log loose, three or four more fell in its place. Each one was as long as my forearm and thick as a loaf of bread. They were unlike any wood I'd ever seen before, and my curiosity was enough to stifle my terror. I picked one log up, tested its weight, and looked it over. The bark clinging to the outside was dark and felt old to the touch; it would crumble, leaving traces of ash on my palms as I slid my hands over it. Instead of typical age rings at each end, these logs had scratches that resembled spider webs. I'm no expert lumberjack, but I could tell the wood was dense, and the thought of being forced to chop all of them to pieces before nightfall didn't exactly instill me with hope.

"Did you get lost back there?" I heard Asclepius call from the front yard. "Time is money, kid."

I would be exhausted from the chopping alone, so I decided to first move all of the logs to the front yard. That way all I'd have to do to grab another one would be swivel my hips a little to the right or left. I could bundle three logs up in my arms at a time (four if I was feeling ambitious) and run back to the front to toss them next to the stump in about two minutes. During my first few runs Asclepius looked at me curiously but eventually he caught on, pulled his hat over his eyes, and seemed to nod off. At first I thought it was impossible, and that somehow he'd found a way to make the wood reproduce asexually, leaving me with an infinite supply of logs. However, after a few hours of scrapes and splinters, the mountain of logs had been reduced to a misfit valley in the front yard. It was as if a tornado had picked up a hundred saw blades and whirled them through a forest.

"Took you long enough."

"Did you enjoy your nap?" I wiped the sweat from my face before it made my eyebrows crust over.

"Not so much," Asclepius concluded. "I can't even leave you alone for a couple of hours without you slacking off."

"Try not to worry about it, it'll get done and I'll even have time to spare."

"Easy for you to say, you won't be the one freezing to death—although that might make a good future assignment for you. Tell me, Edric, how would you like to learn how to avoid frostbite?"

"I'm assuming this would be a trial and error type of test? Count me out; it's spring back in my world."

"Then get your ass in gear before I get bored," he said.

To meet Asclepius's expectations, each log would take three cuts (one to split it down the middle and then another on each half to give a total of four pieces). I placed the first on the chopping block, and with a single, smooth arc of the blade, my first victim cracked—but something was wrong. With contact came sharp pain in my hands that reverberated all the way up to my shoulders. I thought it was my imagination, but the second and third cuts only confirmed it. I could see Asclepius smile from the corner of my eye. Before continuing, I stopped to better inspect the axe.

What I'd thought was the natural grain of the handle was actually small carvings. I couldn't tell what they were (the details were too fine), but it looked almost like children or some other sort of figures wandering aimlessly through a complex maze. Each line had been lovingly cut in such a way that when you squeezed them they'd bite into your flesh. In other words, every time I picked the axe up, every time I tightened my grip, every log that fell under the blade was like giving a handjob to a bundle of razorblades. I wanted to say something—not because I was ready to give up, but because I could only imagine what condition my hands would be in after cutting over a thousand logs this way.

"Don't tell me you need a break already?"

"Nope, I'm good, thanks for asking though." I grinned and turned my attention back to cutting. "If you'd like to bring me something to drink, that'd be swell."

"Less talking and more chopping, you little shit."

I used to believe that through willpower a person could do anything; climb mountains, write books, bob for apples in hydrochloric acid, you name it. But after around fifty logs my resolve began to fall apart along with my dedication. The blisters started small but soon consumed my whole hands. It looked like I got in a boxing match with a hornet nest. The plasma sloshed its way to the tips of my fingers, making the white bumps sag and squish. It wouldn't be long before my skin started to peel off in sheets. And when everything seemed lost, I would look up and see the endless expanse of logs lying in wait, mocking me with their knothole eyes.

I dropped the axe, fell to my knees, and covered my face in defeat.

Ryan
❖

"DUDE, WATCH HIS HANDS," Nate said, nodding his chin towards me. "Don't get sloppy. I'm not dealing with any broken fingers."

My hands were wedged into Edric's armpits, but somehow one of his limp arms had dropped to the ground, and as we walked, the tips of his fingers slid through the sand of the driveway. The skin on each digit was already scraped white and bleeding lightly. The arm looked like it might be dislocated, but I could feel his bones still fit together through his sweaty shirt.

"Do you want to trade ends?" I asked.

"No need," he replied. He took Edric's rogue hand and flopped it over his chest. Edric's eyes never fluttered, he was as passive as a corpse.

"Good thing I noticed before the porch."

"Why's that?"

"Splinters."

Edric

"FIGHT THROUGH THE PAIN! Maybe you've forgotten already, but in the last day you've been both burned up and broken your goddamn leg. A couple of blisters should be a fucking vacation by now! Get over it, sissy!"

To punctuate this he pulled an apple from the tree he was sitting in and gnashed it in ecstasy. The wet smack of his teeth as they pierced the juicy skin sounded refreshing and delicious.

"I'm sorry," I wheezed. "If I finish this, I don't think I'll be able to do anything for days. I don't know how long I'm going to have before they just decide to do away with me. You have to understand. By the time I'm recovered, I could already be dead."

I think I blinked because, before I could process what was happening, Asclepius was standing in front of me with my shirt tangled in his fist. His breath beat down on my face, hot and heavy; I could even see the small red bits of apple peel stuck between his fangs.

"Shut your mouth and get back to work. You told me you trusted me, now you better act like it."

I blinked again and he was back in his tree, but he was no longer eating. Instead, all of his attention was focused on me as he stared unflinching with glassy eyes. I couldn't figure out where I'd seen them before, but I knew for a fact that they weren't human. I sniffled away the tears that never came and returned to my torture.

It still stung to use the axe but I couldn't stop. I worked my way into a rhythm and tried to let gravity do most of the work, stomping on the head when it wouldn't go all the way through. My hands soon became numb to the tight fisted, hot coal feeling of the handle and I began to make good time. Another hundred, another hundred, I forced myself through the motions as fast and as smoothly as I could. In the span of a few hours I had whittled my way down to the last fifty logs.

Asclepius ripped another apple from the branch above his head and launched it at me. I probably would have dodged or caught it, but all of my attention was on chopping. This means I did catch it—but with the back of my head. The brick red membrane split with a luscious smack and I dropped the axe mid swing. I felt my hair, and drew back a wet hand covered in a cocktail of apple juice and blood.

"Is this too easy for you?" he called out from behind me.

"No, this is perfect."

"Are you sure?" he pressed. "You're making good time."

"Doesn't make it any less painful . . ."

Asclepius didn't reply, he was too busy looking for another apple to lob my way.

"Score one for me?" I whispered to myself. My motto in this place was quickly becoming "A victory, no matter how small, is still a victory."

I placed a fresh log on the chopping block and raised my axe yet again. Then, trying to get back into my rhythm before I was rudely interrupted with another apple to the skull, I let it drop.

"Score one? Please, you still have a big fat goose egg my friend," Asclepius grumbled.

This time, instead of a dry crackle as the wood gave way, the log made a wet groan before spraying blood all over the tree stump and the surrounding earth. It happened all at once, sneezing into the mirror with a bloody nose.

"Why'd you stop?"

"It's nothing," I said, wiping the droplets from my cheeks.

I swung again, but this time the blood oozed out with the occasional spurt as if being propelled in beats from an unseen heart. That's when I finally understood: the spider webbing cracks I had seen were veins. It didn't take long before I had to reposition each log back to the middle of the stump because they were trying to drift away on the slick crimson surface. The whole front of me was coated, but as it congealed and dried into syrup between my fingers, my grip actually got stronger and my task became more natural.

The stack shrank, and the blood that poured in waterfalls onto the dirt below began to accumulate past my ankles. It felt warm and inviting, and if it wasn't for the sour copper smell that screamed into my nostrils, I could have bathed in it. With the sloshing tide of blood up to my knees and only about one inch of the stump protruding from the scarlet sea, I turned towards Asclepius with only one word on my lips.

"Finished."

"Almost," he said. "Only one to go. Hurry up and find it so we can move on."

I looked around and was NOT surprised to see that it was NOT bobbing on the surface. That would have been too easy. I moved in little circles, kicking around, waiting to stub my toes on the only thing between me and a bath (and maybe some apples, if I was lucky).

"That's it?" Asclepius said. "After all of this you're just going to half-ass it? How disappointing. I would've thought that you'd learned by now."

I stopped walking and looked down into the ocean of gore, the blurred reflection of my silhouette looking back up at me. There was no avoiding it. I didn't even bother to plug my nose as I leaned forward and splashed down into the perfect silence of the stagnant fluid.

My hands groped around blindly. As dedicated as I suddenly found myself, there would have been no point in opening my eyes. The sweet grass of the field was now acrid seaweed whipping at my face, tangling my feet. I couldn't have been more than three feet from the ground, but I still managed to dive deeper, past the sand into the underworld. My lungs burned and my skin itched but I was desperate, and at last, my fingers wrapped around the final piece of wood greedily. I surfaced.

"Not bad, kid," Asclepius said as he slopped his way over to me. "Now that I think about it, we have enough wood already; you don't have to chop that one. Let's head in for the day."

I spat an ounce of blood through my teeth and onto the front of his shirt.

Ryan

❖

JACOB, IN A NOT SO SUBTLE ATTEMPT to get away from Schafer, ran up the squeaky wooden porch and twisted the tarnished door-knob for Nate and me. The door swung open to reveal the deserted entryway. Disturbed clumps of dust and cobwebs snowed from the ceiling onto the hardwood floor.

"Do you need help with anything?" Wes asked.

"I don't think so," Nate said, "I'll shout if there's a problem. Otherwise, you guys are free, go have some fun or something."

"Thank God," Schafer cried. "I have to piss."

They dispersed in opposite directions, leaving Nate and me to finish the job. We began to march up the tall stairs, easily the sturdiest structure in the house.

"I have a question I've always wanted to ask you," I said.

"Go for it."

"I've known you forever and you aren't from money, so how was your uncle able to afford this place? It's like a movie star's old vacation home. I'm still finding rooms in it."

This wasn't an exaggeration. Had it not fallen into disrepair over the years, Nate could have offloaded it to some Seattle yuppie and made enough to retire from crime, life, and every-thing else. Off of the entryway are two living rooms. One leads to a study (where his uncle stays locked away from the world) and the basement (with full boiler room and servant's quar-ters); the other leads to the kitchen and dining area. Upstairs are four massive suites, each with their own bathrooms. And this is just the main house. There is still the workshop, and other smaller guesthouses and utility buildings scattered throughout the surrounding woods. Unfortunately, if the main house is in bad shape (peeling paint, chipped windows, fried light fixtures), then the outlying buildings are obese in com-parison (collapsed roofs, moldy walls, floors carpeted in broken glass and rusty nails).

It might sound like a waste on paper, but Nate's favorite part of the house has nothing to do with comfort. Instead, he likes the no neighbors, no neighborhood watch, and no questions asked. Being removed from society has its benefits, especially when you're main source of income comes from selling drugs and guns. As a result, both living rooms and the basement are filled with weapons, ammo, narcotics, and the ingredients and equipment to manufacture all of the above.

"How my family got a hold of this place is a funny story—actually it isn't, it's a horrible story—but I'll tell you anyway if you're interested."

"With an introduction like that, how could I not be?"

We reached the top of the stairs and almost caught Edric's shoulder on a splintered board jutting from the wall. We stepped around it and walked down the hallway.

"Back when this place was built in the forties, the guy that bought it was a World War II veteran who fought in the Pacific. But something happened to him over there that mixed his brains up a little bit—and this isn't like today, you'd be hard pressed to find someone who understood posttraumatic stress like we do now. In any event, he must of saw something awful, or something the government didn't want people to know, because they gave him a fat check and he used it to move out here."

The room at the end of the hall was Edric's. It was as far away from the front and back doors as we could manage, and it was nice and quiet, so he wouldn't be able to spy on us or overhear any personal information we might divulge.

"The problem was," Nate continued as we entered the room, "he was all alone out here, and when you're by yourself your thoughts think louder. Eventually he went mad and started to snatch little boys from the surrounding towns, rape, and then murder them."

"I think I'm beginning to understand why you folks were able to afford this place," I sighed.

"We're not even to the worst part yet."

We laid Edric on a stained mattress and positioned his ankles and arms into the new set of cuffs. They weren't metallic like the ones we'd used before; these were leather with soft padding on the inside, the kind you'd find in a hospital. The room looked cleaner and more welcoming than when we'd left (Madison's doing). There were a couple of pieces of antique furniture brought in, including a small nightstand with a vase of fresh flowers in it on top. An old chandelier glittered above us, a festering last note of elegance—of what the house used to be.

"Before we continue, what was this guy's name?"

"Machaon."

"That's weird."

"It's Greek I think. Whatever. That isn't important. In the army, Machaon was a medic and had a pretty good understanding of human anatomy. Eventually he decided, why kill the kids when he could use them as slaves? He started experimenting on them with drugs and even tried to drill holes in their heads to fry out parts of their brains. When they caught him he confessed that his ultimate goal was to train the kids into making friends and tricking them back to his house. This house."

"And let me guess," I rolled my eyes. "This place is haunted now. Is that it?"

"Well that's what people thought. I've never seen anything and I've been coming here since I was a kid. But that reminds me, there's one other reason why no one wanted this house. Follow me."

We shut Edric's door and made our way back down the hallway to a different bedroom on the top floor.

"Remember right before we left when I smeared the tub with that lube?" Nate said, his hand resting on the door to the bathroom. I could hear something moving inside.

"Oh, yeah." I'd forgotten all about it. Planning and executing elaborate kidnappings will do that to you.

"Well, it's time for you to learn the other quirk of this house." He winked and then threw the door open.

I couldn't make out what was happening until he flicked the light on, but when he did, I had to shove my hand over my mouth to halt my gag reflex. Inside the bathtub was a solid ten inches of writing, squirming silver fish. Their legs clawed at the sky as they tried to find anything to grab onto that wasn't their brothers or sisters. They weren't heavy enough to scratch; instead, the only sound came from their slender bodies rolling over one another. It was the sound wrapping paper makes when it's shoved in a garbage bin.

"That's disgusting," was all I could think to say.

"Yeah, not only is this place infested with every manner of bug and spider you can think of, they also act unusual."

"Have you ever thought about getting an exterminator out here?"

"Yeah, I'm sure that would go well," he chuckled. " 'The last time I saw the tarantula it was between those assault rifles and my meth lab over there.' "

"I get it, I get it," I groaned. "Please just get rid of those things, they're going to make me puke."

"No sweat."

He crossed the room and dunked his hand into the mass of feelers and legs to pull the plug, and just like water, they all moved down the drain within a minute. He shook his hand to discard the dozen or so that were still clinging to him.

"Do you want breakfast or should we—" he paused in mid-sentence and stared over my shoulder. I whirled around to see Madison leaning on the doorframe with a contented smile on her face, wearing nothing more than one of my shirts.

"Breakfast can wait," Nate grinned. "Good morning, Maddy. I'll catch up with you guys later."

"Don't wait up," she said, taking special care to trace the inside of her lips with her small pink tongue as she spoke.

IX
Wet Dreams

Edric

❖

"WOULD YOU MIND TELLING ME what the point of that was?" I said.

"Here, clean yourself up." Asclepius tossed me a blanket. "I can't have you dripping all over my humble abode."

Asclepius's house was just what I imagined it would be (if maybe a little filthier). It was a single large room with squeaky wooden planks for the floor, all covered in a layer of sand and dust. Two hammocks bowed from the ceiling in one corner and a heavy iron woodstove with golden flames lolling from its mouth was in the opposite. The only light source other than the belly of the stove came in small streams from the cracks in the walls and ceiling where each board didn't quite meet the next. It was dim but I could still make out the pots, pans, firearms, and blades lining the walls. The only other stick of furniture in the whole room was a magnificent worktable with a scarred top. Sigmund sat at it whittling away at a black, twisted branch; he didn't even notice us. The air smelled like dust and honey.

I ran the raggedy blanket over my face and through my hair. The blood that had seemed so sticky outside dabbed away like water in the warm shadows of Asclepius's shack.

"Why don't you head outside, Sigmund," Asclepius grunted. "Edric and I have some more learning to do."

"It's okay, I don't mind if he just hangs out."

"No, he probably shouldn't catch this next bit," he said.

"But what about all of the blood?"

"He'll be fine, I've taught him well." He grinned. "Sigmund, what did I just say? Get your ass out of here. You're wasting time, go for a swim; it'll be good exercise for you."

The image of sickly little Sigmund lapping his way through the fields, the gore staining his body with every stroke, made me shiver. Sigmund hopped off his stool and waddled through the only door. As it slammed shut, I could hear the waves of blood crashing into one another in the distance.

"To answer your question from earlier," Asclepius said. "The point of the chopping was for conditioning, both physically and mentally. Can you feel the good ache?"

The soft pulse of exertion stung in both of my arms, over my back, and across my chest. My muscles were tightening and rebuilding themselves. It hurt, but in a satisfying way. My expression told Asclepius all he needed to know.

"Ideally," he continued, "you're going to take these bastards out one at a time, that's what I'm training you for. But just in case, you need the stamina to go for more than one round. Get me?"

I nodded. He pulled a heavy knife from its resting place on the wall. It had a thick, black blade with a single edge that ended in a point sharp enough to cut through a rib cage. He tested it with his thumb, drawing blood instantly. He walked back to the center of the room and, pressing the blade to the floor, began to walk in a large circle. Small particles of sawdust leapt into the air from the line he traced.

"And the mental side?" I asked.

"I believe the only way to beat something into your head is practice." He finished his circle and wiped the blade on his jeans. "Think about it, if I handed you an axe right now, you'd feel pretty comfortable, wouldn't you? Like a lot of weapons, axes are just tools in disguise, and the trick to mastering their intricacies is to do the same thing over and over again. You're not trying to be some fancy kung fu master; you're just trying to get a smooth arc out of the head. And when you have a juicy skull placed on a chopping block in front of you . . ."

"I won't hesitate."

"That's what I like to hear! Sadly, not all melee combat is that easy though. If you're in a hallway and you try to fight with an axe, you'll look like a goddamn fool. Like trying to hit one out of the park—but your batter's box is a telephone booth. It just doesn't happen. Before you go back, I want to show you what to do if one of those cowards decides to get in your face."

As he finished, he raised the blade and ran the edge along his whiskers. The ghostly scratch of stubble rang in my ears.

"You mean knives."

"And so, *so* much more, dear Edric. But first, you need to strip."

Ryan
❖

"STRIP," MADISON SNICKERED as our bedroom door shut. It was the first time in the last two days that I didn't mind being ordered around.

"Are you sure?" I teased. "I've been locked up in a car with a bunch of sweaty guys and I haven't even showered yet."

I would have pressed this idea and invited her in with me, but the thought of contorting our way into the filthy stall with the waves of feelers and legs sloshing through the pipes beneath our feet made me bite my tongue.

"That won't be necessary," she said as she grabbed the front of my shirt and pulled me to her. She brought her mouth up to mine and dragged her fingers through my tangled hair.

"Is this just a quickie?" I chuckled. She dropped her head onto my shoulder and snuggled up to my neck. I could feel the flutter of her eyelashes and the subtle tips of her teeth as she nibbled at my collarbone.

"I prefer to think of it as a *thank you*."

Edric
❖

I PEELED MY CLOTHES OFF and stared at the floor. The blood had seeped through the fabric and dyed my skin in streaks of rust. The thin, scattered tufts of hair on my chest, under my arms, and below my waist were still matted with beads of crimson. I thought about covering myself, but I knew it wouldn't be worth it. I would soon need my hands for more important things.

The low light danced in shimmers over Asclepius sweaty skin as he peeled off his clothes one article at a time, revealing more and more scars as he went. There were stitches, gashes, and burns mapped out over his entire chest. On his back were deep imprints in the shape of hands, one of which ended in an old rotten fingernail permanently embedded in his flesh, like someone or something had clawed at him. His member hung limp between his legs and just above it where his pubic hair should have been was the blistered skin of a brand in the shape of an omega. Believe it or not, this last detail actually made me relax; at least he wasn't getting aroused.

"You seem nervous, Edric. Try not to be. The Ancient Greeks believed that there was a power in nudity. I don't know if there's any truth to that, but I do know that if you can effectively fight naked, then no handicap you ever have should be a problem. You need to learn to not be self-conscious, to block out all other distractions and focus solely on survival— solely on killing. Take some deep breaths and try it, let your worries roll off you and melt into the floor."

I closed my eyes and did what I was told.

Ryan

❖

I TUGGED MY SHIRT FREE from the sticky layer of sweat coating my chest. The daylight seeped in from between the slats of the room's one window and threw golden mirages off of my stomach.

"Yeah, I think we'll be able to make this work," she sighed as she backed into me. I wrapped my arms around her stomach and she tilted her head enough for me to sprinkle kisses down her cheeks and onto her neck. "No problems here."

I dropped my hands to my pants, unzipped, and pulled them down. But I was in a hurry and when it came time to step out I almost tripped over my own feet. Madison giggled.

"Take your time, sweetheart, we have *days* to kill. There's no reason to be in a rush."

My boxers followed my pants and soon I was standing completely naked in the center of the room, feeling the rough texture of the floor on the soles of my feet. Her eyes drifted south to my erection. I was already hard, but the way she bit her lower lip curiously with her hips cocked to the side made the anticipation unbearable.

"Did you miss me?" She smiled as she crossed the room.

"Yes . . ."

"How much did you miss me?"

Never breaking eye contact, her petite hand found its way down my stomach until each of her fingertips clasped around my member. Everything from my exodus to Seattle and back faded away at the touch of her skin. My knees started to shake.

"How much did you miss me?" She moved her thumb in little circles over the tip, smearing the translucent dab of pre-cum.

"More than you can understand . . ."

"Tell me."

She released me and stepped away. I did my best to hide my disappointment, but by the way she smirked I could tell she knew everything. She hooked her hands into her shirt and began to pull it over her head.

"It was like sprinting to an oasis in the middle of a desert," I said. She paused with the shirt still concealing her breasts.

"Go on."

"And your heart soars at just the thought that you'll be able to experience that refreshment—letting the water dribble over your face, your lips, your back . . ."

She dropped her shirt to the floor, revealing a pair of light pink cotton underwear, no bra. The lines of her stomach had only recently faded, but hadn't transitioned into the "obviously pregnant" stage. Her perky breasts had also begun to swell, but not noticeably. Each of her small pink nipples was fully erect. From where she was standing I could barely make out the jagged S shaped scar that wrapped over her clavicle from her right shoulder blade. She had received it from a childhood accident involving a barbed wire fence on her father's farm. She had always acted self-conscious about it, but to me, it was just one more thing to love about her. My mouth watered and for a moment I was speechless.

"So?" she grinned.

"So what?"

"Did you make it to the oasis?"

She came back to me, wrapped her palms around my cheeks and we kissed again; her wet tongue teasing mine with every peck.

"It's different," I groaned as I cupped my hands over her breasts, rubbing each nipple with my thumbs. "I was afraid I'd get caught and never see you again. But now that I'm here it isn't like a thirsty man finally finding water. It's more like getting out of jail—or escaping from Hell . . ."

Edric

"**WE'LL BEGIN WITHOUT THE KNIVES,**" Asclepius said as we met in the middle of the ring. "The first thing to remember is that when you're engaged in hand to hand combat, you don't have four limbs, you have nine: two fists, two feet, two elbows, two knees, and a head. I know it sounds like it might hurt, but with your adrenaline pumping, it's better to smash your forehead into their nose and feel a little dizzy if it means incapacitating your enemy. The same can be said for when it comes to deflecting blows. I won't lie, it sucks to take a slash to the arm or hand, but it beats the crap out of eating eight inches of steel in your temple.

"Focus on quick, short strikes with your elbows to their ribs, or their face if you can manage it. The faster you return your arm to its blocking position, the safer you'll be."

We practiced this, circling each other before moving in with a strike. The hard ball of my elbow meeting Asclepius's clammy skin felt incredible. I may have looked foolish, but in my mind every movement I made was as methodical and deadly as a cobra sinking its fangs into a rat.

"It might not seem like fighting fair, but honor doesn't hold any place here. Honor got kicked to the curb as soon as they drugged you and hoisted you into that van. If you knee them in the balls, preferably by surprise, that'll at least shock their system—the same can be said about stomping on their feet."

"But won't that throw off my balance?" I asked.

"Depends on the situation. But if they're barefoot and you're wearing shoes, it might be worth the risk to incapacitate a foot. If you systematically disable their limbs, you'll be able to pick them apart like hyenas on a carcass. Are you getting tired?"

"Not yet," I breathed. "It feels like I took a shot of molten metal, but I'm okay for now."

"If this was a real fight, with any luck, they'd be dead already, but if you end up in a prolonged battle—you might need to tire them out before the final blow."

Asclepius reached one of his hands behind my head and pulled it forward.

"If you do something like this, then you can control their movement or pull their hair." He moved his hand around so that his palm was pressed into the contours of my cheek and jaw. "And this allows you to force your thumb into one of their eyes. If their head doesn't fly back immediately, keep going until you feel a pop. Yeah, it's gross, but no one ever won anything without getting a little dirty."

I smiled. This whole experience was like reading a brochure for a deluxe vacation package. The more I learned, the more I couldn't wait to test it out in the field.

"Now, if you need a break, the best thing to do is come in as close as possible and grip your body to theirs," Asclepius said. He pressed his naked chest against mine, wrapped his thick arms around my midsection so that his hands met in the middle of my back, and slid them up to my armpits. "You see? You can't hit me now. You'll be able to shake me off eventually but that should be adequate time for me to catch my breath. Time is of the essence, but if you don't think you can go on, a little hugging break can save your life."

Ryan

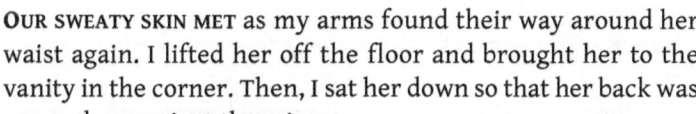

OUR SWEATY SKIN MET as my arms found their way around her waist again. I lifted her off the floor and brought her to the vanity in the corner. Then, I sat her down so that her back was pressed up against the mirror.

"I missed you too," she said.

"How much?" I smiled.

"I could try to explain, or I could just show you."

She reclined backwards, slipping her hands into her panties and pulling them away. They slid down her long, smooth legs. She had shaved her sex since the last time we made love, and with the way she was sitting I could see all of her, open and waiting for me. She pursed her lips and looked up at me with big beautiful eyes.

"I love you," she whispered.

"I love you more," I replied.

Edric

"HOW YOU CHOOSE TO HOLD YOUR KNIFE is going to be the most important decision you make going into a fight." Asclepius picked up the knife he had grabbed earlier and flicked another off the wall for me—it landed point down in the floor at my feet. I crouched, pulled it free, and tested its weight as it moved through the air.

"Knives have the benefit of being both stabbing and slashing weapons," he said. "So at the very least, you have options."

"What does an axe count as?"

"Chopping, of course. Axes don't exactly cut, they pinch."

I took the hilt of my knife in both hands and held it out in front of me.

"This isn't a sword fight, you moron." Asclepius laughed. "Get your second hand off that thing—and don't let me catch you getting pretentious, either; with your fingers stretched out behind the blade, that's a good way to get yourself laughed into an early grave."

I repositioned the knife so that it was clenched in a single fist.

"When knife fighting, you have some leeway with how you choose to brandish your weapon, but for our purposes you're going to learn two. The first is simple. Grip the handle in a fist with the edge facing up and out. This gives you slightly more range than option two, but it's harder to put your weight behind it. Choice two entails flipping the knife over so that you have the blade down, but the edge is still out."

I tried the feel of both and took some practice slashes. My strikes felt weightless after my exercise with the axe.

"These guys that you're up against are amateurs. They might be smart and have some experience, but they don't have the technique," Asclepius concluded. "For instance, it isn't a stretch to imagine that they'll begin the fight by running at you blindly and slashing like a lunatic. Kind of like this . . ."

Asclepius raised his knife and rushed at me. The blade sliced through the air in every direction. I ducked to the ground and rolled past him.

"Good," he said. "When confronted with an opponent who doesn't know what they're doing, just avoid them until they slow down and open up."

I got off the floor and prepared myself for Asclepius's next attack.

"Like I said already, this isn't a sword fight, you shouldn't be deflecting your enemy's knife; instead, you should do quick parries and then cut and stab when you get a chance."

He moved into the center of the ring and invited me to join him. On his mark, I got back into my fighting stance and waited for his move.

He slashed forward past my cheek and I ducked beneath and around it to bury my blade into his hamstring. He kneeled, groping in pain at his leg while I sprang back to my feet, ready to cut his throat and end the match. But before I could finish my strike, his hand shot up and crushed my wrist. I let out a nervous yelp as he brought his knife back around to smack my weapon to the ground. Then, in one motion, he kicked my leg out from underneath me, sending me to the floor. He swung his legs over my chest and looked me in the eye.

"Not bad, Edric, you're a natural."

"Thanks," I murmured, afraid to guess what was coming next.

"Let's finish today's lesson. When you get someone helpless like this, there is a third knife technique I've nicknamed the 'Serial Killer.' I think it was Hitchcock who popularized this one."

He flipped the knife over so that the blade was pointed down at me with the edge inward. From my back I could only see a thin reflection of light off the blade. It was a long sharp sliver floating above my face.

"There are two rules to remember when stabbing someone." He smiled as he dropped the blade into my shoulder. I could feel it rip through the muscles and press into my bone. My back arched violently but Asclepius remained seated. "Be patient; if you go in at a bad angle, the blood will come straight out and get you in the eyes. It isn't sanitary, and it'll make you blind."

I screamed and thrashed, but despite all my efforts, Asclepius wouldn't budge. I was helpless. I couldn't see his face anymore, it was hidden by the shadows; but I was still able to make out his golden furious eyes and his rows upon rows of jagged fangs. He placed the knife over the flat of my stomach.

"The second is that you shouldn't be concerned about making your cuts too clean—it's actually better if you don't." He plunged the knife into my gut and held it there. "Scramble their guts a little, and *twist* when you pull out."

He did just that, first jerking the blade around, shredding the membranes of my internal organs. I could feel the sharp tear of the knife's tip, and then the heat and heaviness of fluids rushing into my abdominal cavity, freed from their homes. He retracted the knife as I vomited a torrent of blood. I could feel my eyes rolling around in my head as I tried to make sense of the blurred world around me, but it was no use.

I blacked out.

Ryan
❖

I SCOOTED HER TOWARD ME, with little squeaks as her flesh slid on the top of the vanity's polished surface. Again, she wrapped her lithe fingers around my cock and guided me in. She'd tightened up, but the building anticipation had made her slick. She groaned as I entered her but placed a hand on my chest to reassure me that everything was okay.

"Take it slow," she breathed in my ear.

I nodded and began to pump my hips. I started slow, barely pulling out and only rotating slightly. When her breathing escalated and I could feel her moist breath on my chest, I moved one of my hands to her opening and massaged her clit with two of my fingers, applying little bits of pressure with every thrust. She moaned, pulled her hair back, and traced her hands over her breasts. When she got closer to her climax she wrapped both of her legs around my waist and began to buck her hips at her own pace. When she came, her eyes fluttered closed like resting butterflies as she let out an elated sigh.

"Let's move to the bed," she said between inhales. "If we're going to keep going, I'd like to be a little more comfortable."

She led me over to the bed and we took our places among the sheets and rock-hard pillows. This time she braced one of her hands against the headboard and caressed the other along her inner thigh. With my erection throbbing and begging to take its place back inside her warmth, I positioned myself behind her and entered in as far as I could go. This time she drew in a quick breath before letting out an ecstatic squeal. Again I found my rhythm, leaving just the tip inside every time I pulled back and moved forward. After another fifteen minutes I could feel her tense up and begin to tighten around me. This time I didn't fight it, and when my head tilted to the ceiling and my nerves let out a final blast of glowing warmth, one thought crossed my mind . . .

Life can't get any better than this.

We lay in bed after, our sweat beginning to dry and our hearts working their way back down to a more casual tempo. The thoughtful silence was broken by a single deliberate knock on the door.

"What do you need?"

"Nothing," Nate replied, "I just wanted to let you know that Edric is awake."

"We'll be out in a few."

I dropped back down onto the bed and turned to Madison. She seemed to be in some sort of trance, staring at a point in the ceiling without blinking. The sanctuary our lovemaking had created seemed miles away.

"What is it?"

"Nothing." She rolled over to face me again. I could still see the rosy tint of her nipples through the sheet she kept over her chest. "I was just thinking, can I meet him?"

"I don't know," I said, then paused. "Is that something you'd be comfortable with? Right now he doesn't even know you're involved. You'd be implicating yourself."

"Oh please," she laughed. "If any of you get busted, all of our lives are over. Him seeing my face won't make any difference. And how long could you guys hide me? He's not an idiot, he's sure to know something is up eventually."

"I'll ask Nate and see what he says."

We kissed one more time and she smiled.

"What is it, cutie?"

"It's nothing, I just missed you."

We both got dressed and met Nate in the hallway. He seemed more anxious than usual.

"How is he?" I asked.

"No reason to be concerned."

"Maddy wanted to know if she could meet him."

"As long as you don't give him any personal details or hints about what we plan to do from here on out, I'm cool with it." He shrugged. "In fact, that's something Schafer brought up earlier."

"What do you mean?"

"He's worried."

"That's nothing new."

"I know, but I can only imagine how bad it's going to get if he's cooped up here for days. His most recent anxiety attack was about how Maddy is the only one who could still be considered an innocent bystander in this whole thing—he's suspicious."

"Whatever," Madison laughed. "If I meet Edric, that should help quell some of this bullshit."

"I hope so," Nate concluded. He flashed a hopeful smile, but something in his eyes wasn't there.

Edric

I WAS PLANNING ON FIGHTING against my restraints. Not to escape of course, it was still too early for that, but instead to see how fast I could slip out of them in case an emergency arose. I was able to deduce that it wouldn't be easy (or impossible for that matter) when someone knocked on the door.

"I hope you aren't expecting me to get that," I called out.

I was anticipating my good pal Schafer to come in with a tray full of milk and cookies—and as soon as he saw my mouth watering, he'd eat them all by my bedside, maybe tossing me a crumb or two if he was feeling generous. Instead, in walked a pretty woman—too old for me but gorgeous nonetheless.

"Great," I grumbled. "I must be dead. How disappointing, I thought I'd last at least a little longer."

She smiled; she must have thought I was joking. When I saw how her demeanor changed after those few words, I thought back to one of Asclepius's first lessons. If I could manipulate this girl, make her think we were friends, then maybe she would cough up some precious information that could aid my escape—and revenge.

"I'm Edric," I said, raising my hand the best I could to try and shake hers. "Pleasure to meet you."

She made an effort to shake my hand (as awkward as it was) and took a seat next to my bed.

"What's your name?"

She hesitated and looked over her shoulder at Ryan who was hovering in the doorway like the schmuck he is.

"I already know all of their names," I continued. "It won't hurt for you to tell me yours."

"I guess that makes sense. I'm Madison," she said. "You can call me Maddy if you want."

She kept smiling even as her eyes traced the cuts and bruises on my face—finally, a real professional. If I hadn't overheard the conversations in the van, I would have thought she was leading this assignment.

"Maddy it is then. So where do you fit into all of this?"

"Moral support."

"Like a cheerleader?"

"I was one when I was younger."

"I bet, you're very pretty."

"Knock it off," she blushed. "What would your girlfriend say?"

"Don't have one," I said. "I was actually working on that before—you know . . ."

"Yeah, well on the bright side, girls like danger. When you go home you can tell them about this and they'll be all over you."

"I suppose I should be thanking you guys then."

She laughed again; I could feel the rage swell in my chest. She honestly believed that we were becoming friends, what an idiot. I wasn't going to be able to continue to pull off the happy-go-lucky illusion for much longer. I decided I should try to sow some seeds of chaos before giving up for the day.

I moved my head in the low light to try and make my eyes look sunken and let out a pained wheeze.

"I'm sorry," I whined. "You seem like a sweet person, and I definitely wouldn't mind continuing this conversation later—but I really need to sleep. It might be the side effects or something, but I have no energy."

"Are you okay?" she asked, startled.

"I think so, I'm sorry, I just need to sleep . . ." I turned away from her the best I could and lapsed into a fake coma.

"What was that he said about side effects?" I heard her say to Ryan in a deadly serious tone. "I want to know everything."

Any other time I would have smiled ear-to-ear and patted myself on the back, it had been even easier than I'd thought. But I was in character, so I managed to stay as passive and still as a corpse until they left the room together.

I would have to thank Asclepius; my skills were improving.

X

Apnea

Ryan

❖

WE WALKED BACK TO OUR ROOM and shut the door. Madison took a seat on the edge of the bed and I pressed my forehead against the doorframe before turning around to meet her gaze.

"This is important," I said. "How honest do you want me to be?"

"Honesty is the foundation of any good relationship," she replied, looking straight ahead. "I'd say our relationship is pretty good, wouldn't you?"

"Damn it, Maddy, I'm being serious."

"I am too. I said before that it felt like you were doing this for me—for *me*, Ryan. So if you guys screwed something up, it's at least partly my responsibility and I deserve to know. What did you guys do to that poor boy?"

"It's not that simple, okay?" I replied. I had known this conversation was going to happen at some point. It's not like I expected that I could avoid the subject altogether and spend the next couple of days fucking and sitting on the back porch sipping iced tea. "It's a long story, and if you really want to know everything like you said, I'm going to need to start from the beginning."

"Well luckily for you," she began, crossing her arms. "I have all day to hear about you and your buddies' adventures. Start talking."

I sat down next to her, took one of her petite hands in mine, and plunged headfirst into my story.

I told her about the dreams. How I'd lost both weight and sleep from the anxiety that crawled through my flesh—that had spun its web between my bones.

"Well if it helps at all," she said, cracking an awkward smile. "You look fantastic."

"Thank you," I said. "I need to finish."

She nodded and pulled me closer.

"You won't hear anymore interruptions out of me, babe. Please continue."

Next I told her about the plan. Even though she was around while Nate put it together and the rest of us went about procuring our transportation arrangements and weapons, we had always played our cards close to the vest. Everything was operating on a strictly need-to-know basis and until now, Maddy hadn't been a part of that circle. We didn't even tell Nate's bedridden uncle, despite our decision to make his home our base of operations.

I explained that while the plan worked perfectly, we still ran into a number of complications. Here I paused until I finally worked up the courage to tell her that I had gunned down a police officer to ensure our escape. My heart was pounding and I'm willing to bet that she could feel its dull pulse in my fingers. Instead of recoiling in disgust and marching out of the room, she kissed me. It's not like it absolved me of my sins, but knowing that I still had her support made me feel light-years better.

Edric had decided he wasn't going to come quietly, I concluded, and Schafer took it as an opportunity to work the boy over a couple of times. The option came up to drug him, and the rest of us were left with the decision to either watch Schafer slowly beat the boy to death or give him a quick shot here and there to help put him out of his misery. I was extra cautious in making sure that it didn't sound like I was rationalizing or supporting this decision, but rather that I thought it was the lesser of two evils.

"And that's it," I said. My shoulders relaxed and Madison sat silent for almost two minutes before she spoke up.

"Jesus," she said. "That certainly is a lot to think about."

"You're telling me."

I covered my eyes and fell backwards onto the bed. The blankets that had felt like heaven before now felt scratchy and rough.

"Honey," she said. "Thank you for telling me. I don't want any secrets between us. Not now, and not when the baby comes, okay? I love you, and as horrible as it is, I think you made the right decisions all across the board."

"Honestly?"

"I swear," she said, nodding. "We've always known Schafer is a little out there. You may have even saved Edric's life. Don't beat yourself up about it, okay?"

"Okay."

"You promise?"

"I promise."

I kissed her on the cheek.

"You're probably bursting with questions," I said. "You can ask whatever you want, girly. I just told you I was a murderer, I don't think there's anything left for me to lie about."

"I don't know," she replied, bringing a finger to her lips. I knew she was thinking, but to me, she was issuing silent directions as she pointed at her perfect mouth: *kisses go here*. "How safe is this drug you've been injecting him with?"

"Not really sure. If I was an expert chemist, sweetheart, I don't think you and I would be here right now. Supposedly they use it in medical procedures all the time."

"You know what else they use in medical procedures? Morphine."

"I know, I know, but I'm kind of hoping the trauma of this whole event will keep him off the stuff, even after we return him to dear old dad. Think about it, if you tried cocaine, but you snorted it while getting raped, would you want to turn around and do cocaine again?"

"I guess that makes sense."

"Plus, we're being careful with how much we give him—half a dose at a time, just enough to make him drowsy. Not even Schafer would risk giving him an overdose."

"Which of you guys have actually done the, you know, injecting?" She asked. There was a hint of hesitation in her voice. I didn't know what it meant and chose not to ask.

"Schafer and me," I replied. "It's not that I wanted to—but I suggested we put him out again and Schafer wanted me to get my hands dirty. Are you okay? You're looking a little green."

"Oh I'm fine," she said. "I hate needles is all."

There was a knock on the door, and despite how soft it had been, it felt like a thunderclap. I hadn't realized that almost our entire conversation had taken place just above a whisper. Madison moved to answer it but I stopped her.

"Allow me, your highness."

"Oh, so I'm royalty now?" she asked. "What does that make you?"

"Why, a member of the Royal House's harem, of course."

"In that case, hurry up. You've yet to meet today's quota, my slave."

We laughed and I opened the door, causing Jacob to jump back on his heels. His eyes darted from paint chip to paint chip, cobweb to cobweb, never coming anywhere close to my face. All the while he rubbed his hands together furiously, like a hypochondriac after they've been given the last squirt of Purell on Earth.

"Hey Jacob," I said. "Why so anxious? Did you think I wasn't going to open the door or something?"

"No, nothing like that." He shot another glance behind him to make sure we were alone. "You guys just hadn't been up and about today, I thought you might want to know what's been going on."

"Did they call about the ransom already?"

"No, I wish. I meant, like, with what's been going on with Schafer . . ."

I knew where this conversation was going, but sometimes, when your brakes are cut and you hit a patch of black ice, you just have to hold on for the ride.

"What did him and that metric ton of paranoid baggage he's been carrying around do now?"

"Nothing—yet," he said, checking over his shoulder one more time. "It's more about what he's been saying."

"Enlighten me," I said, this time checking over my own shoulder to see if Madison was following along. She seemed blissfully ignorant, gently cupping a large, furry moth out of the air before releasing it again unharmed.

"He trusts you enough," Jacob continued.

"Good to see that my stabbing Edric wasn't in vain." Jacob laughed at this before I swiftly added: "That wasn't meant to be a joke."

"Of course not," he squeaked, after a poor attempt at disguising his laugh as a cough. "It's Maddy. He thinks if something goes wrong, she's going to snitch on us in a heartbeat. We're talking about spilling the beans before they even have the cuffs on. He thinks that if we gave her the needle test too, you know, seeing if she's willing to put Edric out, then we could trust her."

I told myself not to get mad, but of course, that never helps. "I've had enough of this," I said. I rolled my eyes and pushed past Jacob. "I'm putting an end to this insanity now before it snowballs out of control."

Jacob put a hand on my chest to stop me.

"I wouldn't do that," he said. He cowered a bit like I was going to hit him, but after a few seconds he realized I was a little more levelheaded than Schafer and relaxed. "It's not that it's not a good idea—it is—but now is not the right time. He's been stalking the halls like he wants to fight someone to help blow off steam. And it can only make things worse now if you oblige him. We knew that this plan wasn't going to be easy, and if someone confronts him, then it's going to jump from tough to impossible."

I didn't like it, but it was true. Getting in a fight with Schafer would be the same as taking the rope that bound our alliance together and running a knife along it until there was nothing left but frayed threads.

"What would you suggest?" I said.

"Give it a day. I think we're all a little on edge from being trapped in the car with each other, and still trying to dial in our emotions after the whole operation. If things aren't better tomorrow, then we'll panic."

It made sense. The anger that had bunched up in my throat moments ago melted and seeped back into the pit of my stomach again, dormant for the time being.

"Thanks, Jake, you're an okay guy," I said, clapping him on the shoulder.

"You too, Ryan. That's all I wanted to say. I'll let you two lovebirds get back to it."

Jacob trudged off down the hall (probably looking for an inconspicuous place to hold up until Schafer's warpath was over) and I closed the door again. I wrapped my arms around Madison and nuzzled into her neck, but she barely responded. She had been listening.

"Something on your mind?" I asked, testing the waters.

"It's nothing."

"Come on, you can't pull that now. Not after that whole 'no secrets between us' speech earlier," I laughed.

"I was thinking about what Jacob said. If it comes up, would I be able to dope Edric?"

"Would you?" I asked, stunned. Her eyes went dark and worried for the first time since our return.

"I have no idea," she said.

"Don't even worry," I replied as she rolled away from me. "I won't let it come to that."

Edric

❖

I WAS STANDING IN FRONT of Asclepius's home again with the light from the sky sinking into evening. The blood that had sloshed waist-deep over the fields before had drained into the sand, creating stagnant puddles of rotting mud and clumping the grass together into tangled masses of scabs. It looked like a giant scalp, smashed in with a stone and left to bleed out. The stiff scent of copper on the wind made me gag. My gasps and gurgles were interrupted by the squeal of Asclepius's front door. He sucked in a deep breath through his nostrils and stretched.

"Evening is my favorite time of day," he said.

"How poetic," I sneered without thinking. Luckily I wasn't within arm's reach.

He had a shotgun strapped to his back and a pistol wedged in his waistband. Both were loaded, I didn't have to ask—call it a hunch. But beyond the sculpted steel, carved stocks, and faint smell of burnt gunpowder, was a ball of fur no larger than an upright cinderblock. Standing alert with its ears perked up behind Asclepius's leg was a puppy. It had tangled black fur on its back like it had just rolled out of bed and a line of shiny silver hair running from its chin down its stomach. I don't know if it was from the sudden jolt of adorable in this otherwise horrific environment, or the need to take a break from the killer developing inside of me, but my heart glowed.

"Come here, boy," I cooed as I dropped to one knee, a hand outstretched. He trotted over to me with his sickle tail wagging and let me stroke behind his ears. "What breed is he?"

"A Shiba Inu, Japan's original hunting dog."

"How did you get a hold of one?"

Asclepius shrugged while the puppy ran in little circles, trying to lure me into playing with its fiercely intelligent eyes. I looked around for a branch or twig I could use to initiate a game of fetch, but gave up when I remembered the nasty traits of the flora in this world. Knowing Asclepius, it was probably for the best that this thing didn't acquire a taste for blood.

"What's his name?" I asked. Asclepius looked down at me like it was the dumbest question imaginable.

"Bullet, of course."

Ryan
❖

BETWEEN SCHAFER'S CONSTANT THEORIES about Madison being an informant for the police and going over the laundry list of all of the terrible things my friends and I had done in our recent history—it had been a long day. Staying in the safe bubble of our room almost the whole time helped make things better though (no silverfish bathtub, no syringes, no ransom, just Madison and I).

The sunset and the ambient sound of my cohorts killing time was replaced by crickets chirping, along with the occasional rustling of something scuttling across the floorboards. I was able to block out the creaks and the groans and focus entirely on the beautiful woman, the mother of my child, lying next to me. We hadn't been talking, just enjoying the feeling of having someone close by.

"What a mess," she sighed. There was no clock in the room, but it had to have been the first thing either of us said in over an hour. "And it's only going to get worse unless we do something."

"What do you mean?"

"Edric. I've made peace with the idea that he's basically in a coma and that it's our fault, but it still can't be very healthy."

I could tell she was sad; it was the way her voice softened at the ends of her sentences. Each punctuation mark was another hairline fracture in her poker face. But there were no tears.

"What would you like me to do?" I asked. It was better that we just cut to the chase. "I've been trying to negotiate this obstacle course between all of my friends alone the last couple of days, I want your help. I want your opinion."

She searched my face before nodding.

"I'll help you anyway I can. You guys snatched him, let me contribute in my own way. Just sleep tonight, honey. If anyone has earned a little R and R, it's you. We'll figure out how to start fixing things tomorrow."

I played with her hair until her breathing slowed and I knew she was asleep. I closed my eyes and soon followed her.

No nightmares.

Edric

I STROKED BULLET'S COARSE FUR and ran my hands over the patch of glossy silver on his belly until Asclepius grabbed my attention.

"Enough of this love fest," he groaned. "We still have training to do."

Bullet looked up, startled, sank away from my hand and skipped back to his original place behind Asclepius. I stood up, ready to face my next test.

"We're going to be moving fast today, so try to keep up." He pulled the shotgun from his back and pumped it once; I could hear the shell slide into the chamber with no resistance. "Follow me."

We went around to the back of Asclepius's cabin, past the mysteriously refilled pile of firewood, and stopped at the edge of an open field. Hovering just above the matted grass were the tops of a few scattered rocks and chunks of debris (there was even what looked to be a shredded airplane wing and a closed door upright in its frame).

"Are you going to make me dodge bullets again? Out of ideas already?"

"No," he said. "The last time we did that it was along the lines of Tag, I liken this more to Hide-and-Seek."

"Isn't Hide-and-Seek just a boring version of Tag?"

"Are you trying to talk me into shooting you?"

"No sir."

"May I proceed?" when Asclepius was sure his threat had me too scared to object, he continued. "What you said is true, you've learned the importance of staying out of sight. That doesn't mean you've learned all of the merits of taking cover, especially in the middle of a firefight. But we're getting ahead of ourselves. Have you ever fired a gun before?"

"Yeah, but it was only a pellet gun."

"Better than nothing. After all, the same basic principles apply: line up your sights, the front one is the most important, take a deep breath, and pull the trigger straight back. If you jerk it in one direction or the other, you're dead. Try to stay out of sight before you take your shot—but you should know that by now. It will always be to your advantage to stay hidden, especially if you're outnumbered. If your target doesn't know you're there, and they aren't doing fucking jumping jacks, you aim for the head. If not, you aim for their center of mass."

"What does that mean?" I asked. Asclepius slapped his palm across his forehead before I had even finished the question.

"Dear God, what are they teaching kids in school these days anyway?"

"Sorry, physics was never my strong suit. I had to pay my teacher off to pass." I paused. "I did the same thing in biology, now that I think about it."

"Their chest and stomach, you idiot. It won't kill them immediately, but unless they're Superman, they won't be shooting back anymore. But these are guidelines, remember? If someone is screaming down a hall at you with a meat cleaver, ready to turn you into a hundred and fifty pounds of prime Grade A bleeding chunks, it's better to shoot than stand around making sure they're between the iron sights."

He tossed me the shotgun and I snatched it out of the air. It was heavy and cold except for a few clammy spots where Asclepius had gripped the stock. I held it to my chest.

"Something you're going to have to get familiar with is recoil. That pellet gun that you used to plink cans in your daddy's backyard is a kitten compared to this twelve gauge. Take a shot at that rock over there."

I brought the butt up to my shoulder and stared down the barrel until the cracked granite surface of the stone came into focus. I held my breath and pulled the trigger. First, there was a loud snap followed by a metallic vibration (I couldn't tell if it was my ears or some loose mechanism inside the gun). Chips of the rock scattered into the air as buckshot scraped across the worn surface and zinged out towards the distant hills and sky. I didn't have time to admire my shot for long though, because soon I could feel a deep ache biting my shoulder. Sometime between aiming and cranking off my shot, I had shifted the gun enough for the recoil to bounce back into my flesh.

"That's going to leave a bruise," Asclepius said. He wanted to laugh but didn't for my sake. "What're you going to do next time?"

"Keep it nice and tight, no room to breathe."

"That's my boy. If you're only firing one shot at a time the kick won't be too much of an issue. But on the other hand, if you're shooting an automatic and aren't careful, you'll be putting bullets in the ceiling—not very helpful, unless you're fighting some sort of giant spider. Even better, a lot of rifles and shotguns have a strap you can wrap around your arm to keep them from flying out of your hands. You can use it if you want, but it isn't necessary. You noticed how your shot did some surface damage but not much else?"

I nodded.

"If you'd been behind that rock, you'd be in the perfect position to spring out and pop the two of us during our reload. That, my friend, is but one of the wonders of strategic cover."

"What about blind firing or firing from the hip like they do in the movies?"

"The rule of the thumb is to just say no, because you aren't John Rambo and you are going to miss. Personally, I'd rather conserve my ammo for when I really need it. Remember though that survival supersedes all other rules, so if someone is trying to make a break for your hiding spot, putting a few over your shoulder might be the best investment you ever make. Let's go check out this door."

We waded out into the field as the red grass brushed past our hips, painting our pants with the final swaths of drying blood. Asclepius called over his shoulder while I did my best to avoid any puddles.

"With cover it all comes down to two factors: material and the size of the rounds it's shielding you from. Obviously stone and metal are the best, but drywall isn't bad either, because it'll stop most buckshot. You can always experiment with unconventional options as well. For instance, bathroom tile is surprisingly good at stopping a bullet. What will they think up next? Also, in some cases, curved and irregular surfaces can be your best friend."

"Why does that make any difference?"

"Ricochets. You heard how your shot deflected off of the rock? Like that, but deadlier. Bullets usually squish flat or shatter when they hit a hard surface, but sometimes they skid or bounce and fly off in a random direction. How embarrassing would it be if Schafer has you pinned down, he fires, then takes himself out?"

"I don't know," I replied. "Sounds more disappointing than embarrassing. Hell, I'd be pissed off if I wasn't the one who finally blasted him."

Asclepius grinned at this.

"I think I'm going to make a killer out of you yet, Edric. I'd be lying if I said I wasn't worried for a little while there. Here we are."

We stood in front of a cream colored door rooted firmly in its frame. Someone had actually taken the time to install it in the ground. Asclepius gripped the ornate brass handle and swung it open.

"Wood, of course, is a different matter. This door is two inches thick and might actually stop some smaller caliber bullets. It all depends on how much of a gambler you are."

He ushered me through the door and grinned when I seemed hesitant.

"I'm not going to shoot you," he said. "If I kill you now, all of this will have been a big waste of my time."

It seemed logical enough, but this was Asclepius. I wouldn't have put it past him to mortally wound me out of boredom. I decided that I didn't have a choice, and in the worst-case scenario, I'd be dead before I realized something had gone wrong. I stepped over the threshold and he pushed the door shut behind me.

"Sometimes the bullet will go straight through, so try to make yourself as little of a target as possible."

He fired a single shot with the pistol through the top of the door. Splinters dusted my hair and the faint smell of smoldering wood twisted its way down my throat.

"Sometimes it'll stop it completely, that one is self-explanatory—but other times you'll get some fragments that push through. They hurt like hell, but it's better than having a piece of lead split your skull. Just try not to catch one in an eye, that's a killer."

He fired a few more shots into the face of the door to illustrate before asking me to lock the deadbolt and rejoin him on the other side. I did as I was told and he shoved the pistol back in his waistband.

"You never ever want to try to take out one of these with a handgun," he said, thumbing the deadbolt. "It'll shatter the lock into a million slivers, and unless you have an axe or some dynamite handy, you aren't getting through. Doors, after all, were invented to keep people out, and they do their job admirably more often than not."

"This, on the other hand,"—he continued speaking while leveling the shotgun at the lock—"is a master key of sorts. The next shot is a deer slug; think of it as a paperweight with a rocket engine on the back. If you have a few of these babies loaded up, all you have to do is say the magic word. What's the magic word, Edric?"

"Boom?"

He pulled the trigger, and like uncorking a bottle of Dom Perignon, the cylinder popped clean out leaving a two-inch-wide peephole. Asclepius lifted his boot and kicked the door open.

"Like shooting fish nailed on a door." He smiled before bending down to examine the hollow where the lock had been. "I like to call these 'mail slots' because you can fit a gun barrel or small explosive through them—or wedge a funnel to pour some gasoline inside. Special delivery! Get it?"

"But wouldn't being next to it when it bursts into flames be a bad idea?"

"That's why you move," he said, ruffling my hair. "We're done here, let's head out."

We trekked back through the field and had almost reached the edge when something caught my eye, something small and twisted huddled behind the rock I had taken my practice shot at earlier. I broke away from Asclepius and crossed the grassy expanse to the stone and peeked behind it.

Stretched out at an odd angle was the body of a boy who couldn't have been older than seven. His skin was pale, like he'd been rinsed in bleach, and the flesh on his face was beginning to pull tight so that it had the texture of an old paper sack. Worst of all were his eyes. They were still bright and filled with fear, like a conscious infant being held underwater. There was no smell. I stood there in some sort of trance until Asclepius's heavy hand landed on my shoulder.

"Don't worry," he said. "He's been here for a while. Your shot didn't kill him."

"Who was he?" I squeaked, sapping all of the remaining air from my lungs.

"I said don't worry about it," Asclepius grumbled. "John Doe? Who gives a shit? Let's head in, we still have business to attend to."

We turned away and continued our trip back to Asclepius's home—but something wasn't right. I could still feel the boy's gaze burning into my back, begging me to return. I couldn't explain it. We stopped near the woodpile. He pulled out his pistol, clicked back the slide and handed it to me.

"One more thing we have to square away before we can continue," he said. "Shooting someone isn't like stabbing, it's far less personal. Depending on the range and flow of the battlefield, you might not even need to look your target in the eyes as their soul leaves their body—but don't get too relaxed. Just because you can push a button to give someone a lethal injection doesn't mean it can't carry the weight of a headsman's axe. For someone with no experience, it's still going to be tough. You need to develop the will to kill. And with that, I leave you to it . . ."

He bowed low enough for me to see the weathered skin behind his ears and stepped to the side revealing a panting, smiling Bullet. The puppy licked his nose unconsciously and grinned up at me, curious what our next game would be. I stared back, and then down at the gun in my hand. It felt like a bucket of ice had been dumped on my head.

Asclepius cleared his throat too loudly for me to ignore and glanced down at his watch. He followed this by tapping his foot rhythmically in the sand. The grit scraping across the bottom of his boot was deafening as twilight strangled the last light from the day. It was like he had invented a new dance. I desperately wanted to laugh at it—but I didn't.

It should have been easy. I'd been training for what felt like months with the sole purpose of becoming a killing machine. But the conditioning, the practice, the lessons, it all didn't mean as much as it should have now that I was the one holding the gun, prepared to make my first legitimate kill. I didn't want to shoot Bullet; but if I didn't, my journey was over. Not to mention Asclepius was still holding his shotgun, and the thought that if I didn't pull the trigger, he would, helped lubricate the whole process. In the end, only one thing determined my decision:

It's not like any of this was real anyway.

I pulled the hammer back so that I wouldn't have to endure the suspense of watching it rise before it slammed down on the next primer. I tried to aim the sights like Asclepius had taught me, but my hands were shaking too much. Instead, I lowered the gun against the top of Bullet's head. I wouldn't miss and be forced to take a second shot. I would make it quick for him. Bullet tried to paw the barrel away a couple of times and tilted his chin upwards to get a better look at the gun. I pulled the trigger.

Click.

The hammer fell on dead air and Bullet immediately leapt off his feet, landed on his back, and pointed all four of his legs to the sky. To complete the illusion, he stuck his pink tongue out of the side of his mouth and breathed a faint, guttural growl—a puppy's death rattle.

"Good boy!" Asclepius called out, and Bullet sprang back up and trotted over to him expecting a treat. I was shaking worse than when I was preparing to pull the trigger not even a minute before. "Christ, Edric, you need to lighten up."

XI
Lavender

Edric

"EDRIC, SWEET VIRGINAL EDRIC . . ."

"Uhhh, that's me?"

"Have you ever been to a bar before?"

As I drew in breath to reply, Bullet raised his head and snarled at some distant, unseen threat lurking in the bloody foliage. Then, he bolted after it as fast as his name implied. Asclepius and I were alone again, and even though I knew it would come off as a sign of weakness, I was crushed to see Bullet go.

"Not really—my father has a shitty one he built himself in the basement of our house, and I take hits off of some of the bottles when I don't think he'll notice," I said. "But to answer your question, no. I've never been to a real bar."

"Never? Huh, I would've figured a rich party boy like you would load the boys up in your fancy European sports cars and hit the old watering hole for a night on the town from time to time."

"You're in my head," I said, exasperated. "I know that some of what happens here transfers out to the real world, so you have access to my thoughts and memories. You know I'm not a 'party boy.' So just cut the shit and let me know where this is going."

Asclepius halted and stood up straighter. He couldn't have stopped more dead in his tracks had he taken a bolt of lightning to the spine.

"Did I touch a nerve or something? Where'd that come from?"

"I'm sorry," I replied immediately. "I don't know."

But secretly I did. I was slowly changing into a different person. The composition of my brain was warping into something darker and beyond my control. My outburst only seemed to confirm that. Even more frightening was this feeling that there was no turning back. Asclepius had said something to that effect before, but I figured it'd just been a metaphor or a turn of phrase. Not something real and palpable. No matter how this whole experiment ended, I would never be the boy I was, playing footsy with girls in my classes and strapping my headphones on for a relaxing walk home; never again. I prayed that after Asclepius was done breaking me down, there'd still be something of my original identity left to salvage among the ruins.

"Earth to Edric," Asclepius said. He snapped his fingers in front of my face. "If you're finished with your existential pondering about how I'm molding you for my own purposes and corrupting your id, I have something I'd like to show you."

Fun fact: when someone is able to read your mind at will, arguing with them is a waste of time and energy.

We walked around to the side of his house and I found myself, for the first time since my arrival, questioning the layout of my imagination. How many sides did Asclepius's house have? From every direction it looked like your basic four-walled shack—but that couldn't have been right, because every time we went for a walk, there always seemed to be new parts of his home I hadn't seen before. Maybe it had as many different sides as I required for my training? That thought should have been comforting (everything I needed could and would be provided for me). Unfortunately, instead of clinging to that idea, I couldn't shake the feeling that if I started at the door and began to walk around the house, I would die of starvation before I ever reached the front again.

On *this* side of the house was an old picnic table with an assortment of copper drums sitting on top. Some of them had begun to decay into Statue of Liberty greens, with crusty deposits blooming on the seams where they'd been hastily welded together. Metallic tubing ran from their tops and curlie-cued into one another. At one end was a crude spout. It looked like a mad scientist's water cooler, or maybe an official Dr. Mengele home chemistry set. Either way, I was hesitant to drink the clear liquid that dripped from its nozzle the way an adder's venom trickled from its fangs. Below it (catching every ounce of the mystery fluid), was a bathtub that had pale gray age rings burned into the sides of the basin from years of either use or neglect.

"This is what you call a still," Asclepius said. He dropped a hand on top of one of the large metal cylinders. Something inside sloshed and echoed through each section of the apparatus. "If you've ever seen an old prohibition or bootlegging movie though, you probably knew that already."

"Do you brew your own moonshine?" I asked as I circled the redneck Rube Goldberg machine. "You certainly seem like the type who would."

"Hardly," he said. He pulled two dusty shot glasses off the table, cleaned them with the tail of his shirt, brought them over to the leaky nozzle, and filled each to the brim. "This is something a little more potent."

He handed me one of the glasses and it made my fingers slick with cold condensation. Then, he raised his in a toast.

"To revenge, a dish that goes down smooth whether it's prepared well done or still bleeding," he said, bringing the shot to his lips. I followed his example, but as I tipped it back, I caught a quick flicker of his eyes transforming into gruesome yellow slits.

It tasted both sweet and sour, and I didn't have much experience drinking, so my natural instinct was to hold it in my mouth as the sweet faded into a burning sensation that numbed my teeth down to their roots. I was about to swallow when Asclepius finished draining his glass and looked at it admiringly.

"Man oh man, that is some *good*, pure hemlock," he said. I replied with a spit take that would have made a comedian proud. "Just kidding, you big baby. It's an appletini."

He reached down to the nozzle and twisted it one full rotation.

"Now we have fresh, liquefied hemlock on tap. Though I wouldn't recommend taking a shot—spoils the appetite. And the nervous system."

I traced the path each transparent drop made as they plummeted into the bathtub below. Every tiny splash sent a fine mist of toxic particles into the air. I suddenly became very self-conscious about how deep I'd been breathing.

"Just by looking at it, I can't tell the difference," I said. "I think I'm going to be sick."

I took a step away from the still. If I was going to be dry heaving with my mouth wide open, there were safer places to do it.

"That's the point, you silly boy. Poisons are like cocktails. All you need to do is find the ingredients and mix. And a lot of poisons, this hemlock included, is clear and untraceable until it's too late."

I tried to picture Asclepius as a bartender, whipping up deadly concoctions as he insulted the dead and dying patrons. I'd have bet my father's whole fortune he'd run the kind of bar that displayed an old lever-action Winchester next to the martini glasses. No one would dare to ask if he kept it loaded.

"Excuse me," I replied. "I find this all kinds of funny. The big bad Asclepius, whose next lesson for me is probably the most efficient way to strangle someone with barbed wire or a chainsaw, thinks that something as clean as poison is a legitimate way to kill someone."

Asclepius continued to stand with his arms crossed. A content smile slithered over his lips.

"Poison isn't clean," he said. "That's something the movies don't show you. A lot of times poison is just as messy as a blade when your victims start convulsing, vomiting, and bleeding out all over the floor. Still funny, little Edric?"

I didn't answer right away; my mind was now occupied with what I would've looked like had it not been a chick drink in my shot glass—my eyes bulging, my tongue swelling until no room remained for oxygen to get down my bleeding throat.

I gulped.

"I see your point," I said. "What if there isn't any hemlock around?"

"That's the beauty of it," Asclepius jumped in enthusiastically. When he got excited, there was no hiding it. "Literally anything can kill if you administer it in high enough doses. Have you ever looked at the instructions on the back of a bottle of pills? You know where it says 'Warnings' in bold print? Yeah, just ignore all of those parts and get ready to have some fun. And from what I can gather, they're basically holding you captive in an amateur pharmacy. Stupid idiots, they might as well of handed you a gun.

"If you'll allow me to take a step back to the hemlock for a moment," he continued. "Everything Mother Nature has cooked up over the years wants mankind dead—and if you're planning to come out on the other side of this, it's better to work with her than against her. The woods around the house you're being kept in are filled with deadly nightshade, you heard your captors say that themselves. It's what they've been using to brew this little nightcap that keeps bringing you back to me. There are also tons of fiddle-back spiders that are loaded with enough necrotoxin to make your skin swell up black until it splits like an overcooked frankfurter. Hannibal used to fill clay pots with asps and hurl them onto the decks of his enemies' ships. If it worked for him, there's no reason it won't work for you."

"It all sounds good in principle," I interrupted. "But I think I'd rather take a more direct approach when I'm finishing them off."

"Then why not give them a taste of their own medicine and drug them? You know, set some to the side while you go to work on their friends? This is, after all, a numbers game. You stand a much better chance if you separate your prey and digest them one at a time."

It was my turn to smile.

"My prey—I like the sound of that."

Ryan
❖

"I HAVE AN IDEA," Madison said. "Say you're at war and your troops have been taking a beating, what do you do to get them back in the fight?"

We were lounging in bed, wasting the day away as the slats of light coming through the blinds stretched out across the ceiling. I moved my hand up her leg and drummed my fingers on her thigh.

"Mead and wenches?"

"You're right," she giggled. "But that's not the answer I was looking for. Everyone is already so on edge the last thing we need is to get them drunk. And do you see any lusty barmaids around?"

"Just my little lusty barmaid."

"I'll pretend that was a compliment."

"Come on, Maddy, I'm busting your balls. What did you have in mind?"

I pulled her down on my lap. Everything in the world was perfect again. The kidnapping, the drugs, even our argument the night before felt so far away.

"If I was leading a campaign and my soldiers came running back to camp with their broadswords between their legs, I'd feed them a hearty meal."

"I follow so far . . ."

"Why don't I cook dinner for everyone? I feel kind of useless sitting around on my fat ass while the boys go out and do all the hard work."

"But I like your ass."

"That's beyond the point—and you're kind of biased."

"Guilty," I said. "But seriously, you aren't useless."

"I know, I know, but I can't help feeling like I haven't contributed. So I'll cook everyone dinner and hopefully that'll get rid of some of this gloom. Let's take the van into town, just a quick trip to pick up some ingredients."

The sun was poking through the clouds, but we dressed in long sleeves anyway (it's not like Washington has a reputation for being rainy). We decided to shower later, because after being confined to the room for so long, we were overcome with an anxiousness to get out of the house.

"I'll tell Nate that we're going, do you want to meet me at the car?" I asked.

"Sounds good to me, but if you can't find him, make sure to leave a note with the time we're expecting to be back so they don't flip out."

I opened the door and was about to head downstairs when I saw Schafer out of the corner of my eye. He was leaning against a water-damaged wall in the hallway like a greaser chilling on a jukebox. He was clearly *too cool for school*—or just drunk.

"Good morning, Ryan," Schafer said suspiciously. How much his tone had to do with the fresh glass of whiskey in his hand, I'm not sure. "Looks like you're in a hurry. Where are you folks off to this fine morning?"

"We're going to run to the market," Madison replied as she appeared in the doorway. She was quick; I hadn't even had enough time to tell him that it is was none of his business where we were headed.

"Oh yeah, what are you planning to pick up there?"

"Groceries," she said, still staying polite. "I'm going to make you guys dinner tonight. I thought it would keep spirits high as we head into the final stretch."

Schafer tossed the rest of his drink back and swished it around his mouth before swallowing it in one strained gulp. I didn't have to be a fortuneteller to know that as soon as he'd finished with us, he was going to head back downstairs and fetch himself a refill.

"That sounds wonderful, Maddy. Nate mentioned that you're a great cook, a real total package," he said. "But I'll tell you what I'm not feeling so hot about. Having both of you off-site at the same time. A situation like that presents itself with just a few too many opportunities for you two star-crossed lovers to run away together, leaving the rest of us stranded here to pick up the tab. Now, say, if one of you were to stay here while the other made a quick jaunt to pick up supplies, that, I suppose, would be a better idea."

"I'm confused," I interrupted. I smiled, but I was being anything but friendly. The venom in my voice could have easily killed small rodents. "Here I was thinking that Edric was the one we were holding ransom."

"Oh stupid Ryan, you never were the brains of this operation. You should know by now that there's a difference between kidnapping and insurance."

"Yeah," I spat back. "I understand the difference between babysitting and hostage situations too. Clear as fucking crystal. Where's Nate? Him and I need to have a talk."

"It doesn't matter where Nate is! I'm the one here! I'm the one you have to deal with!"

I stood there for a second with my shoulders squared. If I killed Schafer, would anyone care? We were already in hot water; hiding a body in the woods wouldn't complicate things much more. But as I considered going back in the room, snapping a leg off a piece of furniture and caving in his skull, I ran into a problem. Jacob and Nate might see the necessity in it (and if they didn't, I could probably convince them), but at the same time, unfortunately, he was still Wesley's brother. Blood is thicker than water, after all, and Wesley was our driver. We were going to need him to make our escape. I changed my approach.

"Look, we just want to get out of here for an hour or two," I started. "If I get permission from Nate, can we not get in a fistfight? Save your anger for the SWAT teams if they show up."

"More like *when* they show up, at this rate." He rubbed his eyes and let out a long sigh. "Nate's not around; him, Wes, and Jake went for a walk in the woods. Too boring for me, but hey, if it's helping them pass the time, more power to them."

"What do I have to do so that you'll let us take off for a few hours?" I groaned.

"Wait right here, I have an idea," he said.

He ran into a nearby room and returned holding a camera that was at least sixty years old. It had a peeling leather finish and enough dust on the lens to transform any photos taken with it into a collage of blobs and shadows.

"Let me take a picture of Maddy and Edric together. She does that, you get your shore leave. Deal?"

"Deal," Madison replied.

"Are you sure?" I said.

"If it'll get us out of the house," she said. "I'll do it."

"She's a big girl, Ryan," Schafer said, trying to scrape as much dust out of the old thing as he could with his thumbnail.

"You know, it's not like that thing is a Polaroid or some rinky-dink disposable camera. You can't drop it off somewhere and have your precious evidence that Madison is guilty as charged in an hour or less."

"If it comes to that, I'll send the whole camera to the police." He grinned malevolently. "Let's get this show on the road."

We made our way to Edric's room; I wasn't surprised to see that he was still sleeping. Madison walked over to his bedside like she was marching in front of a firing squad and stood there awkwardly.

"Come on, Maddy, have some fun with it. This is your photo shoot, after all," Schafer said.

"Just take the picture so I can get out of here."

"Say cheese," Schafer replied, slurring every syllable.

Madison poked her tongue out and flipped off the camera. It was playful, but I could tell that the constant interrogations were wearing on her. Schafer clicked the button, and for a moment, the room was bathed in a ghostly light. Its inner-workings whirred and fell silent again. Edric didn't even stir.

"Are we free to go, officer?" she asked.

"Cute, real cute," Schafer said. He tried taking another sip of his drink, and grimaced when he realized he'd already emptied it. He didn't look at either of us and then stomped out of the room.

"Off to go make someone else's life miserable?" I asked.

We left the house before Schafer changed his mind and drove out on the same road that my comrades and I had taken to Seattle. The grocery store was a half hour away and catered to vacationers and truckers looking for something a little more substantial than gas station sandwiches. It was satisfactory at best, even with the crates of fresh produce and seafood the locals brought in to sell every morning. In any event, it still had the ingredients Madison needed to make her famous stir-fry.

We worked down Madison's list as we stacked the cart high with mushrooms, soy sauce, tofu and shrimp, but I couldn't relax. Every time we passed someone else down one of the aisles, they looked up and nodded at us. Madison thought they were just being friendly, we were from out of town, after all; but that wasn't it. They knew who we were—and they certainly knew what we had done in our little house in the woods.

Edric

"BACK THERE YOU CALLED THIS a numbers game?" I said.

"It's you versus all of them, I'd reckon that's about as clear cut of a definition you could ask for."

We left the still, turned the corner leading to the back of Asclepius's cabin, and much to my relief, we weren't stuck in an endless dimensional loop. I never thought I'd say it, but seeing his magically refilling woodpile (a waypoint that was at least a little less strange compared to the world around it) was almost comforting.

We broke off and made our way out into the brush. Past the splintered door and the rotting remains of the child with the bright eyes, heading straight for uncharted territory. On the horizon was an inky strip of smoke no wider than a matchstick. It looked like the sky was beginning to crack.

"In that case, should I split them up before I start killing them, or vice versa?"

"Your call," Asclepius replied without looking back. "Obviously you're not going to want to take them on all at once, but other than that, it's up to you. I'm beginning to trust your judgment."

He trusted my judgment? How long had it been since every sarcastic word and every disobedient thought was met with a swift smack to the face (or a stab to the gut, or being burned alive, or having my leg dislocated)? Twelve hours? Twelve days? I knew it couldn't have been too long, but all the atropine surging in my blood had made time blurry and sporadic. Was one day with Asclepius still one day? For now, it was unimportant. I'd made progress, and it was gratifying as hell that I wasn't the only one who had noticed the changes taking place inside my head.

"Well, is there anything else you might recommend to split them up other than drugging?" I asked. I wanted to stay in his favor and interested questions seemed to be the best way. Not to mention, I still wasn't too keen on the idea that my success relied solely on my ability to become a half chemist, half shaman with no formal training.

The smoke trail was getting closer.

"You've already started. Schafer hates you, but I'm pretty sure Madison and Ryan both think of you as victim in all of this. That alone is going to make your task exponentially easier. Remember how you manipulated Madison when she introduced herself? We haven't seen the effects of that meddling first hand yet, but it was an admirable start to say the least."

We came to a riverbed that was about twelve feet across. I assumed that it was little more than a drainage ditch, because it was filled with a foot and a half of blood, runoff from the rest of the field. Its surface sat perfectly still as the dunes that lined the shallows soaked up one drop at a time. A rickety bridge spanned the two banks. It was far from structurally sound but, at least we wouldn't be wading today.

"If we set aside the psychology of it, how can I separate them physically from one another?" I continued.

We made our way across. The dark planks groaned and popped beneath our feet.

"Architecture," Asclepius replied. "Solid walls and locking doors are all it takes. If you want to get fancy you could try using fire, but I wouldn't recommend it."

"And why is that?"

I thought I felt the bridge shift and went to grab one of the gnarled railings to steady myself, but stopped when I saw the dozens of crude nails bending out of the wood. Someone hadn't bothered to hammer them down. Instead, I looked past them and into the red below. It looked like something was floating on the surface, foamy and dark. At first I thought they were bubbles or clots, but the longer I stared, the more wings and tiny legs came into focus. They were clumps of dead flies.

"Too unpredictable," Asclepius said. He had already reached the other side and stared back at me. "Fuels like gasoline and black powder can help a little bit, but it's still going to draw a lot of unwanted attention."

I nodded and finished crossing. One more hill and we would be right on top of the smoke. The thin line we'd seen in Asclepius's backyard was now a dense, sooty cloud billowing into the air.

"What's over there?" I asked, dreading the reply before Asclepius had even turned to answer.

"My slaughterhouse."

XII
Dream Eater

Ryan

❖

I SPED HOME HUNCHED OVER the steering wheel. I knew it wasn't smart, but I needed to get away from the suspicious villagers before they showed up on our doorstep with torches and pitchforks. I'd blown through my third stop sign when Madison placed her hand on my shoulder. My muscles relaxed instinctively and I eased my foot off the gas, bringing us almost back down to the speed limit.

"You have nothing to be worried about," she told me. "Schafer is beginning to rub off on you is all. In a few days time, this will all be behind us. It'll just be a bad dream."

"I hope you're right," I replied.

Back home, we brought the groceries inside and unpacked them. Nate (returned from his walk) helped us dig out a pot to cook the rice in and a deep cast-iron skillet for sautéing the rest of the ingredients. Nate and his Uncle were not chefs by any stretch of the imagination, so it took some effort for us to scrub them clean of all of the dust and grease accumulated at the bottom of the pans. It didn't take long for the dank mustiness of the kitchen to be replaced with a sizzling sweetness that hung on the air.

"Dinner is served!" Madison called out to the rest of the house. A faint echo radiated through the melting plaster and crumbling drywall. Soon, four rumbling sets of footsteps followed.

Nate and Wes helped set the table with paper plates and plastic cutlery while Jacob and I assisted Madison in bringing food into the dining room. Schafer was the last one to stumble in. He had the same glass filled with the same amber liquid clenched in his fist, and there was no telling how many rounds he'd gone since our last conversation.

"I wasn't aware that whiskey paired well with stir-fry," Nate said sarcastically. He was nervous, and there was something in his eyes that said we were heading down a path toward hopelessness. No one else seemed to notice though, and before I could pull him aside and ask about it, it had vanished.

"You see," Schafer slurred, "that's why I'm more sophisticated than you. Because I understand that whiskey goes good with everything until we get our phone call."

We sat down and began shoveling food onto our plates like it was the last supper (and for all we knew, it could have been). As the soy sauce was passed around and drizzled over steaming heaps of rice, the mood softened and soon we were chatting and laughing like regular people at a regular dinner table. It had worked. Madison was a genius.

"Nate, would you like to take some in to your uncle?" Madison asked during the first break in the conversation. "It looks like we're going to have leftovers."

"Not if I have anything to say about it," Jacob replied, shoving two shrimp in his mouth at once for emphasis. Wes burst into laughter, showering the tablecloth with rogue grains of rice from the corners of his mouth.

"That's a sweet idea, but I don't think he'd eat it," Nate said. "He's extremely paranoid and will only eat canned food. And I don't know if you've noticed, but this is way too tasty to have come out of a can."

She nodded and cleared her throat to let everyone else know that she wasn't finished yet.

"I have another idea," she continued. Everyone stopped what they were doing; even Schafer, in the process of going back for his third helping, froze with a spoonful of stir-fry halfway to his plate. "Why don't we invite Edric to come down and eat with us?"

The dining room went silent for the first time since the table was set. Jacob stopped eating and instead dropped his eyes into his lap and fidgeted aimlessly. Schafer gripped his glass until his knuckles drained empty of blood, but all the while kept smiling like the room was filled with nitrous oxide.

"I don't know about that," Nate said cautiously. "It's not a bad idea—I just think it might make things more complicated."

"He couldn't make it down here if he wanted to," Schafer grinned. "His legs probably feel like noodles by now. Here's a riddle for you guys, how does a person with noodle legs get down the stairs?"

"How?" Wesley groaned.

"Falling," Schafer said, leaning back in his chair laughing.

"He's going to need to eat something," Madison said through gritted teeth. Her patience was running thin too. "Would there be any objections to me at least bringing him some food?"

"I think that would be fine," Nate said. Nate had known Madison and I way back before we even started dating. If I could see the early signs of her agitation, he probably could too. "Make sure you're the one who feeds him though. Under no circumstances can he be let out of his restraints except for his one bathroom break a day."

Madison agreed, stood up from her chair, and began to walk towards the kitchen to get a free plate or bowl. Wesley caught her by the arm as she passed.

"Maddy," he said. "Before you bring it up to him, on top of the fridge are my sleeping pills. Pop one into the sauce and it should dissolve fairly quickly. He shouldn't even notice the texture with the rate he'll be gobbling this stuff down."

"Wes," I sighed. "Not you too."

"What's the problem, Ryan?" Schafer said mid-bite. "Can't you see my brother is just looking out for us? Sounds like someone doesn't want to be a team player."

"You know it's nothing like that," I said, though in my mind I was getting less and less enthusiastic about being drafted by the Washington Kidnappers. "I just think we're stepping into dangerous territory by keeping him unconscious for so long."

"I understand," Wesley said. "But I thought that maybe, if we sneak him a couple of pills, we could give him both some nourishment and a break from the injections."

"Wait, what's wrong with the injections?" Schafer interrupted. Everyone continued to ignore him. It had become a survival technique.

"It's up to you, Maddy," Wesley concluded. "If you don't feel comfortable with it, no one is going to hold it against you."

The room fell silent again except for the slopping sounds of Schafer gnashing shrimp in his jaws. Madison's eyes fell on me for one sad moment before she came to her decision.

"I'll do it," she said. "One sleeping pill is no big deal. Sometimes I take them if I've been having nightmares."

"That's the spirit," Schafer said.

Madison returned from the kitchen with a bowl and a small orange bottle. She added rice on the bottom, stir-fry on top, and sandwiched a small blue pill between the two. One quick stir and the pill had fragmented into tiny, delicious slivers.

"That was easy," she said. "I'll be back before you can say *Asclepius*."

Edric

❖

ON THE OTHER SIDE OF THE HILL, the tall grass had been cleared away to reveal a dozen steps carved out of the hard-packed earth. At the bottom of the slope sat a shack that made Asclepius's home look like a mansion in comparison. The walls were made up of brittle clay, rotten wood, and dark wire that wrapped all the way around it. It was an attempt to hold it together—the same way a length of rope keeps a maiden pinned to the railroad tracks. The tin roof was well on its way to rusting straight through. At the back corner was a metal pipe spewing smoke, a crude chimney. He had called this place his slaughterhouse, and while the way it was rundown and secluded was creepy, on the surface, it wasn't any more frightening than an old barn.

"It might not look like much," Asclepius grunted. "But what you're going to learn here today will last a lifetime."

He led me down the steps, and as we got closer to the shed, the smoke made the air heavier, like someone had taken all of the light and wrapped it in a black stocking. As the brightness drained out of the sky, the shadows grew and reached out for me. I could still see, but something was whispering in my ear. Something was telling me this place was evil.

Around the side, underneath a spindly tree with razorblade leaves, was a pen holding ten pigs. Each one had long, hazelnut fur the same length as my hair and dull eyes as black as coal. They snorted idly and didn't pay attention to us. Asclepius straddled the barbed wire fence and invited me to join him.

"Did you know that anatomically speaking, pigs are closer to humans than any other animal?" Asclepius asked. He stroked one of the larger pigs behind its floppy ears.

"I thought that was chimpanzees?" I replied.

"Only at the chromosome level," he said, unsheathing a foot-long serrated knife. "You really should start paying attention in that biology class."

He raised the knife and brought it down point-first into the back of the pig's head. There was no squeal of pain, only a hollow pop as the metal stabbed through muscle and bone. All four of its legs buckled before it had a chance to run and dropped flat with a thud. Its nose twitched faintly, searching for its dying breaths, as the fur around its throat became slick with blood.

"Remaining undetected is going to be your best friend during this operation," Asclepius said, dropping to his knees as he continued to stroke the dead animal. He wasn't comforting it, I'm sure it was past that point. Instead he was taking a moment to quietly admire what he'd just done. "You're going to want to learn to kill as quickly and as silently as possible. You might prolong your victim's suffering in some cases, but generally, you want to get in, get out, and be done with it."

He pulled the knife out slowly; I could faintly hear each tooth of the blade click against vertebrae as he retracted it. Once the wound was cleared, three spurts of blood shot into the air and splattered against the side of the shed. It ran back down along the grooves of the wood, making them slick and oily with gore.

"Look, Edric! He's bleeding like a stuck pig!" Asclepius laughed; all of the other pigs had retreated to the far side of the pen. They were watching us now and I swear I could see their boney knees shaking.

Instead of being disgusted, I was excited, and my mind flooded with possibilities. Asclepius had taken something alive, cut its strings, and reduced it to a pile of dead meat in seconds. I imagined doing the same thing to Schafer, and that's all it took to make the bloodshed not only seem worthwhile, but also reenergizing. I felt amazing.

Asclepius put the knife back in its sheath and tossed the pig over his shoulder with no effort at all.

"There's a bag of nails and an old hammer over there," Asclepius said, nodding his chin towards the shack. "Grab them for me, will ya?"

It didn't take me long to find them sitting on top of a flat stone by the front step. I returned to the pigpen.

"What I'm going to have you do," Asclepius said, raising the pig up and propping it against the side of the slaughterhouse, "is nail each of its limbs to this here wall. I know it seems like the nails won't support the weight, but trust me, we're not exactly bound to the laws of physics here."

The nails were like miniature railroad spikes, and without any argument, I went about pinning each foot to the old wood. The bones in each fractured and snapped every time I dropped the hammer. When I'd finished with its legs, I even pinned its tail down.

"Not necessary, but I like your moxie," Asclepius chuckled. Again, he pulled the knife from his belt. "Caution—you will get wet."

He made three quick cuts with three bends of his wrist to form a bloody Y that ran from the pig's chest to its stomach. Then, he folded them back to reveal its insides. A final wave of viscous fluids rushed out of the body cavity, coating me from the shins down. After bobbing for logs, I didn't care much.

Inside was a human skeleton equipped with a full set of muscles, sinews and guts. I took a step back, shocked, and observed the carcass from multiple sides just to make sure my eyes weren't playing tricks on me. Nope, there it was, a human cadaver wrapped in pig's skin splayed out against the wall like Da Vinci's Vitruvian Man.

"Don't act too surprised," Asclepius said. "You should know by now that none of this is as simple as it seems."

"I know," I said. "I'm ready to continue whenever you are."

I don't know what was the bigger shock. Me saying this or that I actually believed it.

"Very good." Asclepius nodded approvingly. "In movies, when commandos go to stealth-kill someone, they slit their enemies' throats. It's not a bad technique, but it also leaves the Nazi or the Communist or whatever a few minutes to gurgle all over the place before they finally bite it. Do what I did instead, take your knife, and shove it into the base of their skull. They'll be dead before they hit the ground."

"What if I don't have the chance to sneak up behind them?" I asked.

"Then you aim for these, kiddo," he said, outlining sections of the throat with the tip of his knife. "These are the laryngeal nerves. Think of them as the superhighway to the voice box. But if you're coming from the front, you're going to need to dig in deep and make it nasty, otherwise they'll be screaming the whole time. And you'll probably need to get a new weapon after because the blade is bound to be dull and stuck in God-knows what when all is said and done."

My eyes scanned the shredded flesh as the gray organs slid out of place. Something, I'm assuming the intestines because they were like pink ropes covered in veins, splattered onto the ground like a bundle of spaghetti.

"I appreciate this," I said. "There's no doubt in my mind it's going to be useful. But what if I don't want to kill someone quickly—what if I want to make them suffer?"

"You're talking about torture," Asclepius said. His voice was level, but his cheeks twitched their way into an unsettling smile. "Aren't you?"

"I guess," I said. "I just want some alternatives to the quick and clean if I end up in a situation where I'm not rushed."

His smile changed. His cheeks tightened and his jaw elongated until each tooth was a good three inches. For the first time since this exercise began, I shivered and realized that the air had become freezing in the absence of light. His mouth returned to normal before he spoke.

"When you set out to torture someone, you're actually taking part in a war of attrition. Who's going to break first, you or them? It takes practice and precision, like a martial art. Luckily though, torture is a lot like poison where it lets you get creative, because almost anything can be used if you have the time to fool around. But if you're trying to get a person to break as quickly as possible, aim for the F.E.E.T."

"Feet?"

"It's an acronym. It stands for fingers, eyes, ears, and toes. People have an inherent fear of being freaks, and if you start to cut them in ways that'll change not only them but how other people see them for the rest of their lives, they'll do whatever you want. Some might even accept that they'd rather die than live without a handful of fingers—get it? Anyway, what are your other concerns?"

"The only other thing I can think of is what are some good ways to get rid of bodies once I'm done playing?"

"Playing? Aw, Edric, I knew I had a good feeling about you from the beginning. My boy, getting rid of bodies is simple."

He was interrupted by a loud thunder crack, and then another and another in rhythm. He looked at the sky and squinted in disappointment.

"Here we go again," he groaned. "Right when things were starting to get interesting."

"What are you talking about?"

A bolt of lightning crashed into the ground nearby and white light burned its way into my eye sockets. It swallowed me whole.

"Don't worry, Edric.

"Edric.

"Edric.

"Edric."

The light faded and became defined by two black strips. It took half a dozen blinks and at least five seconds before I understood I was back in the real world. The lightning had been my door swinging open, focused on my eyelids by the darkness that framed the rest of the room. The thunder had been someone clomping up the stairs. The culprit was Madison, and she was all alone, holding a deep bowl to her chest. Steam wafted over its edge before vanishing in the air like a wraith. Her lithe silhouette hung in the doorframe as the smell of something delicious rolled over me.

"Are you awake?" she said, concerned yet optimistic.

"I think so."

"You were talking in your sleep," she said, pulling a chair up next to my bed.

"I'm sorry," I tried to laugh but it came out as a strained wheeze. "I'm embarrassed. Did I say anything interesting?"

"It sounded like 'bodies' or something, but I couldn't make it out. Were you having a nightmare?"

"I think so," I replied, but left it at that. "What are you doing here? Won't you get in trouble?"

"I had permission," she grinned. She was exceptionally pretty; it was a shame that she was going to have to die with the rest of them. "I brought you some dinner if you're hungry."

"What is it?"

"Stir-fry."

"Who made it?"

"Me, you silly boy," she giggled. "Do you want some?"

It was time to get back into character. I was starving; it felt like my stomach was being scraped empty by a cheese grater, but if I were to simply accept the food graciously, I'd be missing an opportunity.

"I don't know," I said. "I would love to, but the stuff they've been giving me makes me queasy all the time. I feel dizzy, kind of like being on the open ocean."

This was only a half-lie. I could actually feel my body getting weaker and strung out, but I also could have put back a dozen bowls of the stuff Madison was offering me if it tasted as good as it smelled.

She reached out and placed her hand on my forehead. It was soft, warm, and so sweet I almost cried. I wish I had, tears would've scored me some major points in the sympathy department. But as hard as I tried to squeeze them out, I couldn't get a single salty drop to run down my cheek.

"You're warm," she said. "I hope you don't have a fever."

"I've been burning up since they strapped me to this bed," I said, prepping my next lie. "Every time they stick me, it feels like my blood is on fire. It's horrible. Please, don't let them do it to me anymore. I'll be good, I promise."

She set the bowl down and gave me a hug (the best one she could anyway, with my being pinned to the mattress).

"Edric," she whispered. "I'm sorry. I'm so, so sorry. It never should've came to this. I'm going to talk to them and see if I can help. I promise I'm going to do my best. You've been through enough."

She dropped her head into the crook of my shoulder and sobbed softly. I wanted to feel bad for her, even reach down and stroke her hair, but she was literally sleeping with the enemy, and now was no time to be growing a conscience.

She finished crying, got up, rubbed her eyes, and dusted herself off. She was a superhero, returning to her secret identity. No signs of her emotional breakdown remained.

"I should get back downstairs," she sniffled. "Are you sure you don't want to at least try one or two bites, for me?"

"I can't do it," I said. "It smells great, but I'd probably end up puking everywhere and that would only make things worse.

Thank you though, it means a lot—you're my only friend here, Madison."

"It's Maddy," she said. Her lips trembled and tears rimmed her eyes one more time as she turned and left the room.

"Your move," I whispered as her steps faded down the stairs.

Ryan

❖

"HE DOESN'T WANT TO EAT?" Schafer asked, cocking an eyebrow. "What do you mean he doesn't want to eat? The only thing he's been able to handle since we started him on his atropine diet is small bits of bread and water. He should be famished."

"That *diet* is the problem," Madison said. "It's making him sick. Another day or two of this and he'll be dead. Is that what you want?"

"I can think of worse outcomes," Schafer said. "Ryan, reel in your ball and chain before she embarrasses herself."

I almost jumped over the table and dropkicked him in the teeth, but Wes pulled me back down.

"Uh, Maddy," Nate said, trying to derail the conversation before it became an even more devastating train wreck. "What was it that you said before you left? You know, that word you were going to be back before any of us could say it?"

"Asclepius?" she replied. "He was the Greek god of medicine. I thought it seemed cruelly appropriate considering the circumstances."

"Well, none of us could even pronounce it, so I guess you win," Nate said. Droplets of sweat had formed on his forehead.

Schafer stood up, stretched, and left the dining room.

"And where do you think you're going?" I called after him.

"We have a boy awake upstairs who hasn't taken his medicine," Schafer said matter-of-factly. "I thought I'd go play doctor for a bit."

Everyone sat still as we heard the bottom stair squeak under Schafer's weight—and then the second—and then the third. Soon, this sound was joined by a faint scratching, like a tree branch brushing against a screen door in the wind. Madison was digging her nails into the soft wood of the table-top as she stared into space. A small vein pulsed in her temple as blood flooded her cheeks. Before Schafer had time to climb the fifth and sixth steps, Madison bolted out of her chair, sending it clattering to the floor. She hurled herself around the table, shoved Schafer out of the way, and dived into Edric's room. Nate and I followed right on her heels while Jacob and Wes made their way at a much slower pace.

By the time we made it to the second floor landing, the situation had only gotten worse. Madison stood at Edric's bedside, her arms spread wide, ready to be crucified. Schafer was standing across from her, shaking his head out of disbelief and frustration. We'd jumped from a pleasant dinner with friends into a good old-fashioned Mexican standoff in a matter of minutes.

"Get out of my way," Schafer said. "You shouldn't have come here."

He pulled a fresh syringe from his back pocket, raised it to his mouth, and shredded the plastic packaging with his teeth. Then, grabbed a bottle of atropine and jammed the syringe into it with enough force that I could hear the needle clink against the bottom of the glass.

"Please," Edric said from his bed. "I don't want anymore trouble."

"Trouble is what you're getting whether you want it or not," Schafer replied. "Stand aside, Maddy. The boys back here can vouch that if push comes to shove, I have no problem hitting a girl."

Schafer yanked the plunger back and the liquid whistled as it filled the hypo all the way to the top. The room was dark, but I could still tell that the dosage was three, maybe four times what we'd been giving him up to that point. It was an inten-tional overdose, and there was no sense pretending it was anything else.

"You coward," Madison said just above a whisper. "You're not going to do anything to him tonight."

Schafer stopped and examined the needle in his hand. His eyes scaled every millimeter of it, climbing the black measurement lines on the side like they were a ladder. When he reached the sharp metallic tip, he came out of his trance briefly and looked around the room at the rest of us. No one was breathing.

"You're right," he finally said. "Because you're going to be the one playing nurse tonight, sweetie."

His free hand lashed out and grabbed a chunk of Madison's hair, then he pulled her to the foot of Edric's bed one violent tug at a time. She whined and clawed at his chest, but it was useless, she knew she was outmatched.

The look on her face was all it took; I was on him swinging each fist with enough force to demolish skyscrapers. He tilted out of the way of my first blow, but the second grazed off his eyebrow and split it open. I could feel the skin catch, and finally tear across my knuckles.

This got his attention.

He released Madison long enough to throw three rapid-fire jabs my way. The first two landed square with my right eye and the third crushed my throat. I fell hard to the floor and rolled to my back. I wanted to find my footing. I wanted to counterattack. But my body was having a hard enough time trying to take shallow breaths and count stars—fighting back was out of the question.

"Let her go you son of a bitch!" Edric shouted. "You can't even do it yourself, you're relying on a woman to do your job for you. Fucking pathetic."

"Can it," Schafer said before turning his attention back to Madison. "Now Maddy, I know this is all new to you, so let me explain a couple of things. When you've been injecting for a while, you don't want to reuse old holes. That leads to infections. So tonight, we're going to shoot just a little bit up between Edric's tootsies."

"Between his toes?" Wes groaned from the doorway. "That's nasty, man."

"Junkies do it all the time," Schafer chuckled. "And you're becoming our little junky, aren't you Edric?"

"Fuck you!" he said, spitting a fat glob of mucus at his tormentor. He missed Schafer completely, and instead it splattered inches away from my face.

"I won't do it," Madison said. "There's nothing you can do to me to change my mind."

"That so?" Schafer said. He released her, made his way over to me, and pressed the bottom of his boot into my cheek. It smelled like burnt rubber and rotten leaves. "If you don't do it, I'll curb stomp Ryan's skull into the floorboards. Capiche?"

She stood by the foot of the bed with the syringe. Even though my eyes were still rolling around in my skull, I could tell she was staring at me, waiting for me to give her some kind of sign. Waiting to hear me say that we'd make it out of this in one piece.

I couldn't do anything.

She sniffled the rest of her tears away and turned back to Edric.

"I tried," she said, her voice catching in her throat like chicken bones in a garbage disposal.

"I know," Edric said, exhausted. "Get it over with, I'll try not to move. I'm going to close my eyes, if that's okay?"

"That's fine," she said. "Try going to sleep and it'll be over before you know it."

"Let's get this show on the road!" Schafer shouted. He dug his foot deeper and the rubber crosshatch on his sole bit into my flesh. "Ryan doesn't have all day."

Madison spritzed the atropine out one squirt at a time until it was back to an acceptable dosage. She then positioned it above the soft webbing next to Edric's big toe and took the plunge.

"Perfect," Schafer said. He stepped off my face, walked over to Madison, and wrapped his arms around her. "Think of it like dancing."

He took her hand in his and helped her work the plunger. Pulling it out just slightly and then pressing it in again. In and out, in and out; pacing the injection until the syringe was dry.

I limped off the floor rubbing my throat and turned to the door.

"Get out of my way," I told Nate, Wes, and Jacob. They stood there dumbfounded. I don't know if they were shocked that I was up already or if they couldn't believe that Schafer had just forced Madison into drugging a defenseless child. Either way, I pushed past them out to the second floor landing.

My legs were still shaky when I hit the stairs, and I wasn't about to trust the banister with my weight. So I worked myself into a crippled skip, taking one to two steps at a time until I finally hobbled my way into the living room. Once there, I ripped open half a dozen crates of contraband until I found what I was looking for: a brand spanking new Glock 17. As soon as I wrapped my hand around the grip, an overwhelming feeling of calm came over me. I knew what I needed to do to get this operation back on track. I cocked the slide back and a shiny copper round found its way home into the chamber. I headed back upstairs.

Edric's room was just as I'd left it. I decided not to waste any time and tip Schafer off. I raised the gun and aimed at the base of his skull.

"Stand up and step away from her. You have exactly five seconds to do this before I blow your fucking head off," I said.

Schafer's head pivoted around slowly. When he saw the Glock, he shrugged and raised both of his hands. He started to stand up, never breaking eye contact with me. I was already applying pressure to the trigger.

"You going to shoot me, Ryan?" he said. He wanted to be cocky, but no matter how hard he tried, an aftertaste of fear had found its way into his mouth. "Lost a fight and now you want to redeem some of your pride. Is that it?"

"Apologize to Madison," I said.

"Whatever, I did what had to be done."

"Apologize!" I said. "I'm not going to ask you again, you piece of shit."

Schafer was standing three feet away from me, and I could tell by the way he was leaning forward that he wanted to make a lunge for the pistol, but with how shaky I was already, he wasn't about to risk getting shot on the way in.

"I'm sorry," he said. "I'm sorry, Madison."

"Good," I said. "But not good enough."

I pulled the trigger, but my right eye had swollen shut after our first skirmish, so I couldn't see Nate coming in with a punch of his own from my side. He knocked the gun out of my hand before the hammer found its primer and I was re-acquainted with my good friend the floor.

"Sorry, Ryan," Nate said. "But as long as I'm in charge here, I can't have us killing each other."

I groaned. It was the best comeback I could manage while running my tongue along all of my newly loosened teeth.

"As far as I'm concerned," Nate continued, "Ryan, Schafer, you two are even and I don't want anymore of this shit. Let's get out of here and finish dinner."

Jacob left first (he'd been looking for a way out before he'd even arrived in the room), Nate and Wes followed him.

"Try that shit again, and I'll have Maddy inject *you* next time," Schafer said. He kicked me in the ribs as he walked past. It barely hurt with my multiple concussions. When he reached the doorway he added, "Christ, I could use a drink."

As Schafer's footsteps faded, my vision blurred in and out. The heavy thumps of his boots were replaced with the sound of sand and gravel shifting as Madison scooted towards me across the floorboards. She placed her head on my chest, and I smoothed the clumps of hair that Schafer had almost ripped from her scalp. I was drifting off, but before I did I heard Madison whisper:

"Everything is going to be okay. We're almost at the end. Everything is going to be okay."

XIII

"And if I die before I wake . . ."

Ryan

❖

I DON'T KNOW HOW MUCH OF what followed my boxing match with Schafer were dreams and how much was my brain trying to resuscitate itself. I saw Schafer swinging at me in slow motion, and after his blow landed, Nate, Wes, and Jacob hopped in on the action. Everywhere I looked, I was met with another fist, and my eyes, not content to take in one beating at a time, fractured into prisms so that I could see my ass-kicking from every angle. I was surrounded by a blizzard of kicks and punches. It was like I'd pissed off the Hindu goddess Shiva and she wasn't about to let me get away with it.

After the fiftieth time I replayed the same events and knew that I was unconscious, I still couldn't wake up. Every time I'd pinch my wrist or remind myself that I was asleep, I'd get more and more dizzy until I felt like I was spinning down the drain in a maelstrom of silverfish. In one restless night, I'd become an expert on what Christians meant by purgatory.

When my swollen eyes finally pushed themselves open, Madison was already awake and watching me. The worried creases on her face made her more beautiful, like little arrows highlighting her eyes and mouth, extra dimples on her glowing cheeks. It was my responsibility to make her relax; tell her that I was healthy and that today would be different. But what could I say? After everything we'd just been through, how could I even start a conversation?

"You're not supposed to let someone with a concussion fall asleep," I said. It was a pathetic attempt at best.

She sighed and hugged me. I guess sometimes pathetic is good enough.

"Thank God you're okay," she said.

"I wouldn't go that far," I said. I reached up to rub the back of my head, but she read my mind and did it for me. "Did you sleep okay?"

"No," she replied. "I got maybe an hour."

"You didn't have to wait up for me, sweetie," I said. "I'm super tough."

I tried to flex and laugh, but instead I wrapped my arm around my bruised ribs and wheezed. If Schafer attacked us again, I didn't know if I'd have the strength to fight back. Whether we liked it or not, it looked like Nate had been usurped. He wasn't our leader anymore.

"I know the answer to this before I ask it," I said. "Did Edric's dad ever call?"

"I've been up here with you the whole time," she said. "But I haven't heard any cheers from downstairs, so my best guess is no."

"God damn it," I murmured. "Sometimes I think the universe is against us. What about Edric? You hear anything about him today? Screams of anguish, that sort of thing?"

"No, but I meant what I said down in the dining room last night," she replied. "We're killing that boy. It might not be the same as putting a gun to his head or shoving a pillow over his face, but it's going to have the same result in the long run."

"I know."

"And it's not just the possibility of his body giving out on him either. Last night he was running a fever. I pray that those needles we've been using are sterile, because if he has a blood infection—we're taking him to the hospital. No show of hands, no rock, paper, scissors; if he's going to die, you, me, and Edric are taking a ride to the nearest clinic. We could leave him in the lobby, that should give us enough of a head start to get across the border before the entire country comes down on our heads."

The thought of leaving Nate, my best friend for as long as I could remember, behind at the mercy of the legal system was sickening, but Madison was right. I wasn't going to have someone else's blood on my hands. The plan was null and void, and the new plan, one that placed survival of the fittest as the top priority, was about to begin.

"Pack your bags and don't tell anyone," I said. "If things haven't improved by sundown, we're getting out of here."

Edric

I LANDED ON MY FEET, but before I could get my bearings, a polished stone the size of a thumbnail launched straight at my face. I dove into the mucky sand of the pigpen and it flew over my head harmlessly. Asclepius sat on the hog carcass that we'd dissected earlier and continued to toss rocks at the other pigs. Every time a shot connected, the animal would squeal, rear up, and run to the opposite side of its prison. They had nowhere to go; their only options were to either accept the pain or keep moving.

"Your reflexes have improved considerably," Asclepius said in-between chomping chunks out of the inside of his cheek. He spat a line of blood on the ground like it was chewing tobacco. "That'll serve you well."

He stood up and tossed the pig over his shoulder. The nails we'd used to bolt it to the slaughterhouse wall remained deep in the wood, and spread out between them was a grim silhouette, a bloody snow angel.

"Would you mind getting the door for me?" Asclepius asked. "I seem to have my hands full."

We made our way to the slaughterhouse's lone door. It pushed open without a sound, ballerina slippers on a frozen pond. Inside, a large table dyed crimson dominated one corner of the room. My stomach told me that if I were to cut into the grain, it'd be stained straight through to the other side. Above the table was a rough iron bar fixed to the ceiling. Hanging off of it were a number of hooks and cleavers that clinked together faintly. Opposite the table was a rusted woodstove (a twin to the one in Asclepius's cabin) filled with white and green flames. Each individual inferno was lined with flickering sparks. They resembled drooling taste buds. The strangest thing of all though was that there was no dust. Not a single speck. And I could tell from the way that the front door had been oiled that Asclepius came here often.

"Catch," Asclepius said, tossing the mass of dead meat at me when the door closed. I flinched, but recovered fast enough to catch it. To my surprise it didn't weigh more than a child. A clear, thick liquid splashed my shoulder from its open neck flaps.

"You already know how to make the bodies," he said. "So I guess it's time to show you how to get rid of them. First, try shoving that little piggy wee wee wee all the way into the furnace."

I carried it over to the stove, pulled open the grate, and tried to force it into the glowing tongues lapping hungrily inside. I could feel the fire on my hands and face, and I was close to making it fit; but ultimately, the pig wouldn't budge. Its spine was too stiff, its limbs too rigid; Asclepius would have a solution for that though. He always did.

"No go," I said, pulling the pig out of the fire. "It won't fit."

"Unfortunately for you," Asclepius said. "You're going to have to make it fit. If this were a more conventional situation, you'd have a lot of other tools at your disposal; like lye, or acid, or good old-fashioned burying. However, you're not going to have time for that, so all roads will eventually lead to the cremation oven."

He grabbed the pig out of my arms and slapped it down on the table. Then, he reached above his head, fingered through each of his knives and sharp instruments, and eventually decided on a heavy cleaver the width of a loaf of bread.

"Tell me, Edric, what parts of this naughty piggy were keeping you from making us a nice pork supper?" he asked, sliding the blade through the animal's coarse fur.

"Its arms and legs . . ."

"That's as good of a place to start as any."

One at a time, he separated each limb from the body. Occasionally swinging four or five times to peel the skin back, break the bones, and shred the muscle. He never lost his concentration.

"It's like apprenticing in a butcher's shop," he said, wiping sweat from his brow. "Once they've croaked, it's all just meat. It shouldn't be any different from making patties out of ground beef or dicing steak for shish kabob. You only need to cut enough to make it fit, bite-sized pieces. But remember, the smaller the slabs, the faster they'll burn. Any other problem areas?"

"The head and the spine," I said, wondering how much thicker a human arm or leg would be. Wondering if I could take one off in fewer swings than Asclepius.

He swung again, this time in the middle of the pig's back. The skin broke enough for me to see one bright line of blood and the spine cracked like a candy cane snapped in half. I could feel the vibration of the vertebrae shattering in my teeth. Then, he turned his attention to the head, bringing the blade down in long strokes until the skull and brain matter was smashed into gray applesauce. He finished by scraping the goo off the table.

I hadn't noticed the floor because of the dim lighting, but as I watched the viscous waterfall splattering all over our shoes, I couldn't help but stare. The floor was little more than a sheet of dirty Plexiglas, but underneath, staring up at me, were dozens of human skulls. For the first time since entering the slaughterhouse, I smelled something rotting.

"Let's get this puppy in the oven," he said.

I bundled the arms and legs up like they were kindling and dropped them into the flames one at a time. The tongues wrapped around each and groaned with pleasure as the skin was absorbed into its belly. Asclepius picked up the body and folded it into the stove. Its hair caught first, the flames rushing along it like a wildfire blazing across the savannah. We stood there watching it silently as the skin blackened and turned to ash.

"It's kind of pretty," I said absently.

"True," he said. "Moist skin and hair stink to high heaven when they burn though. Keep that in mind before you try this out in the field."

"But it's a quick way to get rid of the evidence, right?"

The pig's ribs glistened through the crisp skin.

"Yes and no," Asclepius said. "It's better than keeping a body out in the open, but cremation only gets rid of soft tissue, leaving you stuck with the bones."

"How's that possible? When someone gets cremated they stick them in a vase."

"Yeah, but that's because you never see the other half of the process. After someone's skeleton has been burned clean, they take the rest and grind it into dust. That's how you get an average sized adult to fit in a cookie jar."

I thought about feeding Madison into a grinder while Ryan was forced to watch, stapling his eyelids to his forehead for insurance. It would make a hell of a grand finale to my killing spree. Unfortunately, I wasn't going to have access to something that handy. I'd have to start thinking up other satisfying conclusions to my story.

"If you don't have access to a rig like this though, you'll have to make due with simply hiding the bodies," Asclepius continued. "Fold them however you need to to keep them out of sight. You'll still have funky joints and tendons to deal with, but overall, a dead body is more flexible than a live one because you won't have to deal with pesky variables like pain and them fighting back. You could always cut their joints to make them more pliable, but bodies have the bad habit of bleeding, and nothing spoils a good hiding spot like a pool of blood."

The pig was gone, up the chimney where God-knows how many of its brethren had traveled before it. Asclepius grinned and a set of fangs poked out from beneath his lips as he patted me on the shoulder in congratulations. I'd done it. I'd survived Asclepius's nightmare boot camp.

"Is that it?" I asked. "Do I get some kind of diploma?"

"Something like that," he said. "You've certainly come a long way, my boy, and I'm proud of you. But we have one last little detail to take care of. One *teensy weensy* detail, and your training will finally be complete."

Ryan

"**THERE'S ONE LAST THING** we need to do," Schafer called out from the second floor landing.

After getting me into bed the night before, Madison had shoved a small dresser in front of the door. Schafer didn't knock, and with one shove of his shoulder, he'd managed to wedge his grinning mug through an open slit in the door. It wasn't enough to get a good look at him, but I could still make out his sweaty hair and sunken eyes. To most people he probably looked like an un-showered drunk, but I knew better. He hadn't been sleeping.

"You have some balls if you think you can walk around giving orders to us today," I said. I was about to pull myself out of bed, cross the room, and slam the door. Unfortunately, my wobbly legs had other ideas. I collapsed next to Madison. "We're sitting this one out, if you don't mind."

"This is mandatory, soldier!" Schafer chuckled. "Meet me in the backyard in fifteen, and bring your cellphones. That goes double for you, Madison. Left, right, LEFT!"

He shut the door and made his way down the hallway, barging into each room and relaying the same information with the same phony drill instructor routine each time. God, I hated that man more every minute. I should have been counting my blessings though, the dresser had done its job. Had Schafer made it all the way into the room, he would've seen

Madison's packed duffel bags. We moved them under the bed just in case. Out of sight, out of mind.

"Do we have to go?" Madison asked.

"No, but we should," I replied. "Let's play nice so they don't catch wind of what's about to go down."

With that, we got ready to face another day in our quaint, decaying home away from home. Getting dressed turned out to be a chore. I was able to stand up and walk without falling over, but I couldn't get a good grip on my pants. After straining for five minutes, Madison sat me back down and helped me put my clothes on—one limb at a time—like an infant. It was degrading, but desperate times call for desperate measures. I got over it quickly.

Once I'd been pampered, we ran into another problem: the stairs. If someone wants a new spin on life, they should try their hand at being handicapped or injured. The world that I'd been traversing for weeks had become a minefield of hazards and inconveniences. Again, with Madison, my crutch, fitted into the crook of my arm, we made our way to the back door.

Outside, the sun hadn't burned the morning mist away and the grass was slick with dew. Everyone waited for us at the tree line, gathered around a hole no bigger than a shoebox. A shovel stood in the earth off to the side, its blade penetrating the crisp pine needles of the forest floor. As we got closer, I smelled rancid smoke.

"How nice of you to join us," Schafer said.

" 'Nice' wouldn't be my first choice of words," I replied.

I peered down in the hole and could make out the orange glow of charcoal reflecting off of the uneven, black walls. Small twigs popped and sizzled in the shallow flames.

"Good morning," Nate chimed in. I refused to look his direction.

"I'd like to go back to bed," I interrupted. "Whatever we're doing, let's get it over with."

Schafer looked straight at me with a self-satisfied grin, but I didn't flinch. He'd taken away enough of my masculinity, no reason to push it. God, I hated that man more every minute.

"Did everyone bring their cellphones?" Schafer asked. One at a time we brought them out of our pockets, nervously searching each other for any hint to what Schafer had cooked up this time. "Good, we're making a sacrifice to the communication gods this morning. I made a funeral pyre and everything. All you have to do is make an orderly line and drop them into this hole one by one."

"I'm not burning my phone," Jacob said. "I just got a new plan. I've been paying out the nose for unlimited talk and text."

"A slap on the wrist," Schafer said. "After Edric is off our hands, you can get a better plan—one with unlimited talk, text, sports cars, and bitches."

"I'm sorry," Wes said. "What does this accomplish?"

"Simple, really," Schafer continued, running his eyes up and down Madison. "No last minute calls—you know the ones, like when we're on our way to Seattle with the package. Calls that detail what kind of car we're driving, or our descriptions."

My blood started to percolate, and with my brain stewing away in its rage-laced broth, I finally understood what Schafer had been doing during the long nights. He'd been thinking of ways to rationalize his paranoia, and narrowing down what bridges he'd have to burn to make himself feel better about it. It didn't matter who he had to drain to achieve his piece of mind, either. He was a vampire in the most literal sense of the word.

"Our only cell will be the one we've setup for special calls. The one we've setup for good news," Schafer concluded.

"And when that call doesn't come?" I asked. It was a risky question, but I had nothing to lose. I'd been treading water even before the ship started sinking.

"It'll come!" Schafer yelled back. He wanted to hop over the fire pit and wrap his hands around my throat. Nate's Uncle could have seen that and he was locked up in the house.

"Schafer and I have been talking," Nate said before he had a chance to pounce. "We think that the note we left is wrapped up in evidence, and the FBI and negotiators are discussing how to proceed from there. That call will come any hour now."

"Well, as long as you're positive about that," I said. The damage had been done. Nothing left to do but wait for it to all come crashing down.

"Okay, I'll go first as a sign of goodwill," Schafer said, clearing his throat and composing himself. "Will that make everyone happy?"

No one replied and he took our silence as permission to continue. He dropped his phone in the hole and soon the plastic began to curl. After a minute, all that remained was a collection of microchips, toxic soup, and stinging smoke. Each of us followed his example until our last ties to the outside world were left boiling beneath our feet.

I'd read about a movement on the internet where lonely people fall in love with cartoon and videogame characters. Apparently the obsession ran so deep that they'd take their digital girlfriends out to movies, celebrate their birthdays, and eventually tie the knot with them. The thought of becoming so attached to a piece of technology, something that wasn't real, always seemed crazy to me. Not the "on-paper" or "in theory" crazy, but full-blown "I talk to my dead mother and wear women's skin" crazy. Still, there we were, a group of full-grown adults holding a mock funeral for our cellphones.

"Ashes to ashes," Schafer said flatly. He grabbed the shovel and dumped shredded clumps of grass and dirt clods onto the embers until the smoke came to a rest underneath the soil. "You are all welcome to return to your regularly scheduled programming."

Everyone turned back to the house and made their way across the lawn. Madison walked on ahead while I hung back with Jacob. He'd become the only other person I trusted. I was about to ask him how he'd been coping since last night, but before the words could leave my lips, they were struck from the air by a scream loud enough to shake the windows in their frames. It belonged to Edric.

"What now?" I sighed. I was too exasperated to even pretend like I cared. Jacob shrugged.

"I'll check it out," he mumbled. "After last night, I want to keep Schafer and Maddy out of that room for the rest of our time here. I think between Nate, you, and me, we can make that work."

"What about Wes?"

"He tries to pretend like he's neutral in all of this, but come on, no one in their right mind would condone what happened last night. I'll give him a heads-up, he should be cool."

"Then you'll hear no arguments from me," I replied as we climbed up the porch and filed back into the house. "Hey, Jacob?"

He stopped and turned around to face me. I was about to ask him to leave with Madison and me. The person who had tried to warn me, who put up with almost as much abuse from Schafer and the rest of the group as I did on a daily basis, deserved a running start. But it was risky, I knew that, and at the last moment, I decided to consult with Madison first. I would leave it to her best judgment.

"What is it, Ryan?"

"It's nothing," I said. "But can you come and find me later today? Alone? I want to talk to you about something."

"Yeah, no problem," he replied. His face softened and for that one second, he knew what I wanted to say. "I'll swing by after things get a little more normal around here."

"Fat chance," I said. "Normal? Here? No way."

"You have a point," he said. "You, me, and Maddy can go on a walk later—then we can talk to our heart's content. Sound good?"

"That's perfect," I said, my mood lifting. Our improved plan was taking shape, and by this time tomorrow, we'd have new lives in a new country. Jacob nodded and headed to Edric's room.

That was the last time I ever saw him.

Edric

WE LEFT THE SLAUGHTERHOUSE, and while we'd been inside, the world had changed. The searing blue sky had faded into an ashen brown and the grass had sprouted up a good twelve feet, growing brittle and dry. The soil was drained into a crunchy mess; every step was like treading on pencil lead. The path back to Asclepius's cabin was overgrown and no longer existed. Sigmund sat up straight in the center of the pigpen, waiting for us.

"What does this say about my state of mind?" I chuckled. Asclepius ignored me.

"Sigmund, get over here. It's time," he said.

He turned to me and pulled his trusty pistol from his belt. I'd never noticed before but the finish on the grip had begun to wear away from use.

"Are you ready to depart? I've got your train ticket right here, and guess what? You're taking the bullet train," he said, waving the gun in front of my face. "Let's climb this rabbit hole, click our heels together, and make peace with Poseidon. It's time to go home. The real world is waiting for us. This is your final test."

He cocked the pistol and I watched the round slide into place; there'd be no playing dead this time. Sigmund stopped and knelt in the dirt, never shuddering, never blinking. A wave of anger hit me. Even when he was faced with his own death he remained completely passive. At the same time, I understood. I would have been just as happy to play along and remain blank during this whole ordeal had I not been enrolled into Asclepius's program. Asclepius handed me the gun.

"Kill him," he slithered. "That's what he's here for, your little sacrificial lamb."

Asclepius moved to my back and his footsteps became echoes. A heavy and metallic smell spiked my nostrils, and I could feel his presence warp behind me. It was twisted, and as my heart pumped in my ears I became too terrified to turn around.

I'd always known that Asclepius wasn't just Asclepius. The shifts in his eyes and teeth had made that obvious since the beginning. But if I whirled around and looked him in the face now, what would I see? There was no sense in considering it. This was my own head, after all, and I knew that he was watching and waiting. If I hesitated or tried something suspicious, he'd be there with an axe, a knife, a set of talons, or rows upon rows of yellowed fangs.

"Kill him," he repeated sweetly.

I brought the gun up past Sigmund's chin and aimed it over one of his eyes. A cruel sense of curiosity and challenge gripped me when I wondered if I could thread the needle and put the bullet straight through his iris.

Only one way to find out . . .

I tried pulling the trigger straight back like I'd been taught, but I jerked it at the last second and sent the round into the ridge of his eyebrow. A water balloon's worth of blood clapped onto my fist and his head snapped back. Somehow, he remained on his knees in front of me. The entry wound (about the size of a nickel) glowed faintly.

"Again," Asclepius said. His tone was soothing but impatient.

I did as I was told. The next bullet went through his forehead and took a chunk of his skull the size of a saltine cracker with it. A blast of light rushed forth from Sigmund's face and pierced the sky as my front was coated with more gore.

"Again!" Asclepius screeched.

I kept firing. With every shot, more bone chips sprang into the air, ripping the world apart with every crack from the pistol. Once the ground was covered with casings and nothing remained of Sigmund's head except a bleeding stump, I felt myself rising into the air. Surrounded by so much light I couldn't open my eyes. I rose up through the ground, through the foundation of the house, and through my mattress until I found myself lying in the same dirty bed I'd been strapped to since my arrival.

"You're my most prized pupil. I'll see you again soon," Asclepius whispered before fading away.

The room was blurry, and only after blinking a dozen times did it start to solidify. My wrists were rubbed raw in their restraints like I'd been thrashing around while I was asleep, but luckily they weren't too swollen. At some point I'd also pissed myself, so my pants were damp and itchy. It was okay though. I was awake. I could figure out the rest later.

That's when I heard it, a hushed rustling like wind through a cornfield. My eyes traced their way up past the wafting dust motes and pluming colonies of mold to the ceiling. Directly above me, squeezed between the rafters, was a spider three feet in diameter. It was covered in uneven tufts of scratchy gray hair and each bony leg ended in a crooked claw perfect for mutilation. Its fangs were the size of butcher knives and it rubbed them together with anticipation, spilling a mixture of syrupy venom and saliva onto the bed sheets. One by one, each of its eight silver-dollar eyes swiveled in their sockets and fixed on me.

I remembered everything that Asclepius had taught me to accomplish my mission. That remaining silent and invisible were perhaps the most important weapons in my arsenal. Still, none of this helped suppress my scream. I knew that everyone had heard me, but it didn't matter, because if I couldn't find a way out of my restraints in the next thirty seconds, I'd be dead.

XIV

Hypnopompic

Edric

❖

"REMAIN CALM," I BREATHED. "Just remember your lessons and everything else will follow. Everything is going to be okay."

The spider unhooked one of its spindly legs from the ceiling and twitched it back and forth. Was it waving at me? Only eight feet separated us, and it could've easily closed the distance in one leap, but no. It was taking its time. I knew that the beast wasn't capable of processing fully-formed thoughts, or even expressing emotions; it wasn't human, after all. Still, somehow, nature had turned this thing into a sadist. I could feel it.

The creature's abdomen bounced rhythmically until a sticky line the thickness of piano wire was anchored to the ceiling. Then, using its back legs for balance, the spider began to lower itself six inches at a time. Its other legs bent out in front of it at odd angles, testing the air.

"Fuck that, time to panic."

The first step was to get my hands free. There would be no quick death if the overgrown arachnid ended up on top of me; I'd never been so sure about anything in my life.

"Punching motions," I recited. Talking myself through the steps relaxed me. "In and out, careful to keep the wrists from swelling."

I slid my right arm up and down in its restraint, fist pumping like I was at a concert. The metal clasp clicked each time, but after ten seconds, I hadn't made any progress. The spider parted its fangs so that I could see down its rotten throat. Something bright glowed in its stomach.

"Why isn't this working?" I wheezed.

I punched faster until the friction gnawed on me. My skin peeled back and I felt the thin cocktail of my sweat and blood buying me breathing room. An ounce of slickness is all it would take.

The spider was close now, flicking its front legs inches from my stomach, deciding what part of me it wanted to devour first. Its warm saliva continued to slosh down my midsection in sticky ropes.

"Damn it, Asclepius," I said. "I knew I'd be on some kind of a time limit, but this is ridiculous. A warning would've been nice."

Even with my burning, slippery wrist, I wasn't anywhere close to being free. It wouldn't be long now. I closed my eyes, ready to die, waiting for the cold emptiness of the other side to whisk me away as the creature ripped through my juicy organs. I gave my arm one last shake.

Click.

The clasp of my restraint popped open. I didn't second guess it or sit around wondering how I'd gotten so lucky, either. I ripped my hand free from its cuff, threw my arm across my chest, and unfastened the left with milliseconds to spare. I rolled out of bed with my feet still pinned, sending me face-first to the floorboards. The spider dove with its claws outstretched into the mattress, flailing violently, searching for anything warm and soft to slice into. Soon, its movements slowed, and after a final stiffening jerk, it was dead.

I worked my way back up onto the bed, which was easier said than done. My hands were swollen and leaking blood from a collection of sores and scrapes. I unbuckled my ankles and stood up to test my legs. They were stiff but ached for activity, the way muscles scream for exercise after a long car ride. Next, I threw a couple of practice punches: jab, hook, jab, hook. I felt good, and was about to toss a few kicks into my training regimen when I caught movement coming from the bed. I whipped around so fast I crashed into a nearby wall.

The spider was changing. It shed its skin and scratchy fur to reveal a skeleton of wrought iron underneath. Its eyes melted into broken glass and bent filaments while the claws faded into tiny, tacky sculptures of hummingbirds and leaves. It hadn't been an eight-legged demon at all, only a chandelier pulled free from its chain.

But at the time, it'd felt like the real thing, and the importance of that couldn't be stressed enough. I didn't know it wasn't an actual spider coming to gobble me up and I still fought back. Not to mention the chandelier would have picked up the slack and impaled me if the spider hadn't. Like I'd said back in Asclepius's world, a victory no matter how small is still a victory. I'd survived the first leg of my journey, and that alone called for a celebration.

Unfortunately, there was no time to break out the champagne, because as soon as the "spider" had gone tits-up, I heard someone climbing the stairs. I was faced with a choice: run straight at the door and hope I hit whoever was on the other side hard enough to knock them out, or rush into the bathroom to remain hidden. I chose the latter.

Even though hiding is a lot simpler than playing tackle football with armed crooks, I cut it close. As I ran on tiptoe across the room, trying to avoid any boards that looked squeaky and loose, I could feel the vibration of my guard's footsteps on the other side of the door. I lunged into the open bathroom and my feet slid on the dusty linoleum, leaving two brilliant skid marks in the filth.

The door squeaked open and I held my breath. I didn't know who it was, and the thought of fighting Schafer with no preparation and no killing experience worried me. I hoped for someone weaker, like Nate or Jacob or Madison. Regardless of who was waiting for me out of sight and less than five feet away, one thing had to come first.

"I need a weapon." My eyes darted around the bathroom, adjusting to the dim light.

The shower rod was hollow, light, and wouldn't work. It'd be like prodding an elephant with a wrapping paper tube. The same could be said for the brittle boards that had collapsed inward from one of the broken walls. Each one would probably disintegrate on impact—not the best quality for a bludgeoning. I was about to give up and go in with my bare hands when a jagged shard of broken mirror clinked into the dirty sink. I picked it up and tested its edge against my thumb. It wasn't as sharp or as clean as I would've liked, but it was good enough.

"What the hell?" I heard Jacob whisper, a slight tremble in his voice.

He stepped deeper into the room cautiously. One more foot and I'd be able to get behind him and shut the door. I let out a sigh of relief. This would be easy; all I'd need was the element of surprise.

"Edric?" he whispered to the tangled mass of bent metal and blankets. "Oh my God, are you okay?"

He moved past the bathroom, never once thinking to turn his head and search the darkness for what lurked inside. I snuck out of the shadows behind him and backpedaled to the door; he was too preoccupied taking stock of the wreckage to notice me, feeling the bunched up sheets for any signs of an arm or a leg. I made sure that I had a firm grip on the piece of mirror, and then closed the room softly with the tips of my fingers.

As soon as he heard the door latch, his posture straightened, and he stopped breathing. I didn't give him a chance to yell or beg.

I swung the shard in one wide arc, throwing my whole body into the motion like a discus champion. It connected with the side of his throat and his skin snapped as the membrane gave way. The shank went in one side and popped out the other, leaving two inches of stained glass protruding from the exit wound. His hands flew to his collar and fumbled helplessly through the waterfall of gore. It amounted to little more than finger-painting away the last clean spots of his neck. He tried to scream, but I'd hit an artery or something, so he was left opening and closing his mouth like a carp in between vomiting spouts of blood. I wanted to get another stab in before he gave up the ghost, but the mirror wasn't having it. It was too slippery and broke multiple times before I could extract it. In the end, he was left with a throat full of ground-up glass.

During this whole ordeal, he never fell down. His knees didn't even shake. And to be honest, I was a little offended. I grabbed him by the front of the shirt and shoved him as hard as I could onto the chandelier. The leaves and hummingbirds ripped through the back of his shirt and into his ribs. Then, after staring into my face with his pupil-filled eyes, he stopped squirming.

I wasn't about to take any chances though. The last thing I needed was for him to wriggle out to the hallway like the snake he was. So I moved my face close to his to check, and wouldn't you know it, underneath all of the bile and blood I could still feel a faint draft radiating up from his lungs. It wasn't just his breath that gave him away either, because with every dying wheeze, a fine spritz of blood left his lips and clung to the stubble on my cheek.

"Oh no you don't," I said, grabbing a sweaty pillow from the bed.

I shoved it over his face and rocked back and forth violently for five minutes. Making sure to smack the back of his head into the tangled iron of the chandelier every chance I got. After this I checked again. The draft was gone.

I dropped the pillow, and with a deep sigh, lounged back next to Jacob. The only sound was the faint drop drip drop of his blood soaking through the mattress and dribbling onto the floor.

"Was that as good for you as it was for me?"

There was no reply, only dead space.

XV

"I pray the Lord my soul to take."

Ryan

❖

"YOU DID WHAT?" Madison asked. "You invited Jacob to come with us? What happened to that whole 'let's play it cool so they don't know what we're up to' thing? He's probably told the rest of the group already. We have to leave *right now*."

"Whoa, whoa, whoa, slow down," I said. She turned to the window and rubbed her stomach furiously, her eyes drifting even further back into her skull. "I didn't ask him anything yet. I thought I'd run the idea by you first—I guess it's a good thing I did."

"You're damn right," she said. "We can't trust anyone now. It's just you, me, and Edric."

"Madison," I sighed. I took her by the hand and brought her over to the bed. Her posture stiffened, but she didn't fight. "Don't say that. Things have been rough lately, but we've still known these people for years and years. We're not some ragtag group of criminals that met up for one last job."

"That didn't stop them from betraying us," she snarled.

"Jacob never betrayed us."

"Don't start. Don't even start with that shit. He turned his back on your friendship the second that Schafer hit you and he didn't step in. Don't be so naïve, Ryan."

We sat in awkward silence, unsure of what move either of us could make next.

"What do you want to do?" I finally asked, my face in my hands. "We have to come to a decision and we don't have a lot of time to put it off. This conversation isn't over, and this isn't settled. Not by a long shot."

She nuzzled up next to me. Deep down, Madison knew that my problems were her problems, the parasitic side to all relationships. She wasn't the type of person to meander around indecision, waiting for someone to take charge and give her orders. She was a killer in that regard. It was one of the reasons why I loved her.

"You aren't going to let this go, are you?" she asked.

"I can't."

"Then cut the bull shit," she said quickly, ready to draw this chapter of our lives to a close. "What are you proposing?"

I hesitated, and I'm ashamed to admit it, but I didn't know the extent of what I was asking for. My plan to include Jacob in our great escape had happened so suddenly that I hadn't had enough time to think it through. Now, faced with making a decision that would lead to either our arrest or death, I froze up. I decided to start by keeping it simple, sticking to the absolutes.

"Later, we're going on a walk with Jacob in the woods. That's already been determined. I suggest that during this walk we try to figure out specifics on how he's feeling about our situation. Coax it out of him naturally. If during this talk we feel like he's looking for a way out, we casually offer him a ride."

"As casually as you can ask a person to throw half of his pool of friends to the wolves," she sighed. "I'm sorry, I know I'm being a cynical dick. It sounds good—as good as it can sound anyway. But it's not just Jacob that's bothering you, is it?"

"What do you mean?"

"Come on, I know you better than anyone," she said. "You still have something on your mind. Out with it already. The suspense is killing me."

It was true. At first, I'd tried to mask all of my sadness and guilt with anger, but I wouldn't be able to hold it back much longer. It was weighing on me, like a smile that tugs at the corner of your lips even though you've been told not to laugh at something that really isn't funny. I missed Nate, my best friend, and I didn't want to live happily ever after if it meant sacrificing him to the twenty-five-to-life gods.

"I've been thinking a lot about Nate too," I said.

"That's out of the question," she snapped. "Jacob maybe, because he tried to warn us before and there's at least a fifty-fifty we can trust him. But come on, Nate was Schafer's wing-man last night, not yours. Telling him that we're planning to leave would be like strapping an anchor to our waists and whistling for sharks."

"Give me one shot," I pleaded. "One more chance to try and force him to be reasonable."

She threw her hands in the air, exasperated.

"Fine, I'm okay with that on the condition that you keep it cryptic, no exceptions."

"How cryptic is cryptic?"

"Vague enough so that he doesn't know we're planning to leave. You're not an idiot, I trust you'll play it close to the vest."

I stood up and stretched. I should have felt better, but instead, there was a creeping in my stomach—anxiety as thick as peanut butter. The only cure would be to put this thing to rest once and for all.

"I'll be right back," I said, squeezing her hand.

"And I'll be waiting," she replied, squeezing back.

Edric

I WASN'T WORRIED ABOUT THE SMELL.

The doors and walls were thick enough to keep the sour stench of stomach acid from drifting too far, and if I had no major hang-ups, I'd be finished before the blood started rotting. But that didn't take care of the mess, and there was the very real possibility that someone would come poke their nose in the door before everything was said and done. No rest for the wicked. I'd have to work fast.

Where to start? I'd practically painted the room in bodily fluids during our dance. The floor was a collage of bloody smears and gory footprints. Littered between these red swaths were tiny chips of mirror, stars in a crimson universe. One wall had even been hit with a slap of vomit during Jacob's death throws. It's what police would later refer to as textbook "signs of a struggle."

It was here, while I was crouched down on my hands and knees, gathering up every little piece of glass and catching reflective glimpses of Jacob's corpse in each silver speck, that it hit me:

Holy shit, I'd actually killed someone.

I froze and felt what little I had in my stomach come chug chug chugging up my throat. My adrenaline fix had been shut off, and searing pain radiated up from a wide gash on my palm. I must have sliced myself open when I stabbed Jacob. What was it I'd said about the shard not being as clean as I would have liked? As I stared down at my wound, I realized that my blood had been mixing with Jacob's, sliding through my veins, ever since our scuffle began. I rushed to the bathroom and puked as quietly as I could.

It wasn't guilt; more like a reality check. I'd been preparing for this ever since they grabbed me, and I thought I'd been conditioned to handle anything. But while I ran around in my dreams, there was one detail that I hadn't given nearly enough weight . . .

Out here, this was real. This was permanent. There were no do-overs, and no time to put it off anymore. The chain of events was already set and it was my responsibility to see it through to the end.

I felt my guts making a break for it again and placed my hands flat on the floor to brace myself. Something, I don't know if it was the water rushing through the pipes or what, sent a tiny vibration up through the tile, like a clothes dryer on its lowest setting. A subtle heat followed the rumbles, and the longer I caressed it, the warmer I felt. My stomach calmed.

"I did a good job," I whispered. "I did what I was supposed to. He's dead, you're not. You still have a job to do."

I wiped my mouth on the back of my hand, picked myself up, and marched out of the bathroom with a renewed sense of purpose.

With my conviction at an all time high, I tugged Jacob off of the chandelier. The iron had cut deep into his back, and it was a real workout to pry him free. His ribs were broken and tangled among the hummingbirds and shattered light bulbs, but with a few pops and twists, his body finally fell to the floor. I dragged him to the back corner and wiped my hands off on my pants.

Next, I did the same with the chandelier; and while it wasn't as heavy as Jacob, it was more unwieldy. It took all of my strength to keep from dragging it across the floorboards. After I'd shoved it in the corner as well, I took a sheet from the bed (the one soiled with dime-sized droplets of Jacob's blood) and used the linen to scrub the floor. From beginning to end, the cleaning took ten minutes. And while I wasn't exactly ready to eat off of any surface in the room, I was satisfied that if someone came snooping, they wouldn't immediately know what I'd done.

Now, what to do with Jacob? Lugging a couple hundred pounds of meat around was a sure way for me to get busted, and fire to cremate the body was in short supply. That's when I got a fiendish idea.

"Jacob and I have almost the same build," I said. "Asclepius never mentioned using a body as a decoy. Maybe the master could stand to learn a few things from the apprentice."

I brought the body back to the bed and tucked it in. The blood that had soaked the mattress caked under my nails as I tried to contort him into a more believable position.

"Maybe I should take up sculpting," I whispered, straining each limb into any direction that didn't immediately scream dead.

I shackled his hands and feet in and completed the illusion by leaving a small bit of hair visible from underneath a clean blanket. Again, it wasn't perfect, but it would be enough if someone took a quick glance.

"For my next trick, I'll magically disappear."

I peeked through the gap under the door and could make out shadows moving down the hall—strike one. Not to mention that was a lot of house I'd have to get through undetected—strikes two and three. The room's lone window was also a no-go because it would leave me completely exposed to anyone out for an afternoon walk. If I put those two together, I was left with approximately zero options.

I was getting psyched up and ready to sprint to the front door when I ran across one aspect of the room I hadn't noticed before. On the far side of the room, past Jacob's corpse, past where I'd dragged the chandelier, set into the wall a few feet off of the floor was a laundry chute.

"I'll have to remember to thank Asclepius again," I said, thinking back to my time in the mines, thinking back to when my leg ripped clean from its socket. I gulped. "Hopefully practice makes perfect."

Ryan

❖

I CROSSED THE LANDING TO EDRIC'S ROOM. I was about to knock, but I heard murmurs coming from the other side of the door and decided to leave it be. Other people would know where I could find Nate, and if Jacob and Edric were having a heart to heart, I wasn't going to be the one responsible for ruining that moment.

Downstairs, Wes and Schafer sat on the living room couch sipping whiskey and squinting at the poor TV reception. The rabbit ears were bent crooked, and I knew that no matter how much any of us fiddled with them there'd be a blizzard on every channel. They didn't look up at me until I stood in their way.

"Hey, I was watching that," Wes said.

I turned around to make sure that my eyes hadn't been playing tricks on me, but no, only static.

"Where's Nate?" I asked.

"Who wants to know?" Schafer replied.

"I do."

Schafer glared but he was in no mood to fight. He knew that if he gave me a simple answer I'd be out of his hair, leaving him to drink and try to decipher scrambled porn for the rest of the day.

"He's on the back porch," Schafer said. "But I wouldn't disturb him if I were you. He's deep in thought."

"Like meditating?"

"Don't be stupid, he just wants to be alone for a bit. Care for a drink?"

He handed me the bottle (now half empty) and I handed it right back. It wasn't that I didn't want a quick hit (Christ knows I could've used one), but instead, my survival instincts had kicked in. It's true that we had crates of contraband and stolen goods lying around, but we had to have been running low on liquor. Every last drop we had would need to be conserved for Schafer, because if he was this bad drunk, I didn't want to be around when he started to come down.

"Thanks, but no thanks," I said. "I have to go see Nate. Talk to you in a few."

"Don't hurry back now, ya hear." Schafer groaned and returned his attention to the blurry moans and scratchy cries of ecstasy.

I walked through the kitchen and caught a glimpse of Nate through the window. He was slumped in his chair, only moving occasionally to scratch the salty trails of dried tears that had stained his cheeks. He was unshaven and his healthy tan had faded to a greasy paleness. Everything that identified him as my lifelong friend had evacuated the premises. Only the shell remained.

But even though my Nate was gone, I had to talk to him. I had to see if he was willing to call this all off and leave with Madison and me.

I took one last deep breath to steady my nerves before exiting the back door. This wouldn't be as easy as I'd hoped it would be.

Edric

EVEN WITH MY CHUTE-SCALING EXPERIENCE, I knew this wouldn't be as easy as I'd hoped it would be. For one, I'd have to climb into the slot feet-first. Nothing new, but working up the nerve to let go and drop into the unknown never becomes anything less than terrifying. Secondly, while easier on the feet than stone, the smooth aluminum that made up the laundry chute walls didn't provide enough grip for a controlled descent. Lastly, the whole thing was filled with spider webs as thick as cotton balls. After going three rounds with the chandelier, this was the most damning of all three.

Once my body was squished inside, I took a peek down past my toes. I could see light, a good sign, but closer observation only made my heart drop. The chute didn't go all the way to the basement like I thought it did. Someone (Father Time or one of my captors) had kicked in the door to the chute on the first floor. Translation: there was no getting around it without a sledgehammer or welding torch.

It looked like I'd be getting off at an earlier stop.

Using the caved-in slot for support, I snaked my feet into the room. When my foot found the floor, I was met with a sickening crunch. Like I'd just infiltrated a potato chip factory. What I didn't hear were shouts for help, so I assumed the room was secure. I wiggled the rest of my body out of the chute.

This room was no bigger than the one upstairs, and it was dominated by a ratty king-size bed. Mismatched furniture lined the walls and the ceiling dipped in the middle from years of disrepair. It was probably used for storage. I looked down to search for the source of the crunching and discovered it immediately. Scattered across the ground as thick as dry leaves along an abandoned cobblestone road were dead insects. Their glossy exoskeletons shimmered in the low light, a meadow of iridescent feelers and claws.

I threw a hand over my mouth, but the surprises weren't over yet. Something stirred in the nearby bed, sending the puffy comforters tumbling to the floor. A shape rose from the mattress, slender, bird-like, and twitched until it was sitting up.

It was human, but barely. His hair had all fallen out, leaving a wrinkled scalp that looked like it'd been mauled by tank treads. His bloodshot eyes sat deep in the pits of his skull. Every other tooth was either crooked or missing and his ribs pressed through his skin, begging to rip free. I'd heard mumblings about this being Nate's Uncle's house from conversations traveling up through the vents and into my cell. I guessed that this shriveled man was him.

"Can you hear it?" he asked. Each word scratched its way out of his throat. "You hear it too, right?

"Hear what?"

Striking up a conversation with this stranger was a bad idea, but I couldn't help it.

"The voices," he gasped. "And the crawling, and the voices and the crawling. They're the same. They're in the walls. They're in the floor. They're all around us. They're coming!"

"Who's coming?"

"Uncle Joe?" I heard Schafer yell from across the house. "Is that you? You need something?"

"Quiet down, I'm not supposed to be out of my room," I hushed him. "Who's coming?"

"You have to get me out of here! He's coming and when he does he's going to do horrible things to all of us!" he screeched.

Our talk was over. As much as I wanted to unravel this mystery, I couldn't have him putting everyone on alert. So, like a robot, I fell back into my routine. I dug through his discarded bedding, found a pillow, and pressed it over his frail face.

Smothering was hardly original, but at times like this there was no sense in trying to fix what wasn't broken. When God gives you pillows, suffocate the son of a bitch.

He didn't fight—didn't even lift his arms in protest as I straddled him and bounced up and down on his clammy chest. Soon his heartbeat muted. Victim number two was on the slab.

I wasn't in the clear yet though. I paused and listened, waiting for what I wanted to hear.

"Whatever," Schafer finally said. "Crazy old coot. Probably just shit himself again. Not my problem."

Close enough. It beat the hell out of running footsteps.

I rolled off the fresh corpse and spied a closed can of kidney beans sitting on the bedside table. I hadn't eaten anything substantial in days, and a growling stomach would be a dead giveaway in a quiet house. I hated kidney beans, but I was stranded behind enemy lines. If I didn't eat now, there wouldn't be another opportunity until after I'd finished them all off. I'd need my strength for the battles ahead. I closed my eyes, peeled the lid back, and shoveled a handful into my mouth, syrup and all. It tasted like mushy pennies.

With my stomach satisfied, it was time to get down to the basement. I pressed my ear to the door, and through the thick wood I could barely make out whispers of television static. I dropped to my knees and peered through the keyhole, making sure no one was waiting for me on the other side. There wasn't.

From my basic understanding of the floor plan (which extended to little more than the laundry chute feeds into the basement), I knew that the door I needed couldn't be far off. I prepared for the worst and gripped the knob.

I pushed the door open one sliver at a time and found myself in a room stacked high with unmarked crates. The adventurer in me wanted to pry the lid off each one, do a little treasure hunting, but I stopped. No more than twenty feet away from me was Schafer gawking at a crusty old television. I could practically smell the sweat running down the back of his neck. Wes was sitting with him though, and even with two kills under my belt, I wasn't prepared to take on multiple adversaries at once. There'd be time for that later. My top priority remained the same—find a way to the basement.

It turned out to be a short trip. Five feet from where I was standing was another door. I held my breath and opened it silently, revealing a set of stairs leading down into the darkness below. I slid inside and shut the door behind me.

I was gone.

Ryan
❖

THE SCREEN DOOR SQUEALED, announcing my presence about as subtly as an air raid siren.

"Hey, Nate?" I said. He continued to stare out into the yard gravely. "Is this seat taken?"

I pulled up an empty lawn chair and sat down. A breeze had picked up since the morning, but I could still smell the remains of our cellphones, tinny and stiff, like battery acid.

"Beautiful weather we're having," I said, trying to force a laugh. Being stranded in the middle of the woods had really degraded my conversational skills.

"For now," he replied in monotone. "It's supposed to rain tonight."

His voice was fragile, and I knew that if I pushed him even a little he was liable to crumble. But if that happened, would I be able to put him back together? Or more importantly, would I be able to before the others noticed? Our discussion was destined to be a tightrope walk from beginning to end. There was no sense in delaying the inevitable . . .

"I wanted to talk to you about something, if you're feeling up to it I mean," I said.

"Take a number," he said. "If it's not Schafer, it's you. What is it?"

"Hey, everything is cool, we're just having a friendly chat," I said.

"What is it?" he repeated.

Maybe Schafer had been right about this being a bad time, but I didn't have very many options to begin with. I pushed forward.

"It's about Edric—no, it's about everything," I said.

"I don't know, man. That seems a little weighty for a friendly afternoon chat."

"I agree, but if we don't figure some stuff out now, we might not have a chance to."

He took this the wrong way. Instead of hearing "we have some details to sort out, some things to get straight" he heard "we've failed, abandon all hope."

"There's nothing left to sort out," he growled defensively. "We're sticking to the plan."

"But things have changed," I said. I would have to choose my next words carefully. "I'm not saying we throw it out, not at all. I'm saying we adapt."

He paused, letting the idea roll around between his ears.

"Adapt?" he said. "I don't think so. There's nothing to tweak, there's nothing to fix. The plan is perfect. I designed it. I'm the one leading this operation."

He leapt up, sending his chair clattering to the porch, arms straight at his sides. He looked down at me with clenched teeth and tight fists. There'd be no convincing him. He was on a crash course, and there was nothing I could do to switch the autopilot off.

"It's okay, Nate," I said, trying my hardest to keep the solemnity out of my voice. It was time to run damage control. "You're still our leader. You have my support until the end."

He leaned up against the porch railing and continued his staring contest with the surrounding forest, his cheeks sagging back into a frown.

"Are you okay?" I asked.

"I'm going to go have a smoke, don't follow me," was his only reply.

"Okay," I stuttered. "I'll catch you later?"

He didn't nod or acknowledge me. Instead, he pulled a Zippo and a flattened pack of cigarettes out of his pocket and headed for the trees.

XVI
Tunnel Vision

Edric
❖

THE STAIRCASE WAS A DEATHTRAP waiting to happen, the side effect of a DIY project from decades past, some person's sad (and probably only) attempt at being a handyman. The steps bowed in submission to years of water damage. It would only be a ten-foot drop to the basement floor, but that doesn't mean that I didn't test every step before resting my full weight on each one.

Once grounded, I took a look around. The basement floor was paved with cracked cement. Stacks of old newspapers, books, and car parts filled most of the room—a hoarders paradise. I'd have to take extra caution when navigating the junk labyrinth. One misstep and I'd be done for.

A sickly vibration shook the foundation, sending a blizzard of dust motes into the air. I stood on my tiptoes, trying to reach the precious oxygen floating a foot over my head. I squinted up at the ceiling and froze. Up past the pinnacles on the newspaper skyscrapers was something tangled among the rafters. Its toxic green ribbed body ran the entire length of the basement, throbbing with life. It was a thirty-foot-long anaconda, waiting to strike and crush me in its muscular coils.

I scrambled into a nearby pile of garbage and came up wielding a dented muffler. I'd taken out a giant spider already; a huge snake wouldn't be much more of a challenge. At least I'd have fewer legs to deal with.

The dust settled to the floor, and the creature flickered in and out of existence, changing shape. It was only a tube, probably hooked up to some long-dead air conditioning unit. I dropped my automotive Excalibur and rubbed my temples.

"Maybe that drug really is messing with my head," I said, lightly smacking my cheeks. "No more of that shit for me. Have to stay focused."

I could make out two doors on the far side of the room, one white and one black. The white one was made of flimsy wood and sat anchored in an even flimsier wall. It hadn't been there originally and was probably erected around the same time the catastrophe that was the basement stairs came into existence.

The black door, on the other hand, was heavy, wide, and crafted from some sort of metal. It was fixed directly into the basement wall and three sturdy jail bars ran along its face. Its patina glistened in the dirty light.

"What is this, a dungeon?" I joked, working my way over to it.

I peered through the bars, and to my surprise, it wasn't a cell but a tunnel. I could barely make out a pinprick of light deep inside. Other than water dripping somewhere in the distance, there was no sound. I wanted to crawl in and begin exploring, but before I got too carried away, I reminded myself that I still had one more door to unlock. My subterranean adventures would have to wait.

"Let's take a gander at what's behind door number two," I said, giving the white door a shove.

It popped open effortlessly and the wall quaked with it. For a moment I was afraid that the whole thing was going to come toppling down, but it held. Inside was an old military cot, a counter with a sink, and a metallic gurney—the kind used for surgery. The lack of ventilation in the tiny room had kept the stifling scent of disinfectant bottled up. It brought tears to my eyes. There was no denying that this amateur ER was creepy, but if I needed to take a breather before I'd finished my revenge, this is where I'd have to do it. It beat digging a burrow out of trash and old newspapers.

But at that moment, a break was the last thing on my mind. I turned my attention back to the mystery tunnel.

I wrapped my hands around the door's cold metal handle and pulled. The hinges bellowed a low groan and chips of rust drizzled the floor. It opened wide, spilling icy darkness over my feet. A draft rushed out past me and my nostrils filled with the smell of wet dirt.

I couldn't tell how deep it went. A hundred feet? A mile? And while I was worried about leaving the house for a prolonged period of time, there could've been something important to help me with my quest on the other side—like an old stash of prohibition era firearms. I knew it was a long shot, but I had to get out of the house for a bit anyway to restore my sanity.

I took a couple of steps inside; the cool mud was comforting on the soles of my battered feet.

"I sure hope there are no bats in here," I said.

Before the last syllable had left my lips, the door swung shut behind me. Trapping me in the black corridor.

Ryan

"**READY FOR OUR PICNIC?**" I asked.

Madison finished rolling a blanket and shoved it into a ratty backpack. Her movements were focused but jittery. I could see it in the way her fingers fumbled with the bag's zipper.

"As ready as I'll ever be," she replied. "Are we really going to go through with this?"

"My mind is made up," I said. "Everything is going to be fine. We're just testing the waters, that's all."

"If that's the case then I guess we should—what is it that Schafer says all the time? Get this show on the road? We're still missing a member of our party . . ."

"I'll find him," I said. "He was headed to Edric's room after our little bonfire. I guess I should start there."

I was about to scour the house for our third musketeer when she stopped me. She'd had a last second change of heart.

"Honey?" she said. "Why not just leave a note with Nate or Wes and have him catch up? I'm in the mood for a little *alone time* before he comes and finds us. I need to blow off some steam."

She kept her mouth tight, but when she moaned "alone time" I caught a quick flash of her slick tongue. For the first time since getting beaten, my crotch stirred.

"There's no hurry," I said too quickly. She giggled. "As long as we get in touch with him before tonight. It might be better to shake him awake and ask him right as we're walking out the door, now that I think about it. That way if he does decide to turn on us, we'll already be gone."

"I'm glad you see it my way." She nodded.

"Oh please," I laughed. "You bribed me with sex, how could I not be persuaded?"

I sprinkled pecks down her neck and pinched her butt. She shooed my hands away.

"Would you quit it? They'll be plenty of that later if you play your cards right."

"And I have a full house, baby."

"Dork," she concluded.

We made our way to the kitchen and fished the leftovers out of the refrigerator, then spooned a couple of helpings into plastic containers—no microwave required. That's the thing about good cooking; it's delicious no matter what temperature it's served at. We placed the Tupperware in the backpack.

"Time to go," she said.

"Not quite," I replied, bending down on one knee and kissing her hand. "Will you do me the honor of letting me accompany you on this romantic jaunt in the woods, miss?"

"Oh lord," she groaned. "If I say yes, will you stop talking like that?"

I kept a firm grip on her hand, and then dove in, attacking it with a flurry of butterfly kisses.

"Ah!" she cried. "Yes, yes, yes, you can take me on this walk. Stop it! It tickles!"

I stood up; and with our arms locked, we headed out to the backyard. Nate was right where I'd left him. Still out by the workshop, pacing, flicking ashes.

"What's the deal with him?" she whispered into my ear.

"Rough couple of days," I said, hoping to leave it at that.

Madison waved until she had his attention. Then, she cupped her hands around her mouth.

"We're going on a picnic," she called out. "If you see Jacob, will you tell him to come find us?"

"Will do," he grumbled, taking another heavy drag from his cigarette. "Don't be out too long. Our call is sure to come any minute."

He stiffly raised one hand to wave, but I pretended not to notice. Instead, I pulled myself closer to Madison as we walked along the fire road, happily kicking pinecones in our path.

"Alone at last," I said.

"The way it was meant to be," she replied.

Edric

"**ONE WAY TRIP?**" I mumbled, feeling around for an emergency latch. I couldn't find one, and searching was useless without a flashlight or lantern. "Hopefully this place spits me out nearby."

I worked my way down the tunnel, testing each step for pits or booby-traps. The cave was manmade, and with the exception of the occasional wooden crossbeam, the walls were constructed from packed mud. Dangling, wiry roots brushed through my hair and against my sleeves. A light breeze siphoned through the tunnel, and the further I walked, the louder it got. Soon it mixed with the wet dripping to create a new sound. Something like footsteps and crying.

There was someone behind me.

I whirled around with my fists raised, but was met with nothing. Just stray fingers of sunlight passing through the barred entrance.

"I have to get out of here before I really go off the deep end," I said.

From entrance to exit, the tunnel was only a couple hundred feet in length. It came to a dead end at a rickety ladder leading up through a crude trap door. I pushed it open slowly, sneaking a look at the world above before committing to leaving my hidey-hole.

I was inside some kind of workshop or shed. Benches and tables wrapped around the room with dozens of tools and pieces of equipment hung up on the walls. Most of the displays were made from disintegrating particleboard, dropping their heavy payloads all over the sandy floor. The walls and ceiling were composed of thick planks hastily hammered together. Despite its age, the structure had held up pretty well, with the exception of a single gaping hole in the roof directly above the trap door.

I was about to do inventory, see what I could use as potential weapons, when I heard someone shout outside. I ducked to the floor and crab walked back to the tunnel. Even if I couldn't make it all the way back to the basement, it would still serve as a pretty kick-ass hiding spot.

When I realized the yells had nothing to do with me, I decided to take a peek. I brought my eye up to a knothole in the rough wall and surveyed the scene. Nate was nearby; smoking and mumbling incoherently to himself while Madison and Ryan disappeared further back into the trees—probably sneaking away for a quick bang on the side. It was none of my concern. The longer they remained unaware of their friend's death, the better.

Time to admire the contents of the shed. It had everything I would need and more: a variety of saws, barbed wire, thick beams, dozens of sharp tools, and even a pair of gas cans. I nudged them both with my big toe, they sloshed in reply. My finale was here somewhere. In pieces, sure, but it was here.

"It's like Christmas," I said. "Not too shabby."

That's when I heard the door crackle open behind me.

In stepped Nate, I guess he was closer than I thought. He was oblivious at first, but when his puffy red eyes fell on me, he stopped.

"Am I losing it?" he asked. He looked down at the cigarette in his hand and watched the embers fade to ash. "Are you real?"

It wouldn't be long until he realized I wasn't a hallucination brought on by his guilt. I looked to the display of tools hung lopsided on the wall, searching for something sharp or heavy within arm's reach. I picked up a can of lubricant and could still feel the weight of the oil inside. I also gripped the handle of an axe, and gently lifted it down from its hook. Whereas all the other tools were coated in grime and cobwebs, the axe head was polished to a shine. Brand new, like it was meant for me.

With both in my hands, I sprinted over to him, dodging workbenches and gardening equipment. He didn't move, his eyes swimming, trying to figure out if this was a nightmare. By the time he found out he wasn't asleep, it was too late.

First order of business was to shut him up. I didn't know how close Ryan and Madison were, or if his screams would reach them. I jammed the nozzle of the spray can in his stupid mouth and emptied it until his teeth clamped down on my thumb. He stumbled back coughing, trying to get an ounce of breath down his quickly swelling throat. He fell back against the wall while his feet fought limply to regain their balance. I shook the pain from my thumb and pressed the blade of the axe to his cheek, lining up my shot. His eyes met mine in defeat, lazily. I lifted the axe with both hands and paused before bringing it down.

"I'm sorry," he wheezed between gasps for air, a brown thick liquid slopping from the corner of his mouth.

"And I'm not."

My aim was perfect. The blade came straight down through the top of his skull and didn't stop until it connected with his jaw, shattering all of his front teeth. He twitched uncontrollably until one of his eyes caved into the ditch that divided his face, quivering in a soup of his own juices. There would be no need for a second swing.

When he stopped moving, I searched his pockets and grabbed a gold lighter. That would come in handy later. Then, I dragged him over to the trap door and dumped him inside.

Two down and four to go. Nate's uncle didn't really count—he was a happy bonus, like finding a prize at the bottom of a cereal box. A nasty bit of collateral damage and nothing more.

"This house is becoming your family's own private mausoleum, isn't it, Nate?" I chuckled, spitting a glob of saliva down into his head wound. I sealed the passage, leaving Nate to finish bleeding out in the dark.

Now I was faced with another choice: who to kill next? I could either ruin Madison and Ryan's walk in the woods or go after the brothers. And while hunting in the woods sounded like fun, it presented too many opportunities for failure. If I didn't finish them both off in quick succession, one could get away. With no hallways to direct them down, all they would need is a head start.

"Best not to keep Schafer waiting anyway," I cooed. "Him and I have had an engagement for some time now."

It was time for the climax.

XVII
Night Terrors

Edric
❖

MY MENTOR HAD SAID that as long as the opportunity presented itself, I was allowed to deviate from quick, clean kills to have a little fun.

The opportunity had most certainly presented itself.

I immediately went to work, devising a plan to destroy Wesley and Schafer on the fly. First, I would have to find a way to pacify or cripple them. Asclepius had said that they were practically keeping me inside of a pharmacy; finding something to put the brothers out would only be a minor inconvenience.

What I was more concerned about was crossing the yard. Yeah, I could have just taken the tunnel to the basement again and tried to force my way back through the door, but that would deposit me into the heart of the house. Moving the five feet between Nate's Uncle's room and the basement had been nerve-racking enough; I didn't think I could handle moving room to room, searching in silence for dozens of minutes. Not to mention I was in no hurry to find out who, or what, the ghostly footsteps and cries belonged to. Just thinking about it made me shiver. There was no reasonable way around it; I'd have to traverse no-man's land.

I pressed my ear to the workshop door. No signs of Madison and Ryan, a good start. It would be a straight shot to the back door. My only worry would be someone seeing me from the broad window that looked in on the kitchen (it was so wide I could see the faucet on the sink bending skywards like the neck of a swan). I would run there, only slowing when I hit the porch to avoid any unnecessary noise.

"Three . . ."

I braced the doorframe for an extra boost.

"Two . . ."

I leaned forward.

"One!"

I exited the shop at high speed, crossing the lawn in a matter of seconds, taking special care to tiptoe over any sharp sprinkler heads. I skipped up the porch and pressed myself against the wall by the kitchen door. I couldn't stay long though, because if Madison and Ryan returned, they'd see me from a mile away. I was basically wearing reverse camouflage.

I leaned over and peered in the window. Through the kitchen, through the dining room, and on the living room couch I spotted two sets of legs. Jackpot. On top of this, the TV was so loud I doubted they'd be able to hear me sneak inside. I tested this theory.

Back home, my father and I kept pills in both our medicine cabinets and on top of the refrigerator. This kitchen didn't disappoint. On top of the fridge sat four prescription bottles. I pulled them down gently to avoid creating medicinal maracas and glanced at each of the labels. I settled on one made out to Wesley that read: "Take one before bed if insomnia persists."

"Sleeping pills," I mumbled. "And not shitty over-the-counter ones either."

The next step was to slip them to my victims somehow. I knew they were both drinkers (Schafer especially), so dissolving them in liquor would be the order of the day. The chemical taste would help disguise the chalky flavor of the sedatives. I'd still have to stalk them though, observe their behavior and wait for the moment when their sweaty hands weren't wrapped around the slender neck of the whiskey bottle sitting on the couch between them.

I fought the childproof seal, twisted the lid off the pills, and glided out into the entryway. I stood over their shoulders, watching and waiting. Reaching down between them would be tricky considering they took alternate hits off the bottle every twenty to thirty seconds, but what choice did I have?

It was time to make my move.

The television unscrambled just long enough for a blonde bombshell to run her hands through her hair.

"Like that," she moaned. "Like that, like that."

Static swallowed the image again and my hand crept over the back of the couch. Schafer snatched the bottle without looking, brought it to his lips, and returned it.

"Put it in there," she continued. "Faster!"

I was now elbow-deep, inches from the top of the bottle. Spit shimmered along the rim.

"I'm close!" she shrieked.

I gripped it with my fingers and pulled it back up, a human claw machine. I kept it at an angle during its ascent, making sure not to rub the tinkling glass against the course material of the cushions.

"I'm there! Oh my god!"

I didn't know how many pills to use. I needed the brothers knocked out while I finished setting up—but I couldn't risk a coma. Still, I decided to overcompensate. Wesley would have built up some kind of a tolerance to the stuff if the prescription was really his, and it's not like I was spoon-feeding them whole pills. I dumped half of them into the amber liquid and sloshed them around to help them on their way.

Schafer started to shift his shoulders, like he wanted a drink. If I tried putting it back now, we'd definitely bump elbows. But I couldn't wait around and have him discover the bottle was missing either. So, I went with my only option, dropping the bottle back on the couch between them. Booze droplets spouted out the top and splattered Wesley's shirt.

"What the hell, man?" he said, trying to wipe the stains away.

"Cry baby," Schafer chuckled as he took another swig.

He looked down at the label, like something sour had crossed his pallet, but then shrugged and continued drinking.

Over the next five minutes they drained the bottle until there was nothing but a powdery sludge caked to the bottom.

The television crackled and blacked out. The brothers soon followed.

Ryan
❖

AFTER WALKING HALF A MILE, Madison and I pulled off the trail and setup in a clearing. The trees were dead; their rigid limbs outlined the sky. Thick, billowy sheets of moss had shed from their trunks, leaving a green carpet on top of the brittle leaves. We spread out our picnic blanket and lounged on top. I'd never been more comfortable, yet worried, at the same time.

"Are you hungry?" she said, unpacking our meals. She laid them in a row in front of us, correcting the corners so that they made a perfect line.

"Kind of," I replied. "I feel a little sick."

"What's wrong, babe?"

"I'm thinking again."

She set the food down and hugged me. Being isolated outside of the house I felt free to speak my mind, no longer afraid that someone might hear me.

"Well then knock that off," she laughed. "Be happy! We're going to figure this out."

"What do you think is going to happen?" I asked. "To us? To everyone else?"

She sat up straight and looked me in the eye, still radiating a caring aura, but her tone was deadly serious.

"I don't know what's going to happen," she said. "But what I do know is that we always do what we have to to get by. I'm going to be a mother; you're going to be a father. And no matter what it takes, we are going to live happily ever after, together. If we have to, you and me will shoot our way out of here."

I paused; her intensity had caught me off-guard, but I actually felt better. I knew with her by my side we could do anything.

"I'm afraid things are broken, that they're going to be different," I sighed, venting the last of my inner demons, praying that she kept one more small vial of emotional holy water on reserve.

"Things are going to change, I have no doubts about that," she continued. "We're not going to take it lying down, though. We're going to fight to be normal again. We're going to fight to give our child an average life—albeit across the border."

I let out a deep, genuine laugh.

"I'm sorry. I guess my brain is a little scrambled is all," I said.

"Well, luckily for you, I have just the antidote for that," she purred.

She pushed me down onto the blanket and straddled my hips.

"What about Jacob?" I asked.

"I don't think he's in any big hurry," she said, her tongue snaking along my ear. "I haven't even seen him since this morning."

As she stripped my pants off, I stared up into the blackened canopy. The twigs and branches shifted in the breeze, blending, making shapes. When the wind died down, the limbs remained merged together to form a grizzled face watching over us as we made love on the forest floor.

Edric

"**WAKE UP, KIDS**, the show is about to start," I said, slapping Wesley and Schafer's cheeks. Their eyes opened groggily.

I'd moved them both to the work shed (Asclepius's conditioning had done wonders for my cardio) and tied them to a pair of old chairs. They were facing one another, bound and gagged. I stood between them like a ringleader underneath the big top.

Wesley looked disoriented, but Schafer was pissed. He'd ingested enough meds to kill most men, but as soon as he laid eyes on my grinning face, he was wide-awake.

"Not bad for a beginner, huh?" I asked him, pulling the gag from his mouth.

"Is this some kind of joke?" he replied, shaking away any lingering side effects. Warning: use of this drug may lead to mutilation. "You haven't won yet."

"Is that so?" I said as I moved over to Wesley, grabbing him by the shoulders. "Let's see what your brother has to say about that."

I pulled an eggbeater hand drill from my back pocket, a cruel, primitive thing with a jagged bit and red handles. I pressed it to the soft dimple above Wesley's ear. A muffled cry escaped from behind the oily rag crammed in his mouth.

"I'll be honest, it's a little rusty. It might not spin as fast or as effortlessly as it was originally intended," I said.

"Get away from my brother!" Schafer growled, hopping in his chair.

"Or what? You'll kill me? Please," I replied. "You couldn't kill me if you tried. I've been playing you this whole time and you were never even close."

"Edric," he breathed. He was straining so far forward against the ropes constricting his chest that the blood drained from his face. "If you go through with this, there'll be no second chances for you. I will ride your corpse all the way to Hell."

"Save it," I said. "And a word of advice: don't fight your restraints, it's only going to get you more tangled. Don't go anywhere either, you're next."

I pressed the bit into Wesley's flesh and he thrashed for every millimeter of it. My hand found the crank and I started to drill. Unfortunately, for Wesley or for me I'm not sure, it kept locking up.

"Told you this wouldn't be easy," I said. "I'll never crack the skull at this rate."

"You bastard!" Schafer screamed, continuing to fight.

I hit gold. Blood leaked out over my hands and wrists, making the knobs slippery. Wesley's eyes rolled back into his head.

"I do believe that look of retardation means we have reached the brain cavity," I said, continuing to work the drill in little circles. "This blood makes a fantastic lubricant. Anyway, don't worry, he won't die immediately. He still has a while to go before he bleeds out and his body starts shutting down. Enough time to reflect on his life choices at least—well, the best he can now, anyway. My guess is he doesn't even recognize you. Who's that, Wes?"

I pulled the drill from the side of his head and pointed it at Schafer. Something gluey and pink clung to the tip.

"I think I'm going to give you a special kind of lobotomy," I said, turning back to Schafer. "The kind where you go in through the eye to reach the frontal lobe. I saw it in a movie once."

Schafer worked all of his strength into one last tug. He brought his arms up and ripped free from the restraints, splitting the chair down the middle. He looked at me with gritted teeth, and more hatred and anguish than I'd ever seen before.

He was free.

Luckily, conscious enough to talk and conscious enough to fight are two different things. By the time he'd recovered from his wobbling knees, I'd already ran past him, out the door, across the lawn, and back into the house. I collapsed up against a wall in the living room, catching my breath and contemplating my next move.

Did I screw up? Had I lost perspective? Maybe a little, but I wouldn't make that mistake again. The war wasn't over yet.

A dazed Schafer was a good start, but I'd still need something if I wanted to finish him off and remain in one piece. I spotted a long extension cord bundled up behind the TV. What it was doing there I'll never know, but it would make a handy tripwire. Keeping one end in its outlet and the other in my hand, I sat back down next to the kitchen doorway.

Schafer kicked the back door open, putting his foot through the screen. Then, he yanked a butcher knife free from the block. The blade vibrated metallically as it sliced the air.

"Here Edric, Edric, Edric. Come out, come out, wherever you are," he said. "I'm not going to kill you."

"Oh yeah?" I called out. "Then what are you planning to do with that knife, big boy?"

"Just make you into a more agreeable person," he said. "Maybe slide it into your spine a little so you can't run or fight back anymore. That's the ticket. We'd get along fine then."

"Tell me something," I said. "Did you stay with Wesley as he died? Or was getting revenge more important?"

That did it. His awkward footsteps rumbled across the linoleum. When his shadow passed through the door, I pulled the cord taut. Timber! He face planted on the nasty Persian rug and the knife bounced free from his hand.

I scrambled over the top of him, reaching for the blade, but before I could get a good hold on it, he planted his boot in the center of my face. My nose cracked and I felt hot sticky blood splash my cheek and run past my lips.

Schafer closed the distance between him and the knife by crawling and snatched it up. He sprang to his feet and swung it at me in a wide arc. At the same time, I reached down to the couch and grabbed the neck of the liquor bottle, right where they'd left it, and swung back. They met in the air in a glassy explosion, raining slivers down in the room like shrapnel from a grenade. When the final pieces had clinked to the floor, we stood across from one another, bloodied, the knife in his hand, the sharp stump of the bottle in mine.

"I always thought that it could never end any other way between us," he said gruffly.

"Bull shit," I replied. "You just still can't fess up that I played you like a fiddle."

He thrust forward and I easily dodged, bringing the bottle down into the soft skin behind his elbow. He screamed and fell back clutching his arm, gore pulsing from behind his fingers.

"I have to admit," he said, wincing. "You're better than I thought."

"Thank you–you're *worse*."

He dove in again. This time I rolled past him and slashed at the back of his knees. The glass shredded the fabric of his pants effortlessly and he dropped, only supported by the knuckles on the hand that wielded the knife. I gutted that elbow too, and kicked the blade away as he limply sprawled out across the floor.

"What was that you said about making me a more agreeable person?" I panted, standing over the top of him. The only response was gurgles.

"You'll have to speak up, I can't hear you."

"I said do your worst!" he spat.

"I plan to," I said. "But first, I have a couple of things to get out of the way that will make this whole process tick by more smoothly. Be right back, don't go too far."

I kicked him in the face, ran upstairs, and yanked one of the curtains in my room free. Then, I entered the crate room and sifted through boxes until I found a handful of wrapped syringes. I returned to Schafer and spread the curtain out on the floor next to him.

"I know you're a little *hindered* right now, but if you can help me with this at all it will be very much appreciated."

I grasped his sides and rolled him over onto the ever so absorbent curtain. Surprisingly, it was harder than moving him to the shed—more dead weight.

Get it? I made a funny.

"Whew, you're a heavy one," I said, wiping sweat from my forehead. "Any last words?"

He looked up at me with a dark light in his eyes. A dull shimmer glazed his irises. Was he crying?

"Please . . ."

"What was that?"

"You've already killed my brother, what more can you do to me?"

"We're about to find out," I said as I unwrapped one of the syringes. "You seem to think there's something left that we can do, otherwise you wouldn't be begging like this."

"Help!" he screamed suddenly. "Somebody help me!"

"Everyone is gone, you idiot," I said. "Why do you think I waited so long for this? Why do you think I'm taking my time?"

He eyed the needle again and gulped.

"We should get started," I continued. "Ryan and Madison could be back from their walk soon and I'm going to need to clean up after we have our fun."

"Why?" he asked as I climbed on top of him.

"You're not really asking that," I sighed. "You're just trying to stall me."

There was a quiet moment of understanding. Then, he swallowed his pain and glared up at me.

"I knew it all along, you aren't an innocent victim. I should've killed you when I had the chance."

"Finally, something we can both agree on."

I brought the syringe down into his throat, straight through the Adam's apple, and back up in one smooth motion. His head bucked and he spat a line of blood into the air. I did it again, this time twisting when I retracted it. The second stab had been so violent it bent the end of the needle. No worries; I unwrapped another.

I went through four syringes this way. I didn't stop until nothing remained below his chin but spongy, red, meat.

"We're almost done, big boy," I said. "And if you keep behaving yourself, I might give you a lollipop when this over. Probably not, but it doesn't hurt to try."

Using the butcher knife, I slit the front of his shirt open, revealing his naked chest. I picked the broken liquor bottle back up and pressed it into the flesh above his heart. "I hope that alcohol disinfected the glass," I said. "Because this is a very delicate procedure."

I dug the shards into his sweaty skin and twisted back and forth. Grinding in a circle, it tore through him like a cookie cutter carves moist dough. I removed the greasy skin flap and stuck it to his forehead. Next, I smashed the bottle down again and again through the gap, shattering ribs with every swing. When I'd finished breaking through, I gave his heart a quick couple of superficial jabs, and then sat back and watched as his abdominal cavity filled with blood.

The Big Bad Schafer had been defeated.

I sat in silence, absorbing the calm of the empty house—the house I had emptied--as my bloodlust faded. Soon the windows shook and the floorboards groaned. The vibration carried Asclepius's voice.

"I'm proud of you," it said.

"Thank you," I replied. "That means the world to me."

I was ready for a victory nap before launching into the final act, but first I had to clean. I scrubbed the blood and picked up the glass. Working under Asclepius, in constant fear of physical retribution every time I screwed up, had given me a talent for going over things with meticulous detail. When I was finished, the room was cleaner than it'd been before the battle had even taken place.

I dropped the knife into the curtain with Schafer's corpse, rolled him up like a human burrito, and tossed him down the basement stairs. I buried him underneath a few armfuls of garbage.

Should I have said something? My greatest adversary had been slain. A warrior deserved a warrior's sendoff, right?

"He lived like trash," I began. "And to trash he returned."

I stumbled into the poor man's ER and blew my nose into the sink, forcing out clots of mucus. There was no question in my mind—it was broken—and not even a minute after this evacuation had taken place, the skin on my face tightened until my right eye was swollen shut. I didn't want to think about the medical reasons for that. I was too tired.

I plopped down on the surgical gurney and stared up at the ceiling. I'd come a long way, but my most magnificent accomplishments were ahead of me. They would have to wait until sundown.

"Only two left," I recited in a lullaby. "Only two to go, and then I'm finished."

XVIII
R.E.M.

Ryan

❖

WHEN WE RETURNED, Nate was no longer out back smoking and someone had demolished the screen door. Its aluminum frame was bent and a large hole opened wide in the center of the wire mesh.

"What does this mean?" Madison whispered. Her eyes darted around nervously, inspecting shrubs and trees for signs of an ambush.

"I don't know," I said. "Something isn't right. Stay quiet and stay close. Let's find someone."

There was no note on the kitchen table, the fridge, or either of the doors. The van still sat in the driveway undisturbed, and with the exception of the screen we had passed on our way in, nothing was out of sorts. The TV was unplugged, but that just seemed smart. Calling the wiring in this place "dangerous" would have been a compliment to the electrician and the last thing we needed heading into the final stretch was a fire. Other than that though, there wasn't even a hint as to what we'd missed. It was like a ghost story, the kind where an entire village vanishes during the night.

A light bulb glowed between my ears.

"Edric," I said, heading for the stairs. "If he's still here, then maybe he heard something."

I opened his door and snuck a look inside. He was still bunched up beneath the covers, sleeping the day away. I should have woken him up, but I couldn't bring myself to do it.

He'd been through enough, no need to pile more on his plate with another interrogation. I returned to Madison.

"Call me stumped," I said, taking a seat in the dining room. "Any thoughts?"

Somewhere in the house a clock ticked, what little precious time we had to solve this mystery draining away.

"Do you think they got the call?" she asked. There was a ring in her voice that was somehow both skeptical and filled with hope.

"I doubt it," I replied. "If that was the case, why would Edric still be here?"

"True," she sighed, resting her chin in her palms. "What are the chances that they're off to retrieve the money and they ditched us here, red-handed, with the hostage?"

"Vegas odds? A million to none. That wasn't part of the plan and Nate seemed pretty damn set on sticking to it. Plus, they know how sick of them we are. What would stop us from snitching on them immediately? From turning ourselves in and cutting deals?"

Madison ran through all of the other possibilities she could think of, reviewing her mental Rolodex. She shook her head.

"None of this adds up," she concluded.

"Preaching to the choir, babe."

"Wait a second," she said, breaking the unnerving quiet with a snap of her fingers. "This is perfect. Let's just leave."

I frowned and gave her a sideways glance.

"Why are you looking at me like that?" she asked.

"I just thought up one other scenario."

"Yeah?"

"Yeah, and it isn't a pleasant one."

"Well, let me in on it," she said. "We're partners in crime now, no secrets."

In truth, you always keep secrets from your partners in crime because you never know when someone might flip on you—but I neglected to bring this up. Now was not the time.

"I think this might be a test," I said grimly.

"A test? What kind of test?"

"A loyalty test—they're waiting nearby to see what we do when we're left to our own devices."

"Hold on just a second. Schafer said that burning our phones was the last thing he needed to trust us."

I rolled my eyes.

"Did you really think that someone as twisted up in their own paranoia as Schafer would just drop everything because of that stupid barbecue?"

She looked down in her lap disappointed, fiddling with her nails.

"You're right, I guess I'm not cut out for this criminal business after all," she said. "And if we fail their test?"

"Who knows, they could be waiting out in the ditch by the side of the road with guns right now."

"Do you really think they'd do that?"

"After the last couple of days, I wouldn't rule anything out."

A sad quiet passed between us. All of our plans for the future were trapped in this house, and they kept getting dragged back no matter how much we clawed our way towards civilization.

"What should we do?" she asked. Her lips trembled.

"What can we do? We spend the night—and if we feel safer in the morning, we leave. Preferably with them still in bed."

"I don't like it," she said. "Can't you just go through the contraband and see if any guns are missing?"

"They have so much shit in there," I interrupted. "And Nate isn't the kind of person to keep a stock list. It'd be impossible. Baby, I don't want to spend another second in this place either, but we have to. Twelve more hours and we'll be gone—I promise."

"Will you stay with me tonight?" she whimpered. "Keep me close?"

"I wouldn't want it any other way."

We climbed the stairs hand in hand as twilight seeped through the front windows. Our room, our only peaceful sanctuary, was warm and inviting in comparison to the empty claustrophobia of the rest of the house. We prepped for bed.

"Should we take Edric some dinner?" she asked, systematically removing each piece of jewelry and placing them one at a time on the dresser.

"No, I think Jacob had that handled before they all ran off," I said.

"You sure?"

"Yeah," I lied. "He told me to leave it to him for the rest of our time here, thought it would make everyone get along better."

"For what it's worth, I know you were right about him," she said, slipping into a nightgown. "He's a good guy."

"What convinced you?"

"Nothing specifically, just a feeling."

We crawled into bed together and I wrapped my arms around her, pulling her warmth into my chest. I kissed a strand of hair draped across the back of her neck.

"Ryan? We're going to be together forever, right?" she asked.

"Hell or high water," I replied.

"What if I die?"

"Then I'd come with you. You're going to need someone to help carry your bags in the afterlife."

"And what if someone kills me?"

I took a breath and gave her one final kiss.

"Then may God have mercy on that poor bastard when I get my mitts on him."

Edric

I COULD HAVE TAKEN THEM BOTH right there as they slept—stabbed, or shot, or burned them alive. I can't say how many times I played it out in my head. But no, I'd prepared something much more special for these two. I crept back out onto the landing, keeping one eye bent around the doorframe at all times, waiting. Four hours passed, but something told me to remain resilient. It was coming.

I saw everything. I saw Madison toss and turn. I saw her climb out of bed. I saw Ryan's fingers grasp at nothingness in the empty void her body left behind.

She took two steps towards the bathroom before it was her turn to see everything. She saw my pale, bloody face. She saw my malnourished frame. Last but not least, she saw my rifle. I'd picked it up on the way in case I thought she needed a little extra incentive to go along with my plans. It was tough to choose just one gun though; they'd built a regular armory downstairs. Ultimately I decided on a beat-up Mosin-Nagant, probably pulled off some stiff in one Eastern European conflict or another. It had a smooth, slanted magazine that swooped back to the trigger. Someone had carved "Don't say a word, Momma's going to buy you a mockingbird" around the stock. Letters all made from nothing but straight lines.

I raised a single finger to my lips and ushered her out to the hallway. What choice did she have but to follow?

"If you scream," I said. "I'll ruin that nighty of yours. Blood is hard to wash out."

"Edric?" she asked, frightened and confused. "What are you doing? What happened to you?"

I could feel humming in the bottoms of my feet, lifting me up, making me braver.

"Nothing happened to me, I chose this."

"But you said I was your only friend."

"And I'd like to thank the Academy."

A tear rolled down her cheek. It gathered what little light was in the room and glittered.

"You have your whole life ahead of you. Please, don't shoot me."

"I don't want to shoot you, but I won't hesitate if you leave me no choice."

"You can leave," she pleaded. "I'll pretend like I never saw you. Ryan and I were planning to help you escape tomorrow morning anyway. No one will know."

"Help me escape? God, you must think I'm pretty dumb. But yes, no one will ever know what happened here. Have you figured out where all of your friends are yet?"

She put two and two together, and her eyes widened. The tear was soon joined by a torrent of cold sweat. I gave a single satisfied nod.

"But we didn't hear any gunshots?"

"There's more than one way to kill a person," I replied simply.

"What have you done?"

"Only what was necessary—nothing more."

I placed the barrel to her forehead, mostly just to relish her reaction.

"I'm pregnant," she blurted out. "Please let me go."

I loosened my grip on the rifle.

"You're pregnant?" I began. She nodded enthusiastically, the worried creases disappearing from her face. "Then why didn't you say so?"

I brought the butt of the rifle around in a flash, splitting her eyebrow open. She fell to the floor reeling, unconscious.

Of course she was pregnant. I'd known that since the first time I laid eyes on her. That was my ace in the hole. That's what was going to make tonight's events into a tragedy of Shakespearean magnitude.

I let the gun fall loosely on its strap, knelt down, and carried her away. I held the last domino in my arms. The only thing left to do was give it a little flick, and then watch all of the rest come tumbling after.

Ryan
❖

"RYAN!" I HEARD MADISON SCREAM, but it wasn't the terror in her voice that made me fly out of bed—it was the pain that resonated beneath.

"Louder!" Edric shouted, punctuating her cries with the crack of a gunshot. "Your hubby needs to rise and shine, and you sleep a little heavier after you've taken a beating. Trust me, I know from experience."

Their voices were distant, drowning beneath a haze of sleep.

"She was right here two seconds ago," I said, rubbing her side of the bed, searching for signs of her body heat. "How could I have been so stupid?"

"Ryan, hurry!" she said again, followed by two more gunshots.

Where could they be? I heard them clearly, but the shots were far enough away that I couldn't feel them in my chest. Clear but far, not many barriers to ricochet the sound waves in between—not many walls.

They were somewhere outside. They had to be.

I slid open the window and poked my head out into the muggy night air. Crickets chirped as the moon drifted behind a cloud, bathing the yard in complete darkness.

"Madison, where are you!?" I yelled so loudly my voice chaffed my windpipes. "Answer me!"

"Out here," she wheezed. "I'm not going to last very long. I need help."

At the back of the lawn, swallowed by the shade of the trees, I could make out her white nightgown flapping in the wind, suspended three feet above the ground. The night didn't allow any other details—but it was enough. I could figure the rest out later.

I forced my feet into a pair of shoes, then sprinted down the stairs in nothing but a long-sleeved shirt and pajama pants. I burst through the kitchen door, my muscles fueled with icy panic.

I tore into the forest and came face to face with my wife. Her back was pressed up against a sturdy wooden beam planted in the earth. The nightgown that had been pristine when we laid down for the night was now smeared with streaks of blood. Nothing pronounced, she wasn't soaked; it was more like finding bedbugs in your sheets. Spun all the way around her, keeping her afloat, was a lengthy coil of barbed wire, each spine nipped at her veins begging to be fed. Her feet dangled above the ground helplessly, giving the occasional involuntary kick. A strange smell that I couldn't place wafted up my nostrils and strangled my lungs.

"Ryan?" she breathed.

"I'm here, sweetie," I said, trying to find a way to untangle the yards upon yards of jagged metal. "Don't move, okay? I'm going to get you out of here."

"Edric did this to me."

"I know."

"He's killed everyone . . ."

I was in too much of a hurry for this to register. All I could think was my wife is going to die, my wife is going to die, my wife is going to fucking die and there's nothing I can do about it.

What was that smell?

"He's out there somewhere waiting for you," she continued. "He's got a gun."

"I don't care. Fuck!" I screamed, unable to find a way to unravel the mess without ripping Maddy to shreds.

"Honey, my shoulder really hurts," she said. "Can you look at it for me?"

"Yes," I said, my voice cracking as I suppressed the sobs. "Whatever you want."

I peeled back the top of her gown, revealing even more blood. Instead of circling around her body like the rest of the wire, this section passed through the skin below her clavicle and out the other side. The sick son of a bitch had actually threaded the barbs through her scar.

"It's fine," I lied, trying to remain calm even though stars were bursting in front of my eyes. "I'm going to go get something, I'm going to get you down, and then we're going to get you to a hospital. Everything is going to be okay."

"Do you think the baby is fine?" she asked deliriously.

I gagged and my knees buckled. I found myself in the shadow of her swollen belly, unable to answer for too long.

"The baby is fine," I whispered. "You're fine, I'm fine. We're going to live happily ever after. I'll be right back."

"Don't leave me!"

"I have to, baby, but I'll be back in less than a minute. I promise. I promise."

I turned away before she had a chance to convince me otherwise. I ran back into the kitchen and grabbed a knife (another one was missing, I hadn't noticed it before during my sweep). I was suffering from shock; I actually believed that I'd be able to cut her down with it.

As I stepped out onto the back porch again, a loud whoosh rushed along the perimeter of the yard, engulfed in flames that licked the tops of the trees. A dragon had captured my princess. That strange smell I hadn't been able to place before was gasoline.

I ran back towards the forest, but the fire was faster. Madison screamed as the flames spread to the post she was strapped to, eating their way along it. Her feet came next; as they thrashed in pain, the wire peeled the flesh clean from her shins.

"Ryan! Help me!" she screeched over the roar of the chaos.

I tried to dive through, but the inferno was too intense. I stood there, eight feet away and completely helpless. Our eyes met for the last time as her tears evaporated from her cheeks faster than she could dispense them. Sparks leapt onto her gorgeous hair, I shut my eyes, and collapsed to the ground.

The screams faded to ash.

Edric

IN BETWEEN THE WAVES OF FLAMES, I wrapped the halo at the end of the rifle barrel around Ryan's head. I visualized firing, sending chunks of his skull and brain all over Maddy's exposed feet, a final sloppy kiss.

Until death do us part indeed.

But right as I was about to pull the trigger, I had an epiphany. I wanted him to feel it. I wanted him to know that I was the one who took everything away from his perfect little life. If my shot hit its mark, he'd be dead before the bullet even ripped the skin off his face.

I reset my sights on his lower back. That was better.

Like Asclepius taught me, I held my breath, preparing to exhale and send the round into my prey less than thirty yards away. I rubbed the cool metal of the trigger against the pad of my index finger, getting it nice and snug, ready for war. I steadied my nerves one last time . . .

I dropped the rifle to my side.

Wasn't it better to let him live out the rest of his life in misery? He'd be a pathetic exile with no one to run to, no one to love him. Maybe he'd take the initiative himself, and instead of coping with the pain, go back into the house and blow his own head off before the flesh had boiled clean from Madison's bones.

It was a risky move, but what could he realistically do to me? Back home I'd be surrounded by security twenty-four seven, and even if he did get to me somehow, I'd be ready. I'd beaten him before.

I didn't want to live the rest of my life looking over my shoulder though. So just in case he got any ideas, I sprinkled a cherry on top.

"Hey Ryan?" I called out. He didn't move. "I'm leaving now, but don't think about coming after me. If I ever get even the slightest whiff of your sweat, I'm going to come back and do the same thing to you that I did to your bitch. Remember that."

I turned and took my first step away from the flames. My revenge was complete. The curtain closed, I took a bow, and caught a stray rose in my teeth.

It was time to go home.

XIX
Among the Ruins

Edric

❖

USING THE SHADOWS OF THE TREE LINE, I made my way to the front of the house. Even though Ryan was destroyed, I wasn't about to risk him rallying one more time and flying at me in a blind rage. It's always better to be safe than sorry.

My feet crunched through the gravel of the driveway, and for the first time in a while, I noticed how sore they were. I would've killed everyone all over again for a new pair of shoes.

This pain meant escaping on foot was a stupid idea. I'd pass out before I even hit the highway. The van would be an all around better choice, but that meant I needed keys—thanks for not teaching me how to hotwire, Asclepius.

The thought of going back inside made me woozy. Maybe this had something to do with being surrounded by bodies. Upstairs, downstairs, it didn't matter. Dead eyes would be on me at all times. Maybe I was starting to lose it—maybe it was more than just a house . . .

"I'll be quick," I said, talking myself into it. "In and out, like the rest of this mission."

I pushed the door open and stepped inside. They hadn't bothered to hide the keys during any of their fits of paranoia. They hung on a ring in the kitchen below a placard that read "God Bless Our Happy Home." I snatched them up, dropped them in my pocket, and took one last look out the window above the sink. Ryan's crumpled figure was outlined against the backdrop of flames. He hadn't killed himself in desperation yet. I hadn't given him enough credit.

I passed through the living room and morning shined through the open door—the light at the end of my tunnel. Before I took those final steps, I had to figure out what to do with the rifle. I wanted to take it with me, but I wouldn't exactly look like an innocent victim if I was caught packing. I worked the bolt, snapping back and forth, ejecting the unspent rounds onto the couch. Once it was empty, I tossed the gun back into the opposite room, the one piled with crates.

That was it. I was ready to leave this place behind forever.

I climbed into the driver's seat and the car rumbled to life. The fluorescent orange needle of the fuel gauge traced all the way up to half a tank, more than enough to get to a phone. The view staring out over the dashboard was a million times more appealing than the one from the floor in the back.

As I shifted the car into drive, I was overcome with optimism. Life was going to be different from now on. Innocence was overrated anyway.

I pulled away from the house and set my course for Seattle.

Ryan

❖

IT STARTED TO RAIN.

The flames that had wrapped around the yard like a viper vanished into white smoke. I stayed on my knees in front of Madison's blackened body, letting the ashes of her charred gown caress my cheeks as they wafted to the ground in flecks. Her hair was completely gone and her eyes were shut. The flesh up to her chest was charred with dark streaks, yet barely blistered—almost like I could pull her down, scrub her off, and she'd be as good as new. Her stomach was bright red and her bellybutton protruded out, like one of those cheap plastic meat thermometers that pop when your meal is finished cooking.

I wish I could say that she looked peaceful strung up like an angel, but there wasn't one goddamn peaceful thing about it.

Somewhere in the background I heard the van start and kick up dust as it headed down the road. Edric had left, and I chose not to follow. I didn't stay close to Madison during her final moments; I could stay close to her now.

I looked down. I still had the knife clenched in my fingers. I rolled my arm over and pressed the blade to my wrist. Only one thing left to do. I would be with Madison again in less than ten minutes if I didn't apply pressure. The blade shook and vibrated into my arm and up to my ears.

"Get up," a voice said. "Be a man and get up!"

"I can't," I wheezed. "No reason to."

I must've been crazy. I was talking to my imagination, an angel on my shoulder.

"You're just going to let him get away like that?" it asked.

"I don't want to."

"Then go and get him!"

"He's already gone!"

"So?" it asked—I didn't have a good reply to this. "My money's on that he'll never make it to the highway. Now, if that were true, then would you go teach him a lesson?"

"Then he'd only be a hop, skip, and jump away," I said, calculating the distance.

"Precisely—so, would you?"

I remembered Madison's screams and the way the fire toyed with her before running its fingers up through her hair, the way I liked to when we made love. Edric was the one responsible for this. He was the reason I was alone.

"If I catch him, then revenge will be too nice of a word for what I'd do to that boy."

"Excellent," the voice cooed. "Then you better get a move on."

With my sense of purpose renewed, I made a new plan. I ran track in highschool, but somehow I didn't think that would help me compete with a car. I'd need a vehicle. To my knowledge, Nate's uncle didn't own one, so that avenue was closed. But there was something else. Something I'd forgotten . . .

Nate's old Triumph in the side yard, the one I'd seen before we kidnapped Edric. It was my last chance for closure.

I rushed around to the side of the house and there it sat, still tangled in the weeds, a few years from being completely reclaimed by nature. I dragged it from its resting place. The grass under the tires was brown and dead; no new life had sprouted there in decades. The bike felt fragile in my hands.

"This is never going to work," I groaned. "Look at this thing."

"Don't say that," the voice continued. "Go through the steps, that's all I'm asking. I'll take care of the rest."

I nodded. I owed Madison at least that much.

This story wasn't over yet.

Edric

I WAS TWO FOOTBALL FIELDS OUT of the driveway when something cold curled in my stomach. I lost my grip on the steering wheel and the van came to a stop, stalled on the side of the road like a dog that leaps from the bed of a pickup truck during rush hour.

"Shit." I cranked the key again and again. "Not now."

Something drew my gaze over my shoulder, out the back window, up to the house. My hands, moving on their own, tugged the wheel around, trying to make a three point turn.

"No," I said. "What is this crap? There's nothing back there."

I ripped my hands free and twisted the key again. The motor started as I let out a sigh of relief.

"Close call," I mumbled, pulling back onto the road. "No more surprises, please."

Ryan

FUEL ON, CHOKE UP, and the bike was in neutral. I tossed one leg over the seat and tried to squeeze the clutch. It was rusted solid. I pumped it with both hands, shattering the crispy rot until I could work it with only one. Gritty flakes of rusty metal stained my pant leg.

"We're halfway there," I said. "Don't fail me now."

I hit the gearshift like I was trying to smash through the surface of a frozen lake as my child drowned beneath. The bike gave a dull groan.

"Come on, you son of a bitch."

I hit it again, the engine tinkled and popped, brushing off the cobwebs, coming back to life. I was Dr. Frankenstein lifting my beast into the lightning-fractured sky.

"It's payback time!" I stomped again. "You killed my wife!" —and again—"You killed my child!"—again. "I'm going to take you apart one piece at a time!"

Smoke as dense as pea soup fog poured from the exhaust. I caught my breath as sweat slid down my back and into the seat of my pajamas.

"Call me crazy, but I think this thing is long overdue for a smog check," I said, rocking the bike back and forth, adjusting to the strange balance.

I tucked the knife into the back of my pants and got comfortable on the shredded seat. I revved the engine; it purred like a chainsaw ready for an amputation.

"I'm coming, Edric!" I shouted. "Ready or not, here I come."

Edric

I DIPPED THE VAN INTO ANOTHER TURN and continued forward. For someone with no formal driving experience, I'd caught on quickly. When I got home and settled in, my first goal was to go out and get my license. I might even ask my dad to get a van just like this one for my first car—or maybe an Escalade—or a Porsche.

Wait, no. My first goal was to pass around the story of my escape, get laid, and *then* I could turn around and get my license. If I timed it right, I might be able to christen my new automobile with some screwing in the backseat, a true maiden voyage. That was a better idea.

And I'd get to sleep in a real bed!

It wouldn't be long now. I could see the highway. I'd made it.

Then, something shot in from my peripheral. I probably could've avoided it under normal circumstances, but my eye on that side was still out of commission.

It's funny, in those split seconds before the crash, all I could think was: motorcycles aren't supposed to fly.

Ryan

❖

IF HE WAS TRAVELING AT THE SPEED LIMIT, I'd never catch him on the cycle's flat tires. The fact that they were completely bald didn't help much either. Nate had said that if things fell apart, we could escape along the old fire trail that led back to the main road—the old fire trail Madison and I had wandered down not even twelve hours earlier. I had no idea how the bike would handle it, but it was better than nothing.

I gave the engine one more practice rev and bolted past the tree line, skidding on the moist earth. The dim headlight made the shadows of the potholes that marred the surface of the road elongate into the gloom of predawn. The bike bucked and tried to twist out from underneath me every time I hit a bump or a pinecone got kicked up into the spokes. Bull riding would have been less hazardous.

The trees thinned, and I noticed a rumbling echo that wasn't radiating from underneath me. I looked to my side and caught shots of the van rapidly between the columns of trees, individual cells in a film reel. It was Edric. I'd managed to catch him.

The trail edged closer and closer to the road, they'd crossover soon. I would only have one shot.

I lined the bike up the best I could and fought to keep it steady, the muscles in my arms ached from gripping the handlebars. Random pieces of the engine left a trail of nuts and bolts behind me as the frame shook apart.

"Just a little further," I shouted. "Almost there!"

I hit the gas and screamed towards the car in a wheelie that I didn't know the motorcycle was even capable of. I dove off into the dirt as the machine left the ground. The bike made a perfect arc over the edge of the embankment, bounced into the road, and landed straight through the van's windshield.

Edric, shitting himself I imagine, overcompensated and jerked the van into the drainage ditch on the side of the road. The vehicle bounced once, ripping its front axel clean off the body. Steam puffed out of the grill as the ticking in the engine slowly died away.

I wasn't sure if he was still armed or not, so I took my sweet time down the slope to the driver side door, waiting to see if he would lunge out, firing like a classic last stand in a John Woo film. Minutes passed and nothing moved. I decided to take a chance.

I beat on the dented door until it popped open. Inside, Edric was bloodied and bruised, but breathing. He was sprawled out across the seat on a bed of broken glass, each eye shut but flicking back and forth beneath the lids, dreaming.

As I stared down at him, the panic that I'd felt racing down the fire trail melted back into rage. I scooped him into my arms.

He would be at my mercy now, and I wasn't going to let him get away again.

He would understand despair.

XX
Phantasmagoria

Edric

❖

I WAS UNCONSCIOUS, BUT I HURT EVERYWHERE.

I was still trapped in the cab of the van—didn't have to be awake to know that. I faintly remembered the windshield shattering, leaving the road, and rolling over something that made me smack the top of my skull into the ceiling.

Should've worn my seatbelt.

Whether from the blood loss or head trauma, I found myself slipping back into my own head, back into the endless fields of Asclepius's world. But it wasn't the same. Each step I took dropped me in a new location—his cabin, his slaughterhouse, his mines. I needed to find him. I needed to wake up and get moving. But no matter where I searched, I found nothing but emptiness. He'd picked up and moved on. I was alone.

When my tipsiness faded, I was in the forest again, my butt planted firmly in the tall grass and twigs at the base of a tree. There was a cut on my forehead, and a small trickle of blood ran down along the crooks of my nose. I reached up to brush it away, but I couldn't. Someone had bound my arms and chest violently to the tree with a scratchy length of rope. The fibers burned every time I breathed. It was a full-body tourniquet.

"Here, let me help you with that," Ryan said, appearing from my side.

He bent down to clear the blood, but instead of wiping me clean, he landed a blow between the eyes. I was still awake, but the dizziness was back. He shook his knuckles out.

"You have a hard head," he said matter-of-factly. "That won't save you though. Nothing can. Not your barbed wire, your gasoline, or even that rifle. It's just you and me now."

"That was a pretty nifty trick you pulled with that motorcycle," I interrupted. "Who trained you?"

He screwed up his face and swung again. It'd be sweet dreams if this kept up.

"You're delirious. Snap out of it, I want you awake for this."

He pulled a knife from behind his back and waved it in front of my face in smooth strokes. I could tell he was a newbie. A ribbon dance would have been more intimidating.

"Look, you've had your fun," I said. "You really don't want to do this, it's obvious with how flashy you're being. If you honestly wanted me dead you would have slit my throat in the car instead of going through the hassle of dragging me up here. But it's cool, let me go and we'll call it even."

"Even?" he said. He tried to laugh to let me know how absurd the idea was. What I got instead was a psychotic chortle. "No, we won't be even until I get answers and my pound of flesh."

"Answers?"

"Now, Schafer I get, believe me I do. I almost punched his ticket myself," he said, tears pouring from his eyes. "But Madison, why her? We trusted you!"

"Oh, you want to know why I killed everyone. She was sleeping with the enemy—and you were either with me or against me." I shrugged. "Pretty simple stuff."

"She wasn't your enemy! She'd never done anything but look after you."

"Yeah, look after me—also look at me as you guys stuck me with God-knows what again and again. We're going to be here a really long time if you don't listen to the answers I give you."

"You piece of shit. You're going to be sorry . . ."

"Well, I'm not going to apologize," I said. "It seems we're at a stalemate, so let's get this over with."

"Get it over with?" he asked, tasting the words as he spoke, savoring each. "No, Edric, we aren't going to just get this over with. I'm going to keep you alive for as long as I can manage. You have many terrible things to atone for, and guess what? Today, I'm your judge, and your sentence starts now."

Ryan

❖

"I HAVE TO ADMIT, I'VE NEVER DONE THIS BEFORE," I said, sickness overwhelming my determination. "I've carved plenty of jack-o-lanterns though. How much harder could this be?"

"Never done this before? Gee, I never would've guessed. Fuck you, Ryan," he spat. "This is your fault. You never defended your woman once. You're a failure as a husband and a father."

He was right, but my mind was made up. Killing him wouldn't make me feel better, but it'd be a start.

"Enough talking," I said.

I shoved the blade in at the base of his swollen socket, and as the metal sunk deeper, the eyelids peeled back. Even with the knife stuck halfway inside his face, his pupil swallowed up his iris. It twitched left and right, trying to escape the pain until I cut it free. The dead thing bounced off of the slick blade and rolled into his lap. He leaned forward vomiting, fighting for breath.

"No comebacks?" I asked. "Don't tell me you've used them all up? We still have one to go."

He mumbled something, and when I leaned closer to check, he lunged forward and almost caught my ear in his jaws.

"You're a tricky one," I laughed. "Maybe I'll take your tongue next to teach your smart mouth a lesson."

I grabbed his scruffy cheeks and traced the tip of the blade over his lips, leaving a path of translucent eye fluid. The upper, the lower, then both. His fight had shriveled up, but I wasn't finished yet.

"No, I really had my heart set on the eyes first, we'll stick with that plan," I continued. "Christ, here I am talking about plans again. You'd think I'd have had my fill of those things by now. Plus, if we keep your tongue a little longer, I get to listen to you beg for mercy."

"Why my eyes?" he squeaked. "Of all things, why are you taking my goddamn eyes?"

"I don't know, Edric, why did you burn my wife at the stake, huh?" I asked. "Because it's fun, that's why! I'm going to rip your fucking eyes out, and then let you run around the forest. Let you see what it's like to scramble around for a bit. Then, when I feel like you've learned your lesson, I'm going to take your hands and feet and leave you for the crows."

His features smoothed and his mouth hung open. A bead of sweat rolled from his temple, picking up rivulets of blood during its descent along his jaw. His lone eye spun before focusing on something distant, like he was looking through me and out the other side—peaceful but horrified. Another one of his mind games—and I wasn't going to fall for it.

"Edric?" I chuckled. "You look like you've seen a ghost."

"What's that?" he asked. Every syllable trembled its way out of his mouth, like trying to drink and talk at the same time.

"I'm not falling for that. I'm not as dimwitted as Schafer. I've caught on to your tricks."

"No, Ryan," he said, shaking more violently. "What the hell is that thing?"

"Drop the act!" I screamed.

"Kill me now," he breathed while fighting his restraints. Maybe he'd finally realized he was about to die, because the calm and defiant Edric had transformed into a panicky mess in a matter of seconds. "I know you want revenge, and I understand where you're coming from. Just do it. Kill me, I'm *begging* you, if you have even one compassionate bone left in your body."

Something cold ran up my flesh, pricking each goose bump with a long sliver of ice. Edric wasn't faking, and that's when I realized that during our entire exchange, our voices had been the only sound in the forest. No breeze through the branches, no birds serenading the morning sun, and especially no raindrops dappling off the crisp spring leaves. I slowly turned to face what Edric had been staring at.

Bugs and spiders, millions of them, marched along the ground and down the trunks of trees. Their compound eyes sparkled in the red glow of sunrise, a wave of tiny, shimmering prisms. Snakes sprouted from the ground and ravens clutched at branches with serrated talons.

We were surrounded. Above, below, and on every side, we were surrounded. We'd been cutoff from the rest of the world.

Even more frightening than this was the six-foot orb of dark smoke that hovered above the insects, pulsing with understanding and purpose. A dozen rogue swallowtail butterflies flapped their wings around it.

Before I could raise my arms to fight or spin my legs around to run, it was on me. Engulfing me in a choking, toxic cloud. I tumbled through the air, hope drained out of me until I was bone dry. I traveled up a searing vortex of black.

I would never get my revenge.

My story was over.

Edric

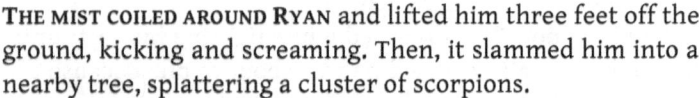

THE MIST COILED AROUND RYAN and lifted him three feet off the ground, kicking and screaming. Then, it slammed him into a nearby tree, splattering a cluster of scorpions.

As he fought for breath, his arms raised from his sides. The smoke began to slowly pull them back behind the trunk, snapping his elbows like popsicle sticks. I could see ragged tendons and loose muscles through the shredded flaps of tissue. The thing did the same to his legs. Twisting until his kneecaps split the skin and dropped to the forest floor like discarded softballs. After this, it released him to the ground with a thud. The angles of his ruined limbs made it impossible for him to lay flat. He wasn't dead yet, but I was sure a highlight reel of his life was projecting onto his eyelids.

Then the mist turned to me, darkened, and took shape. It stood eight feet tall with outstretched shoulders, resembling more of a crucifix than a man. Its head was a collection of white glowing sockets housing no eyes and a mouth lined with fangs that made garden shears look pathetic. Its skin (if you could call it that) was like a combination of soot and oil, and seemed to be in a constant cycle between the creature's head and where it pooled on the ground.

"Tell me, who do you think I am?" it asked. Its voice was booming, yet hollow and cold, an echo in a cemetery.

I wanted to give a smartass reply like the heroes always do in the movies. I don't know, buddy, the Spirit of the Forest? But no, I was too busy trying to stay focused—trying not to slip into shock.

"Asclepius?" I asked weakly.

"Asclepius?" it repeated before a thoughtful pause. "I guess you could call me that—but my birth name is Machaon. We're one and the same though, pick whichever suits you best."

"Thank you for saving me, Machaon," I said, stumbling over the pronunciation. "Can you get these ropes off me? I'd like to go home."

"Home? Edric, you *are* home. Your new home is with me."

His arm, which was little more than a wispy trail ending in a lone claw, reached out and tickled my chin. It felt like having warts burned off with liquid nitrogen.

"What do you want with me?" I cried out, struggling against the restraints. I was too terrified to remember my training. "I killed them all, wasn't that enough? Can't you just let me go?"

"Let you go?" the thing laughed like sludge being sucked down a drain. "Never, little Edric, I need you. These simple creatures that I've inhabited for decades—the insects, the arachnids, the reptiles—have grown quite stale. I need a fresh, young host. One that can help *satisfy* the things I've hungered for during my long sleeps beneath the floorboards in my humble home. I've been waiting a long time for someone weak and willing enough to accept me into their soul."

"Into my soul?" I wheezed unconvinced. "What are you talking about?"

"It means exactly what it sounds like. Did you think that you could've accomplished all of those murders on your own? I've been sinking inside of you since they took you home from school that day."

It was sickening but it made sense. I wasn't a cold-hearted killer—but I'd still enjoyed snuffing each candle. And the crueler I was, the better I felt. I vomited again.

"Now, Edric, you're going to rip free from your chrysalis and blossom into a social butterfly. We're going to need plenty of playmates in our little cabin in the woods, after all. I'll need you to go out into the world and make some friends."

"Please, anything else."

"I guess I could make you a pig?" he said, smiling.

I remembered the pigs from my training. The ones we'd meticulously dissected on my quest to become the perfect killing machine. They'd been Asclepius's failed protégés all along—the ones too weak to do what he'd asked of them in the end.

"Fuck you!" I screamed. There was nothing left for me, I wanted to go out fighting.

"Aw, there's that fire that I fell in love with, good boy. But time is short, and I long to feel you from the inside. Brace yourself, you're going to feel a little pinch."

His whole body dissolved and the smoke trickled into my gaping eye socket, but instead of feeling cool and dry like I'd expected, it was as slimy and thick as gravy. I finished choking him down—the only thing that remained were the swallowtails clinging to the front of my shirt. A yellow and black spider the size of my face with bony legs fought its way through the mass of creatures, crawled up my front, and chewed each one into slippery pieces.

"Let's go have some fun, Edric," Asclepius echoed in my brain. My arms flexed and the ropes split like they were made of pasta. The sea of insects parted for us. I took one last look at Ryan's dying body, and we left the woods.

There was a magnetism bringing me back to the house. I fought the tugging with every step, lurching away with the last drops of my remaining willpower. But it was hopeless. Even though I could regain control over myself for a minute at a time, each step I took away, I'd take two back towards Hell.

"Don't fight," he said. "You'll come to want this as much as I do. Trust me, I've been inside your head. I know what lurks there."

That's when I got my last idea, and it was a doozy. It would be tough, there was no doubt about that, but I knew deep down that I could do it. I could do anything.

I would only have one shot at a happy ending.

I made my way up the dusty road, past the creaky porch, leaned up against the front door, and fell inside.

I'd been saving my strength during the trip for one last push. In the entryway, I yanked away from the wraith's hold, and smashed into the room with the contraband. I found a single syringe and filled it to the brim with atropine; droplets squirted out the top, letting me know that I had enough. I climbed the stairs to my room.

Was it what I wanted? No, of course not. But did it beat a secluded lifetime of brutal, sexual slavery? Hell yes. Hell yes a million times.

I positioned the needle over the bulging vein in my neck and steadied my hand.

"What do you think you're doing?" he growled.

"Lesson one," I whispered. "Being self reliant, breaking away from you."

I pushed the plunger and felt the dreams pour into my bloodstream. Everything disconnected, everything was melting out of reality. It was a perfect conclusion.

I wanted to collapse into the bed I'd been shackled to, my bed, but I couldn't stand the thought of cuddling up with Jacob's blood-soaked body. Instead, I dropped to my knees and looked up at the room's lone window as the sun rose high into the sky. The red glow of the morning washed over me. My heart pounded, fighting the drug with every pulse, and the magnetism of the phantom receded to a deep dizziness. It was working.

Again, I could hear the humming.

Something dropped on to my shoulder, then again and again. I used my last bit of strength to look at the ceiling. The rustic exposed beams had been replaced by millions of black widow spiders devouring one another. It was raining legs and fangs. The wallpaper bubbled and split. Cockroaches crawled out of every orifice like sweat through a man's pores.

The humming continued, louder now. Asclepius was close, hovering around me, waiting for my body to break.

The floorboards groaned and peeled back, revealing dozens of black snakes. The rats followed them; their yellow, rotted teeth the only color in the wriggling, scratching wave of darkness. Everything formed a semicircle around me, a reverse eclipse on the floorboards, ready to pounce.

But I didn't see the fangs, the claws, the eyes. I didn't smell the death, the rot, the decay. My entire focus was on the window, the glowing square of gold in front of me—the portal to outside. I could barely make out the tops of the trees standing resolute against the coming day.

The room faded to black, but there I stayed, kneeling in my own private box of light.

My new home.

SERVA ANIMUM CASTELLUM CUSTODITUM · HORTUM BENE CURATUM · FLUMEN NON OBSTRUCTUM ·

Did you enjoy the book?

We welcome all feedback and queries.
Villipede.com

Acknowledgments

❖

In the time that it has taken from outline to physical publication of this book, I've wracked up debts even more intense than my student loans. There are no words in the English language that can properly express my gratefulness, but I'm going to try. If the following people ever need help with the disposal of a body, I'm your guy:

Team Villipede: Matt Edginton, Alandice A. Anderson, and Sydney Leigh, for their long hours and faith in this project. I was about three rejections away from shoving it in a crate and getting "top men" to bury it in a warehouse somewhere when they gave me the thumbs up. Also the painfully talented Mikio Murakami for designing a cover so hypnotically wonderful the book practically sells itself . . .

. . . but just in case it doesn't, buy a few more copies.

My parents and grandparents who continue to support me even though they weren't "allowed" to read any of the stuff I was publishing for years.

My sisters/best friends, Kathleen, Amy, Emily, Rebecca, and Gwen, for teaching me the art of hand-to-hand combat with their constant ambushes.

My literary superhero, Sandra Hahn, for listening to me read the whole book out loud from beginning to end and only falling asleep a couple of times.

The entire staff of the University of California, Riverside creative writing department (including the ones who don't like me very much). Special shout-outs to Susan Straight, Mike Davis, Victoria Barras Tulacro, and David L. Ulin.

Writer friends, Koren Zailckas, Kelly Braffet, Matthew Stokoe, Monica Drake, Anne Rainey, A. R. Kahler, John Everson, Benjamin Kane Ethridge, Kurt Fawver, Alexandra Kleeman, and Max Booth III for their query letter prowess, kind words, and just being nice to me in general.

Finally, infinite gratitude to Hideo Kojima, Fumito Ueda, Suda 51, Shinji Mikami, Ken Levine, Akira Yamaoka, Clint Eastwood, Jackie Chan, Park Chan-wook, Guillermo del Toro, Alex Garland, Quentin Tarantino, Takashi Miike, Haruki Murakami, Karen Russell, Stephen King, Joan Didion, Bret Easton Ellis, Cormac McCarthy, Donna Tartt, and Amy Hempel. Thank you for helping me escape the desert for hours at a time and inspiring me to write the things that I do.

Stephen Williams is a janitor in a small desert town where the only thing to do for fun is catch rattlesnakes. He holds a degree in creative writing from the University of California, Riverside where he won the Chancellor's Performance Award for excellence in fiction. His work has appeared in numerous publications, including Menacing Hedge, Sanitarium, Underneath the Juniper Tree, and Goreyesque. Currently, he serves as an editor for Rind Literary Magazine. *Among the Ruins* is his first novel.